**She was only trying to help out a friend, so how could she be in danger?**

Restless, Cait decided to check on Turtle Creek Winery to be sure it had been secured. She hurried upstairs to change her clothes; grabbed her keys, shoulder bag, and sunglasses; and went downstairs, where she found Niki spread out on the cool kitchen tiles. She secured the house and then went to the Harts' RV to let them know where she was going. Finally, inside the garage, she settled behind the wheel of her Saab.

Five minutes later, she pulled into Post Lane, waved to the neighbor working in his yard, and then parked in Sadie and Luke's driveway. The house was partially shaded by large oak trees, while the long wraparound porch looked cool and inviting. Cait wasn't expecting trouble, but she wanted to make sure no one was sniffing around the house or winery while her friends were away.

She tried the doors of the house and, finding them secure, headed to the back. She stood for a few moments to admire the lush green vineyard before trying the doors to the winery. As she reached for the door handles, she noticed one door was cracked open. Adrenalin surged through her body.

Cait listened, but all she heard were birds in the trees. She inhaled deeply and then nudged the door open with her toe. The hinges creaked as she pushed it.

She heard a metallic click—the sound of a pistol being cocked. Then another click.

Realizing she wasn't alone, she turned her head at the slightest hint of movement—a muffled sound, maybe feet hitting the cement floor. Thoughts rushed through her mind, like storm clouds passing over the sky.

She was on her own.

She could be in serious danger.

Cait Pepper, owner of the Bening Estate vineyards, and navy SEAL Royal Tanner return to help friends who recently acquired a vineyard in Livermore, California. Sadie, an Amish girl, and her husband, Luke Sloane, are excited about their new adventure of owning their own vineyard until agents from the Drug Enforcement Agency knock on their door. When Luke bought the property, he neglected to check the previous owners' background and didn't know about their drug connections. Desperate to save her friends from danger and embarrassment, Cait is torn between helping the Sloanes or the actors in her Shakespeare Festival. Will Cait's cop skills be enough to save the Sloanes from the drug dealer—and the DEA—while avoiding another tragedy that could put her Shakespeare Festival in peril?

## KUDOS for *Vineyard Prey*

In *Vineyard Prey* by Carole Price, Cait Pepper is the owner of a California vineyard, which she inherited from her aunt, and where she holds monthly Shakespeare Festivals. She is also a retired cop. When friends and fellow vineyard owners Sadie and Luke Sloane, Cait's neighbors, start getting mysterious threats, Cait puts her cop skills to use to help them. Thinking the threats were most likely meant for the previous owners, Cait investigates and is appalled at what she finds. There are some bad people out there, looking to get paid what they are owned, and they don't care which vineyard owners they collect from. Price is an accomplished author and knows how to craft a story. This one—a cute, clever, and fast-paced cozy mystery—will keep you enthralled all the way through. ~ *Taylor Jones, The Review Team of Taylor Jones & Regan Murphy*

*Vineyard Prey* by Carole Price is the third in this talented author's Shakespeare in the Vineyard Mystery series. Our heroine, Cait Pepper and her navy SEAL boyfriend RT, become entangled in the criminal underworld when they try to help Cait's neighbors, new vineyard owners Luke and Sadie, because strange things are happening on their property, and they are being threatened. In addition to helping investigate what is going on at the neighboring vineyard, Cait is also trying to keep up her aunt's practice of holding Shakespeare plays in theaters on her property. But as the bodies pile up, Cait finds she has stumbled into a little more than she bargained for when she set out to help Luke and Sadie. Told in an informal and interesting voice, and filled with enchanting characters, an intriguing mystery, and plenty of fast-paced action, *Vineyard Prey* held my interest from the first page to the last. ~ *Regan Murphy, The Review Team of Taylor Jones & Regan Murphy*

# ACKNOWLEDGMENTS

On the home front, much love and gratitude to my husband Cliff and daughters Carla and Krista for their support and encouragement. I would be amiss if I didn't include Shilo, my precious mix terrier, who sits by my side while I plot another mystery.

Thanks also to my critique group of early readers who offered encouragement and constructive criticism: Ann Parker, Penny Warner, Staci McLaughlin, Janet Finsilver, and Colleen Casey. Special thanks to the officers of the Livermore Police Department. My many years there as a volunteer has afforded me opportunities to learn and understand how they function.

Finally, thanks to Black Opal Books and acquisitions editor, Lauri Wellington, who offered me a new home after my other publisher dropped their mystery line. Also, thanks to extraordinaire editors Reyana and Faith and cover artist Jack.

# Vineyard

# Prey

*A Shakespeare in the Vineyard Mystery*

## CAROLE PRICE

*A Black Opal Books Publication*

## DEDICATION

*To my niece Cathy Lynch and her husband Bob, and in memory of their chocolate lab Niki.*

# Chapter 1

Under a blazing morning sun, Cait Pepper stood on a bluff overlooking the Livermore valley in northern California. She watched Royal Tanner duck to avoid a low tree branch as he advanced toward her. She was impressed that, at forty-one, tall and lean, with black hair and intense blue eyes, he'd kept himself in such fine shape. Cait wanted to reach out, take his hand and ask what he was thinking when he looked at her with that half smile, his eyes hidden behind his sunglasses. Instead, she turned her camera toward the valley floor as she thought how her life had changed so drastically in three short months.

She felt his warm hand, strong and familiar, close on her shoulder. "Did you know Brushy Peak is regarded as sacred ground by generations of indigenous Californians?" RT asked. "It lies at the center of a network of ancient trade routes. Many tribes called this place home—Ohlones, Miwoks, and Yokuts."

She glanced up at him. "Aren't you a fountain of information?"

He held out a folded paper and grinned. "Most park districts offer maps and information. You should carry one."

"Smart aleck." A long-time hiker and ex-cop, Cait hadn't found time lately to enjoy the great outdoors she valued. Until now. Through no fault of her own, she'd lost control of her life when she'd inherited her Aunt Tasha's Livermore Bening Estate, which included two Shakespearean theaters and a vineyard. Her new responsibilities had left little time to explore her surroundings, but at the urging of her new friend, Ilia Kubiak, a local professional photographer, she'd agreed to join him and RT on a hike up Brushy Peak before the actors arrived in a couple of days for the July Shakespeare festival.

Ilia, who had been stopping periodically along the way to take pictures, jogged into view with Niki, Cait's chocolate lab, at his heels. His professional camera dangled around his neck. "Hey, Cait. Wasn't I right when I said this was the perfect place to de-stress?"

Niki bounded up to her, with an expectant wag of his tail. "Yes, you were," she said. Cait bent down and stroked her dog. "But I can't linger. There's a lot to do. The actors will be arriving soon, and I want to be ready when they are. I'm looking forward to meeting them and enjoying another play." She straightened up, snapped his and RT's picture before they could object, and then swung her camera around, and zoomed in on the thousands of wind turbines dotting the landscape along Interstate 580.

"Ready to head back?" RT asked.

She nodded. "But I'm coming back up here as soon as the festival ends." She started down the trail ahead of the others. When her footing slipped, she grabbed hold of an old oak branch covered with bright green moss, in time to keep from tumbling off the steep path. As the trio walked single file for a while, they skirted sandstone outcroppings as they approached the parking lot. When they reached RT's Hummer, Cait pulled her Columbus, Ohio, PD ball cap off, shook out her curly black hair, grabbed a water bottle from her backpack, and drank deeply.

"There are other places we can hike," Ilia said. "Let me know when you've got some more free time."

"You should take him up on the offer, Cait," RT said. "You've been stuck in your house too long."

"I will when I can," she said.

They drove in comfortable silence until Ilia asked, "So Cait, when do the actors arrive?"

"Tomorrow or Friday," she said. "I expect to see Ray Stoltz tomorrow, if not sooner. He'll want to make sure I haven't overlooked anything at the theaters—burned-out light bulbs, exposed wires, empty water bottles, not enough coffee, and anything else he can dream up."

RT chuckled. "Ray pushes your buttons to see your reaction."

"Ya think?"

Ray was a seasoned stage manager. On good days Cait ignored his jesting, but not so much when things turned stressful. The festival ran the first weekend of every month, May through September. This weekend would be Cait's third festival since she inherited the estate and, hopefully, the easiest.

"I'm sorry the play *Royal Family* had to be canceled," Ilia said.

Cait nodded. "Me too. The male lead suddenly took ill." She took another drink of water. "It did free up the Blackfriars Theater, though, which turns out to be a good thing. I had a call from the Theater Arts Department at Las Positas College. They were looking for extra space to rehearse. According to my aunt's notes, she encouraged interaction between the college and her festival, giving students of the arts opportunities she never had."

Tasha, a retired Shakespearean actor, had built the theaters soon after she and her husband bought their house just outside of town.

After their unfortunate deaths, Cait inherited the estate, reluctantly resigned from her law enforcement job in Ohio, and moved to Livermore, California.

The trio returned to the house to find Marcus Singer, Cait's newly promoted assistant manager, and Sadie Sloane,

Cait's friend from college, who had recently relocated to Livermore, sitting at the kitchen counter.

Sadie, almost as tall as Cait's five eight, slid off her stool and gave Cait a hug. "I hope I'm not imposing on you by dropping by too often." Her hair, the color of a new copper penny, sparkled under the fluorescent lights.

Cait assured Sadie she was always welcome. "Where's Luke?"

Luke, Sadie's husband, was an investigative reporter for *Outside Magazine*.

"In Santa Cruz, getting our house ready to sell."

Cait opened the freezer, took out three chilled glasses, and then filled them from the pitcher of iced tea sitting on the counter. She handed one to Ilia, one to RT, and picked up the third. The icy touch of the glass felt good against her hands. She slid the glass across her forehead, enjoying the sensation on her hot skin. "Sadie, I'm sorry you have to give up the house you love on the coast, but from what I know about the winery business, you'll be busy twenty-four-seven, and little time will be left for anything else." She sipped her iced tea.

A frown crossed Sadie's face. "I suppose."

Cait set her glass down. "You're not sorry you bought the winery, are you?"

"No, but—" Sadie reached into her purse, withdrew a folded sheet of paper, and handed it to Cait. "I found this on our property."

Cait opened the paper. Her heart lurched as she read the note. And then she read it aloud. "'No cops! Pay up! We're watching.'" She looked up. "My God, Sadie, this is a threat, or at least a very mean prank. Do you have any idea what it means?"

"No." she said, her voice near a whisper.

"What does Luke say?"

Sadie shook her head. Her hair fell across her face. "I haven't told him about the note. I didn't want to upset him while he was in Santa Cruz."

Cait blinked in surprise. A dozen questions popped into her head. "Why not? He isn't in any trouble is he?"

"No! Of course not. I mean—we've only been here at the winery three weeks. The note had to be meant for the people who owned the winery before us."

"Who are they?" RT asked. "Are they still in town? Can you contact them?"

"Pamela and Vince Harper, a brother and sister. I don't know where they are. They seemed nice, maybe a little eager to sell, but then we were eager to buy. Luke's always wanted to follow in his parents' footsteps and own a winery. He grew up in the business and knows it well."

"May I see the note?" RT asked. "Where did you find this?" he said to Sadie, when Cait handed it to him.

"Taped to the winery's door," Sadie said. "When Luke left for Santa Cruz, I stayed behind to get the house organized. This morning I noticed the cat food I'd put out last night for Minnie hadn't been touched and went looking for her. That's when I saw the note on the door at the winery."

"When were you there last?" RT asked

"Not since Luke left."

RT frowned a little. "How long has he been gone?"

"Two days. He should be back tomorrow."

"And you hadn't gone to the winery during that time?"

"No. I had no reason to."

"So the note could have been on the door at least a couple days," he said. "Are you open for business yet?"

"No. We'll be advertising our opening in a month or so."

"Noticed anyone wandering about the property?" Cait asked.

"No, but I've stuck pretty close to the house. It's larger than our house in Santa Cruz and needs some work."

Cait had only been to the Sloanes' winery once since Sadie and Luke moved in, even though it was minutes from the Bening Estate by car. She'd never met the previous owners. She looked at Marcus. "Did you know the Harpers?"

Since Marcus was born and raised in Livermore, she thought it was a possibility.

He ran his hand through his blond spiked hair. "Nope. Lots of wineries in Livermore. I prefer beer."

Cait sighed. "Right." She then turned back to Sadie. "This note needs to be taken seriously, whether it's meant for you or for the Harpers. You have to show it to the police."

Sadie bit her lip, looking nervous. "I'm sure you're right, but I'd rather wait until Luke's back."

"No, Sadie. Call him now," Cait insisted. "Tell him about the note and say that you're going to the police. If he argues, tell him I made you. I'm on friendly terms with one of the detectives. I'll go with you."

Sadie reached in her purse for her cell phone and hesitated. When Cait crossed her arms and stared at her, Sadie sighed and called her husband. "Luke? When are you coming back?"

While Sadie walked around the kitchen talking to her husband, Cait spoke softly to the others. "I can't imagine Luke would know what's behind that note."

Sadie tucked her cell phone away. "He's coming back, but agreed I should go to the police now."

"That's good, Sadie. You never know what lies behind notes like these. It could be nothing, or it could be something."

Cait fervently hoped it was the former, for her friend's sake. Unbidden, the words scratched in block print with a heavy hand on the note rose up in her mind's eye and sent an unwelcome shiver down her back.

*WE'RE WATCHING.*

# Chapter 2

C ait drove to the police station, past vineyards stepping their way up terraced hills or blanketing fields in tidy rows. Ahead of them, a dozen or so hardpedaling bicyclists in bright yellow jackets turned off onto Mines Road, toward the steep climb to Del Valle Regional Park. She glanced over at Sadie, who had been quietly looking out the window.

"Detective Rook is easy to talk to," Cait said. "You'll like him."

"I'm sure you're right, Cait," Sadie said. "I'm worried about Luke. He's been looking forward to having our own winery and starting a family. If anything goes wrong...or we lose the winery—"

"You won't." Cait turned into the police station lot and parked. "We're here."

Detective Ace Rook stood at the kiosk in the lobby at the Livermore Police Station when Cait and Sadie walked in. Dressed as if headed to court in a blue suit, pink shirt, and blue tie, he greeted them with a friendly smile. After introductions, the detective led them to a private interview room and closed the door.

"Have a seat," he said as he pulled out a chair and sat across the table from them. "May I see the note?"

Sadie reached into her purse and handed it to him. "It doesn't say much."

Rook looked at the note. "It says enough. It's clearly a threat, but from whom?"

Sadie shook her head. "I assume it's meant for the winery's previous owners."

"From what Cait told me on the phone, you recently purchased the place and are now living there with your husband." He set the note on the table. "Where's your husband now?"

"He's on his way back from Santa Cruz," Sadie said. "We're selling our house there and he had to meet with the realtor. He agreed with Cait that I should bring the note to the police."

Rook pulled a pad and pen from his jacket pocket. "When did you purchase the winery?"

"June first. We moved in on the fourteenth."

"What did your husband do before you became winery owners?"

"Luke's an investigative reporter for *Outside Magazine*, but he only free lances now."

"What's the name of your winery?"

Sadie's dimples flashed off and on as she talked. "It was listed as Spring Haven Winery. After we bought it, we changed it to Turtle Creek Winery."

Rook showed no recognition to the name. "And the name of the people you purchased it from?"

"Pamela and Vince Harper. They're brother and sister."

Rook looked up. "Interesting. How did you hear the winery was for sale?"

Sadie folded her hands on the table. "Luke saw it on Craigslist. He'd been researching wineries for sale for a while, but most were larger than what we wanted or could afford. His parents own a winery in Napa."

Rook smiled. "So this isn't an entirely new venture for your husband since he's familiar with the business."

"No, but we thought it would be awhile before we could afford our own."

"I hope it works out for you. I'll make inquiries about the Harpers and the sale of the winery and get back to you," Rook said. "How can I reach you?"

Sadie gave him her cell phone number, the landline at the house, and Luke's cell number. Rook wrote as she recited them.

"I'll hold on to this note," He reached in his pocket and handed her his business card. "Let me know if anyone contacts you or threatens you in any way." He stood and reached over to shake Sadie's hand. "I'm glad you came in."

Cait smiled. "Thanks for seeing us on short notice, Detective."

Rook hesitated. "One more question. Any chance someone's playing a joke on you or your husband? Maybe a friend or family member?"

Sadie shook her head. "No. I can't imagine anyone we know who would do something like this." Outside the station, she turned to Cait. "I like Detective Rook. Thanks for coming with me."

"It's going to be okay, Sadie," Cait said, but she felt uneasy.

Sadie had left her Amish community to further her education and immerse herself in what the Amish called the English world. *How will she handle the note that threatens their dream of owning a winery? That note didn't get on the door by itself*, Cait thought. She liked Luke. In fact, she had introduced him to Sadie back at Dennison University when he visited his cousin Samantha. Sam, Cait's best friend and roommate, was now an ER doctor in Columbus.

Cait drove Sadie back to the house for her car. Sadie promised to call when she heard from Detective Rook. Cait waited until Sadie turned her BMW around and disappeared down the driveway. She thought about calling Samantha, but then decided to wait until she heard from Detective

Rook or Sadie. It might look as if Cait was unsure about Luke's innocence.

Niki jumped on Cait when she walked in the back door. RT sat at the kitchen counter with his cell phone to his ear. He turned and winked at Cait while continuing to listen to the person on the other end of the line.

Marcus came out of his office behind the kitchen. "I researched Spring Haven Winery and the Harpers," he said. "Brother and sister, as Sadie said. The Harpers bought the winery two years ago after the owner died. Apparently, they did okay and had a talented consulting winemaker. I wonder if he'll continue with Sadie and her husband."

"Luke studied chemistry and viticulture at U.C. Davis," Cait said, "and has worked at his parents' winery in Napa since he was a kid. It wouldn't surprise me if he already had employees lined up to work for him." She took a chilled glass from the freezer and filled it from the iced tea pitcher left on the counter. "I hope they make a go of it. Sadie plans to bring a little of her Amish culture into decorating the tasting room. She makes beautiful quilts."

RT tucked his cell phone in his jeans pocket. "What did the good detective have to say about that note?"

"He's going to make inquiries about the Harpers and the sale of the winery," Cait said. She tilted her head. "You looked pleased while you were talking on the phone. I assume it wasn't a call to report to duty." The dreaded phone call always weighted heavily on her mind. Being a SEAL meant RT could be ordered back any time. Before now, they'd never spent more than a couple of days together since they met in April. That RT had been here four days was a luxury, an opportunity to get to know one another better. Cait didn't know what it meant for the long haul and chose not to think about it.

RT grinned. "Were you worried?"

*Always, where you're concerned.* She shrugged. "I'm getting used to having you around."

The smile slid from his face. "Yeah, me too." Then he

quickly shrugged. "It was good news. I sold my fourth children's book—*Secrets from the Bottom of the Sea.* I read the draft to Mindy, my toughest critic. She loved it, but then she's partial."

Cait leaned in and gave him a hug. "RT, that's terrific. Maybe you should retire from the Navy and write full time." *And then what?* she thought. *Settle down in San Diego with his six-year-old daughter Mindy while I remain in northern California? Maybe fly up here a couple of times a year?* "I don't know how you find the time to write when you're traveling all over the world, and under such dangerous conditions."

"Stolen minutes, here and there."

Marcus slapped him on the back. "Congrats, RT!"

"Thanks."

An awkward moment passed before Cait said, "I better check the Elizabethan theater. Ray could pop in any time."

"Want help?" RT asked.

"I'd like that." She reached into her backpack for her cell phone. "I love the new app on my iPhone. It links the house and the theaters so I can manage and monitor each one. Easier than the key chain modem where I had to race around to unlock and lock the theaters. It should make Ray happy." She opened the back door and Niki ran out ahead of her.

"Remind me what this weekend's play is about," RT said as they walked along the brick path and through the rows of cypress trees.

She smiled, as RT put himself out there to try to understand Shakespeare. "*Twelfth Night* is a romantic comedy. The plots and subplots are woven together like a tapestry. Toni Behren has the role of Viola, disguised as a boy. She played Ophelia in *Hamlet* last month, remember? And Betsy Ryder will also return as Lady Olivia, a rich countess. I don't know any of the other actors."

"I remember Betsy. She played Lady Macbeth."

Cait glanced at RT. "That's right." When they reached the trellis gate, Cait dug a penny from her pocket and dropped it into one of the terra-cotta oil jugs flanking the trellis.

"What'd you do that for?" RT asked.

"Fumié said it's for good luck when walking under a trellis." She pushed the squeaky gate open, ducked to avoid trailing ivory roses, and entered the theater courtyard.

"Did she also say its bad luck to oil the rusty gate?"

Cait poked her finger at his chest. "No, but maybe that's something you could do while you're here."

RT grinned, grabbed her finger, pulled her close, and whispered in her ear, "I have better things on my mind."

Chills ran through Cait, despite the blazing sun. She wrapped her arms around his neck, responding to a need that only RT could satisfy, until what sounded like coughing caught her attention. She backed away from RT and straightened her T-shirt.

"There you are," June Hart said, as if she'd just arrived. But Cait thought she knew better. "Marcus said you were headed to the Elizabethan Theater. What do you say we plant something for Ray to find so he won't be disappointed if there's nothing to complain about?"

Cait laughed. "I love it."

Niki rested his paw on Cait's foot and looked up at her with warm brown eyes.

She reached into her pocket for a treat and gave it to him.

"Poor Ray," RT said. "You ladies go ahead. I'll call my mom and talk with Mindy. She can't wait to start school in the fall and share my books with her classmates."

"She's a lucky little girl to have you for her dad," Cait said. "I feel guilty you're here and not with her." Her inability to have children had been the biggest contention in her failed marriage.

"You've nothing to feel guilty about," RT said. "Mindy likes you and wanted you to have a dog for protection. She chose Niki for you."

"And I'm grateful." Cait smiled, remembering the one time she'd met Mindy. "Maybe your parents could bring her here again so she can play with Niki and see how the dog and I bonded."

"Good idea," he said. "I'll make my call and then help Marcus finish packing boxes for the move to your new gift shop. Thank God, it's finally happening." He winked at Cait before walking away.

"Sorry for the interruption," June said as she watched RT.

"No, you're not, but it's okay. We had a terrific hike this morning, normal for a change."

"Marcus told me about the note Sadie found at her winery. Do you think it's a serious threat?"

"Yes, or a sick joke. Detective Rook is looking into it. It's hard enough Sadie's been shunned by her Amish community and no one's allowed to speak her name. And now this at their winery—it isn't fair."

June shook her head. "I hope Sadie's not as fragile as she looks."

"She isn't, at least not anymore. I was a sophomore at the university when Sadie started as a freshman. I became her mentor. She has a photographic memory for anything she reads. Reads it once and never forgets. It wasn't discovered until a teacher encouraged her to continue her education beyond the eighth grade. That's as far as the Amish attend school. Sadie thinks it's because she has the ability to organize certain types of information, rather than possessing eidetic ability, but she's never been tested."

"Goodness, think how handy that would be for Shake-spearean actors."

Cait laughed. "June, you're a natural at remembering lines. Your conversations are riddled with quotes, most I admit I don't recognize." She used the app on her iPhone to unlock the theater. As she stepped inside, her eyes swept over the sun-drenched open-air theater, the empty two hundred and fifty seats, the small orchestra pit, and the stage. She inhaled a deep breath. *It's mine. Now if only I can manage to keep it running—*

"Coming?" June asked from half way up the stairs to the stage.

"Yes. I was thinking about *Twelfth Night*. It's the most musical of all of Shakespeare's comedies and will be the first to use the orchestra pit." She hurried after June. "Maybe you could do a walk-through out here while I start back stage."

June tucked loose strands of blonde hair into the clip on top of her head. "Oh, sure. I'll catch up with you," she said as she retraced her steps.

Cait ducked behind the red velvet curtain and stepped into the green room. She reached for the light switch. Her gaze swept the room before focusing on the monitor mounted on the wall in front of twin sofas. The actors relied on the monitor to let them know what was happening on stage and for their cues to go on. She turned it on to make sure it worked and then walked the perimeter of the room, stopping to erase the white board of notes from last month's play. She continued to the corner where the coffee was kept. She had purchased Keurig Brewers for the theaters, along with several variety packs of coffee and tea. She felt the actors deserved a good cup of gourmet coffee that could be made fast.

She moved on, bypassing the stairs to the loft, and stepped into the wig and makeup room. Lighted tables were lined against the wall. She checked that all bulbs around the mirrors worked before opening the closet doors. Most of the wigs had been stored in a trunk in the loft, but a few rested on Styrofoam heads on one long shelf in the closet. She thought it a little disconcerting to see all those disembodied "heads." She remembered a couple of the returning actors, including Toni Behren and Betsy Ryder, preferred to clean and care for their own wigs. Satisfied the room was in order, she moved on to the dressing rooms where June joined her.

"All's good out front," June said. "To tell you the truth, I'm looking forward to the actors' return and all the hustle and bustle, even Ray's snarly temperament." She glanced around the room. "Must be dead here in the winter." She clapped her hand over her mouth. "Oh, Christ, forget I said that. Maybe quiet would be a better word."

Cait hadn't thought much about the off-season since she hadn't been there in the winter months. "I guess we'll find out." She bent and picked up a stray program from last month's festival and briefly scanned the list of actors.

"What's that?" June asked.

"An old program." She tossed it in the trash but couldn't help wonder if Actors' Equity would be extra attentive during the festival to ensure their actors were safe during this month's festival. Not that they didn't have reason to be concerned. The last two festivals had turned deadly.

"Let's finish up in here before I starve to death," June said.

"What about hiding something in plain sight for Ray to find?"

June grinned. "Already done."

౿ఎ౭఼

"The boxes are ready to go," RT said when Cait and June walked in the back door. "Ilia called. He and Fumié are on their way."

Eager to have the gift shop out of the house and in the courtyard where it belonged, Cait smiled. "I can't believe it's finally happening. The shop will open for business this weekend."

"Then let's get going," Marcus said. "There's a riding mower in the garage and a small trailer to hitch onto the back. A couple of trips should do it. You gals can carry the small stuff."

Cait shot him a look. "Are you saying we're weaklings?"

Tasha believed everyone deserved a second chance in life and had hired Marcus as her secretary after he was re-

leased from prison for robbery. Times were tough for Cait
when she inherited the estate. It had taken a while for Marcus to accept her and for them to come to a mutual understanding, but he felt the need occasionally to assert himself
as a tough guy.

Marcus raised his hands, palms out. "Whoa. I didn't say
that."

Cait smiled. "Just checking."

One side of RT's mouth curled. "What are you going to
do with the two empty rooms?"

"You kidding? An office for me and a dining area," Cait
said. "Stanton Lane said I could buy whatever furniture I'd
need." As the sole trustee of the Bening Estate trust, all ex-
penditures went through Lane for approval.

"I'm going to feel a hell of a lot better knowing strangers
won't be running through the house," RT said. "Can't imagine what Tasha was thinking when she turned those two
rooms into a gift shop."

"Probably her only option at the time—"

A loud banging at the back door interrupted Cait. "Mov-
ers reporting for duty!"

RT opened the door for Ilia and Fumié and greeted them.
"Hey."

"Glad you're here," Cait said. "Anyone interested in
grilled ham and cheese sandwiches before we start?"

Cait's cell phone buzzed. She reached into her jeans
pocket and glanced at the screen. "Sadie? Everything
okay?"

"Luke's not home yet and there's a black car parked in
the driveway. I can see two men in it. I couldn't reach Detective Rook."

Cait looked at RT. "Don't open the door, Sadie. RT and I
will be there shortly."

"What happened?" RT asked when Cait ended the call.

She grabbed her backpack and keys. "Sadie's alone at
the house and two men are sitting in a car in the driveway."

RT reached into his pocket for his keys. "I'll drive."

✌✍✌

RT turned into the Turtle Creek Winery at the end of Post Lane. Cait wasn't surprised to find Sadie standing in the driveway, even though she'd advised her to stay in the house. "What happened?" she asked Sadie as soon as she got out of the Hummer. "Why are you out here?"

"I wanted to know who those men were and if they were looking for the Harpers," Sadie said, "but they left as soon as I came out."

"That wasn't a smart thing to do," RT said. "Did they say anything?"

Sadie shook her head. "You made the trip for nothing."

"Where's Luke?" Cait asked.

"I don't know, maybe he got tied up with the realtor—oh, here he comes."

A white Fiat convertible pulled into the driveway. Luke Sloane jumped out. "What's going on?" He nervously ran his fingers through his wind-blown light brown hair. "I couldn't break away from the realtor."

"Two men were parked in your driveway for a while," Cait said. "Sadie called us when she couldn't reach Detective Rook. Whoever it was left as soon as she came outside."

Luke stared at Sadie, stunned. "Why would you do that? They probably wrote the note."

"I know. I'm sorry, but I thought if they were looking for the Harpers I could tell them they didn't live here any more."

"Luke, this is Royal Tanner, a friend of mine," Cait said. "RT, Luke Sloane." As the men shook hands, she asked, "Luke, have you any idea who might have written that note or who those men are?"

"No, of course not," Luke said. "As Sadie said, they're probably looking for the Harpers."

Cait liked Luke or she wouldn't have introduced him to

Sadie, but the note had made her wonder about Luke's background. Even though his cousin Samantha was her best friend, she only knew what Sam had told her about Luke. Cait was anxious to talk to Detective Rook. She wouldn't be surprised if Rook had done a background check on Luke as well as the Harpers, as she would have done if she were still a cop. *Never leave a stone unturned*, she thought.

"I hope I never see those men again," Sadie said, "but I wish I could have talked to them so we could put an end to all this craziness." She held her hand up to shield her eyes from the sun. "Would you like to come in for a cold drink?"

Cait smiled. "Thanks, another time. We're in the process of moving the gift shop into its new home." She looked at Luke. "Stop by the police station as soon as you can. Detective Rook would like to meet you."

"I will," he said. "Thanks for helping Sadie."

"I don't like it," Cait said to RT as they drove back down Post Lane. "I doubt this is the end of it."

"Yeah," he said, frowning. "It stinks."

*Chapter 3*

B y the time Cait and RT returned to the house, a load of boxes had been taken to the new gift shop waiting to be unpacked. Marcus flipped a couple of grilled ham and cheese sandwiches onto plates and handed them to Cait and RT. "Kept these warm for you."

"How did I ever get along without you?" Cait asked.

"Yeah, yeah." He wiped his hands on a towel and looked at her. "Been wondering—has there ever been a time when you haven't been involved with other people's problems? I don't mean as a cop, but—"

"As a concerned human being?" She shrugged. "I guess helping people is what I've been put on this planet to do, standing up for those who have been struck down." She bit into her sandwich to change the subject. Praise embarrassed her. "God, this is so good." She licked at the cheese oozing out the sides of her sandwich.

"What happened at the Sloanes' house?" Marcus asked. "Were those guys still in Sadie's driveway when you got there?"

"Nope, gone," RT said, then he bit into his own sandwich.

Cait sat quietly, eating her sandwich, her mind on Sadie's bold move to approach the two men in her driveway. Cait hadn't seen Sadie often after college, but they'd kept in close touch. She did notice Sadie had lost a lot of her shyness. "Maybe the Harpers owe money and those men came to collect."

"Sounds like a reasonable explanation," RT said, "but they've taken the wrong approach. If the previous owners still owed money, it should be handled in court. Leaving a threatening note stuck on a door suspiciously smells of fraud. Now it's a police matter. If the Sloane's are involved—"

Cait's head jerked up. "No way—they're the innocent party here."

"I hope you're right," RT said. "Detective Rook will discover if anything is squirrely when he does background checks. In the meantime, let's finish moving the boxes to the gift shop." He wadded up his paper napkin and tossed it into the trash. "Great sandwich, Marcus. Thanks."

An hour later, all of the boxes had been moved and set on the ground in front of the gift shop. The gray weathered shingles gave the shop the appearance of an aged building. The peaked-roof one-room shop had a skylight, making it appear larger than it was. A small window at the back that Cait had requested faced Mount Diablo. Inside, the walls were covered with open shelves.

Cait's eyes swept the theater complex—the Elizabethan and Blackfriars theaters, the small outdoor stage, and the new gift shop. Marcus had surprised her with an engraved sign he'd made for above the door—*Ye Olde Curiosity Shop*.

"Marcus and Fumié designed the perfect shop for the space available," June said.

Cait nodded. "They work well together. I'll miss Fumié when she leaves." She watched Fumié's long black hair fall across her face as she leaned over to rip tape from one of the boxes. Fumié Ondo, a graduate of UC Davis, would soon be off to Santa Rosa to attend school to become a park ranger.

"We'll all miss her," June said, "but she'll be back. Her family's here." With her hands on her hips, she sighed. "Ready to attack those boxes?"

"Sure." Cait's cell phone buzzed as she started across the courtyard. She glanced at the screen. "It's Detective Rook. I'll catch up with you."

"I hope it's good news."

"The sale of the Spring Haven Winery appears to be legit," Rook said. "I need more time to look deeper into the Harpers' background, but so far I don't see anything that would affect the sale of the winery to the Sloanes. By the way, Luke Sloane called and told me about the car parked in their driveway."

"Good. He's a great guy, Rook. I'd appreciate a call if you learn anything more about the Harpers. That note had to be meant for them, and they should be made aware of it and about the men who parked their car in the Sloanes' driveway." She tucked her phone away and started toward the gift shop.

"Hey, Cait! Hold up."

She turned and saw Jim Hart hurrying toward her. "Were you expecting company?" he asked.

"No. Why?" She glanced over his shoulder but didn't see anyone behind him.

"I was in the garage when I heard a car coming up the driveway. I didn't recognize it so I watched and waited to see who it was. Funny thing though, no one got out. Whoever was in the car sat in front of the house for a couple of minutes and then turned around and drove off. Odd, if you ask me, but maybe they realized they had the wrong address."

The back of Cait's neck tingled. "How many were in the car?"

"Two. I saw someone in the passenger seat as they turned the car around."

"What color was the car?"

"A black SUV Toyota. Possibly a Highlander. Sound familiar?"

She briefly closed her eyes and drew a deep breath. *Could it be the same car that was parked at Sadie's house? Were RT and I followed when we left?*

"Cait, do you know who those people are?"

"Not exactly, but I'm going to find out." She looked over her shoulder. "I have to find RT."

"There he is," Jim said, pointing to the shop.

RT stood outside the door. He looked up when Cait called him.

"A black car was in front of my house," she said as she ran toward him. "Jim saw it. Want to bet it's the same guys seen at the Sloane's house?"

"June told me about that car," Jim said, "but I didn't connect it to the one I saw out front or I would have approached it and taken down the license plate."

Frustrated, Cait admitted, "I didn't even look to see if we were followed."

"No reason you should." RT's tightly clamped jaw told Cait he hadn't checked for a tail either.

"I have a security system and cameras at my winery in San Diego," RT said. "Check with Sadie, maybe they have outside cameras."

"I will, after I call Rook."

Rook answered immediately. "What's up?"

"A black car like the one in the Sloanes' driveway showed up here a few minutes ago," she said. "No need to speculate any longer. This is serious. Whatever is going on, Sadie and Luke are caught in the middle. And now maybe me, too."

"Are you sure it was the same car?" Rook asked.

"You think it's a coincidence two men in a black car show up here after we left the Sloanes? Jim Hart saw them. They sat in front for a couple of minutes, never got out, and then took off."

"No, Cait, I don't think it's a coincidence."

She frowned. "No way are Sadie and Luke involved in whatever is going on. I'd bet my life on it. I'll do everything I can to get to the bottom of this."

"I'll check the Harpers' background," he said. "Ask the Sloanes if they met the Harpers or if they know what their plans were after the sale. I'll contact the realtor who sold the winery. They should know how to reach the Harpers."

"I'll call Sadie. Let's hope they have outside cameras." She disconnected the call.

"What do you want to do, Cait?" RT asked. "Do you want to go back and talk to the Sloanes?"

She shook her head. "I'll call. They need to know we were followed."

eↄeↄ

The Sloanes didn't have outside cameras, but they did have spotlights at the house and the winery building and would leave them on all day and all night for a while. If the men in the black SUV returned, the lights might deter them from going onto the property. The Sloanes had briefly met Pamela and Vince Harper when they first toured the property. Frustrated, Cait didn't know what else she could do for her friends at this time.

Meanwhile, she had the weekend festival to think about. Ray Stoltz, the stage manager, would be there tomorrow and start issuing orders if the Elizabethan theater didn't meet his standards. Not that Cait was afraid of Ray. He wasn't exactly a teddy bear like June thought he was, but he liked to test Cait, to find fault even when there wasn't anything to complain about. That's why June planted a surprise for him to grumble about, but she hadn't told Cait what it was so she would show surprise, same as Ray, when he discovered it. All Cait knew was it was "hidden" in plain sight.

By five o'clock, the gift shop was ready for business. June helped Fumié until all of the shelves had been filled and the gifts priced for sale. Cait had requested a small table be set inside the door for a credit card machine. The shop couldn't hold more than half a dozen people at a time, but she loved it. She took one last look out the back window at Mount Diablo before locking up. The shop wasn't part of the security system and required a key to unlock it, but Cait saw no reason for anyone to break in.

Jim and June returned to their RV. Fumié and Ilia left to take in a movie downtown. Marcus returned the tractor and trailer to the garage before leaving to visit his mother in a Tracy retirement center.

While walking back to the house with RT, Cait wondered what Rook had learned about the Harpers and was tempted to call and ask, but hesitated because, when she was a cop, she was frustrated when pushed for answers she didn't have.

"I've learned when you're too quiet, you're up to something," RT said. "You're worried about the Sloanes and want to help but you don't know how. Right?"

"Yes. There's nothing I can do until those men act first. That's what worries me—not knowing what they'll do."

He took hold of her hand. "Maybe nothing. If they didn't recognize Sadie when she went outside, they might realize they have the wrong people and leave the Sloanes alone. But if they did recognize her—"

She pulled her hand back. "I told you, Sadie and Luke are the victims of mistaken ID."

"Then why were we followed here?"

Cait had wondered the same thing. "I don't know. Maybe they think the Harpers moved here."

"To the Bening Estate? That's what the sign says at the foot of the driveway in big, bold letters."

"I know. I'm grabbing at anything for an explanation. Nothing makes sense."

He reclaimed her hand. "Want to go downtown for dinner?"

She perked up. "Yes! I'm starved."

ფოფფ

Half an hour later, they were strolling through downtown Livermore until they settled on the First Street Alehouse. With baskets of beer-battered fish and chips and mugs of cold beer in front of them, they relaxed at an outside table. Conversation surrounded them, along with foot and car traffic, but Cait loved it. She also loved being with RT. He'd pulled his chair closer so they could hear each other talk.

"We should do this more often," he said.

"I agree," she replied and took a sip of beer.

RT talked about his daughter Mindy and the next children's book he was writing. Cait talked about *Twelfth Night*, the romantic comedy playing that weekend at the Elizabethan Theater. No one mentioned the situation with the Sloanes, but Cait couldn't put it out of her mind for long. Community life was a natural extension of home life for the Amish. When a catastrophe happened, they were not alone to face the problem. But Sadie had been ostracized from social contact with her community when she left. All she had now were Luke and Cait.

It was after eight when Cait and RT left the Alehouse and started back to the parking lot where RT's Hummer was parked. As they were about to turn down an alley, Cait noticed a black SUV idling in a parking space near where they had been seated at the restaurant. Cait froze.

"I see it," RT said. He took her hand. "Keep walking."

"Are we crazy? I'm sure there are lots of black SUVs in town," she said.

"I'm sure there are."

They cut between the buildings to the rear parking lot. Cait half expected to see the same black SUV waiting in the back, but she didn't. Still, her eyes swept the lot as they headed to RT's car.

RT unlocked his Hummer and they got in.

"Go around the block and down First," Cait said. "I want

to see if that car is still in front of the restaurant. If so, I'll get the license plate."

"It was idling. I'm sure it's gone," he said.

"Humor me, okay?"

RT was right. The car was gone and Cait was disappointed.

They drove slowly through town and then headed back to the Bening Estate without incident or seeing another black SUV on the road. "What do you want to do?" Cait asked after they let Niki out.

"I'll walk around outside with Niki," he said. "I won't be long." He pulled her close and kissed her neck, her ear, and then her mouth. "That's a promise." Then he left.

He didn't fool Cait. She knew he was concerned for her and for Sadie and Luke. He would walk the grounds as a safety check like he always did when he was there, but usually he'd go out around eleven o'clock. It wasn't even ten. *Maybe he plans to call Detective Rook and ask about the background checks on the Harpers*, she mused.

Her cell phone beeped. She answered without checking the screen. "That was a short walk."

"I don't usually walk at midnight," the voice on the other end responded, "but hey, I'm game."

"Shep!" she said. "Hi." Detective Shepherd Church had been Cait's mentor after she graduated from the police academy in Columbus, Ohio. Soon they became partners and best friends.

"The line goes both ways, kiddo. I'm thinking you've got company. Is it your favorite SEAL?"

Cait pulled out a stool and sat on the edge. "How'd you guess?"

"Your voice changes when he's there. Have you decided to marry the guy yet?"

"What? I tried marriage. Once was enough."

"So you say," he said and changed the subject. "It's about time for another Shakespeare festival, right?"

"Yes. *Twelfth Night* is this weekend at the Elizabethan

theater. The other play at the Blackfriars was cancelled due to the lead actor's unexpected death from pneumonia."

"Sorry to hear that." He hesitated. "Cait, I have too much vacation time accrued and am being forced to use part of it. I'm thinking a trip to California and golf at Pebble Beach. In a week or so. Will your SEAL still be there? I wouldn't want to create a problem for you."

She laughed. "No problem. RT's never been able to stay here this long, so I doubt he'll be here. If he is, I'd like you to meet him."

"Is he the jealous type?"

"I haven't known him long enough to find out. Seriously, Shep, come. I'd love to see you."

"Okay. I'll let you know when." He hesitated again. "Everything peaceful out there, no more problems?"

She went to the refrigerator and filled a glass with iced tea. "Remember Sadie Miller? My Amish friend from college?"

"Sure. You took her under your wing and became fast friends."

She sipped her tea. "She and her husband, Luke Sloane, bought a winery in Livermore. They only live five minutes from me."

"That's great, Cait."

She set her glass down on the counter. "It is, but Sadie and Luke might be in trouble." She explained about the note left on the door at their winery and about the men in a black SUV who had turned up at the Sloanes' and then at her house. "And it's probably the same car we saw in front of the restaurant where RT and I were tonight. I don't think that's a coincidence."

She heard a long sigh from the other end of the line. "I know you. You're going to do your darndest to investigate and help your friends."

"I have to, Shep. You would do the same."

"You're right. I assume Detective Rook is looking into it."

"He's doing what he can with little to go on," Cait said. Shep and Rook had talked on the phone a month ago when Cait became a target for revenge after shooting a thief two years ago while she was still a cop in Ohio, but the two had never met. She glanced at the clock on the wall: ten o'clock. "It's midnight there. Why are you working so late?"

"I wasn't. Look, I'll let you go. I wanted to let you know I'm coming out there."

"There's an apartment on the second floor of this house. You can stay there if you'd like. I use the master bedroom on the third floor."

He chuckled. "Thanks, but no thanks. Wouldn't want to ruin your reputation."

"Funny. There are nice places to stay across the freeway. Can't wait to see you."

"Be safe, Cait."

There was a loud banging on the back door. "Cait! Open up!"

Startled, she turned to see RT through the window looking like a thundercloud.

She opened the door. "What the—"

"I couldn't get through on your cell phone," he said. "I thought something happened." Then he saw her phone in her hand. "You were talking on the phone?"

She shut the door behind RT and Niki. "Yes, but I didn't hear a call-waiting beep."

"Damn. I'm sorry," he said. "I ran around to the front to see if that black car had returned." He pulled out a stool, sat down, and released a big sigh. "I worry a lot, about you and all the people hanging around here during your festivals. It's beginning to affect my job."

Cait stood still, sure RT was going to say they couldn't see each other any more, and that she was a distraction he couldn't afford in his line of work.

"My home's in San Diego. You're in northern California." He passed his hand over his face, as if struggling to make a decision about their relationship.

Seeing this big, tough navy SEAL baring his feelings tore Cait apart. How had a relaxing evening turned into an emotional rollercoaster?

Her pulse racing, she asked, "What do you mean, RT?"

"Christ, Cait, I...have feelings for you." He jumped up, grabbed her around the waist, and kissed her long and hard. His kiss left nothing to the imagination. Then he pulled back. "I had a call while I was out."

Her heart sank. The dreaded call. That would explain RT's intense outburst.

He pressed the heels of his hands to his eyes. Cait recognized exhaustion when she saw it and felt sorry for him.

"Can we go upstairs now?" he asked.

# Chapter 4

C urled next to RT, her head resting on his bare chest, Cait agreed he should go home and spend time with Mindy before he had to leave on his next assignment. The emotional turmoil she felt left her feeling restless and sorry for herself. Whenever a crisis arose, the dreaded phone call came and he had to report for duty. It wasn't fair. Then Cait's self-pity disappeared in a wash of guilt as she thought of his young daughter and how she must feel every time her daddy had to leave, and then about the long drive ahead of RT from Livermore to San Diego. He'd left his 1970 vintage Airstream trailer and Hummer at Cait's place the last time because of the urgent call to report back immediately. Detective Rook had driven him to the airport.

She wound a finger through his black curly chest hairs. "Why not fly to San Diego? Leave your trailer and Hummer here like before. You'd have more time to spend with Mindy."

He kissed her neck, her lips, and mumbled in her ear, "I can't. I've been given a grace period to get home. The next call should come a day after I get home, but it could be a week. And I don't know how long I'll be gone. Depends on where I'm sent."

*How can you live this way?* she wondered. RT never

talked about Mindy's mother except to say she wasn't in the picture, and he'd had sole custody of his daughter from birth. Cait closed her eyes and tried to visualize what country RT might be sent to and for what purpose—Israel? Syria? Afghanistan? Navy SEALS lived in a private world. If he left his trailer and Hummer in her parking lot, at least she'd see him again when he came to pick them up. Gripped with fear for his safety, she snuggled closer, afraid to let him go.

৩৩৩

By nine Thursday morning, RT was gone. Cait's last view of him was from the top of her driveway, where she stood with Niki at her side until the taillights of RT's trailer disappeared from view. She finally dragged herself back to the house where June and Jim waited. They'd said their goodbyes to RT earlier and had stayed inside the house to give Cait and RT a final private moment. Marcus perched on the edge of a stool in the kitchen, his head hung low as if he'd lost his best friend.

June forced a cheery smile. "What do we do now?"

A sharp rap on the back door answered her question.

Cait opened it to find Ray Stoltz tucking his shirttail into his jeans. "Hey. You're early," she said.

"Saw RT on his way out. Seems like he's always leaving."

"That's right," June said before Cait could answer. "And now we can look forward to his return. So what's your plan for today, big guy?"

Ray arched his eyebrow at June. "A walk-through at the Elizabethan, of course. I admit I'm glad there's only one play this weekend. Simplifies matters."

"Don't get too comfortable," June said. "A group of students from the local college are going to use the Blackfriars Theater, for rehearsals, and they might want your professional advice on anything from building scenery to stage presence." She glanced at Cait. "Cait and I would be happy to tag along on your walk-through. You know, in case there's a problem at the Elizabethan theater."

Ray frowned. "All this sweetness and light makes me nervous. Not expecting trouble, are you?"

"Perish the thought. Why would you think that?" June asked.

"Hmph."

"There *are* a couple of surprises," Cait said.

Ray glanced at Marcus. "You know what they're talking about?"

Marcus looked up. "Beats me."

Ray looked at Jim. "You?"

"Nope."

Cait opened the door. "Then let's get to it."

Niki lay sprawled in the sun, but perked up when Cait stepped out.

Ray hesitated. "You got the keys to the theater?"

"Don't need them," Cait said, as she pulled her cell phone from her jean's pocket.

Ray rolled his eyes but remained silent as Cait and June exchanged smiles.

The gate to the theater complex squealed when they opened it. "A little WD-40 would do wonders for that gate," Ray said.

"Got any on you?" Cait asked.

"Do I have to do everything around here?"

"My, aren't we in a cantankerous mood today," June said, obviously enjoying herself.

As they approached the Elizabethan Theater, Cait touched an app on her iPhone and then opened the side door. "Enter."

Ray stood there, staring at Cait. "How'd you do that?"

"You gotta keep up with technology, Ray," Cait said. "I can now control the theaters and the house from an app on my phone. You and the actors can come and go as you please. But let me know when you're leaving for the day so I can lock up."

He nodded. "Miracles never cease." He went inside the open-air theater. With one foot on the first step leading to the stage, he paused. "You ladies going to follow me around like a couple of hounds? Why don't you amuse yourselves while I check the place out? If I need you, I'll let you know."

"I'm sure you will. Where's Jay?" Cait said. "I thought you and your brother did walk-throughs together, you know, in case one of you missed anything."

"He'll be here," Ray said. He climbed the steps to the stage and disappeared behind the curtain.

"Do you think he'll find what I planted?" June asked.

"You never told me what or where it is, remember?" Cait glanced up at the stage. "You going to tell me what this mysterious plant is you so ingeniously hid in plain sight?"

June grinned. "Ah. What's the one thing that makes Ray's blood boil?"

Cait could think of several things, but thought back to last month's festival and came up empty, then to the first time she'd met Ray shortly after she'd arrived in California to take over the festival. Her mouth dropped open when she knew she'd hit the jackpot. "Weapons—the lost or misplaced props."

"Good. What else? Think about *Twelfth Night*."

Tired of guessing, Cait sighed. "I give up."

"Coins, jewels," June said. "Lots of coins are exchanged in this play. And lots of bling going around as gifts." She shrugged. "I didn't want to tamper with the boxes of the real props. They arrived earlier this week so I dropped a few of my own cheap pearls on the floor. Ray won't know the difference but his reaction should be interesting."

"I don't know, seems like a cruel joke," Cait said. "Let's hope he doesn't fall or go ballistic."

"Son of a—"

A loud bang, like a door slamming, drowned out the rest of Ray's exclamation.

Cait and June exchanged looks and then charged up the stairs to the stage and behind the curtain. Ray stood calmly in the middle of the green room tapping on an electronic notepad in his hand.

"Is there a problem, Ray?" June asked innocently.

Ray looked up. "What? Nope." He continued writing and then slowly began to walk around the room—touching each leather sofa, straightening a coaster on one of the end tables, a lamp—before stopping to switch on the monitor mounted on the wall. He grunted as he turned it off and on and then tapped keys on his notepad.

"Uh...Ray," Cait said. "Everything okay? We thought we heard you yell—"

"Nope, so far so good."

"Hey, Ray," someone yelled. "You in here?"

Cait turned to see Jay, Ray's brother, step around the stage curtain. As soon as he entered the green room, something crunched under his feet. A confused look crossed his face. He stared at the floor, did a little skip to avoid stepping on whatever was rolling around, and then reached down to pick one up. "Holly crap," he sputtered. "Pearls? Where did these come from?" Then he glared at the women. "Wait a sec. No one had better be tampering with our props."

Ray stabbed his finger in the direction of Cait and June, his lips slightly curled up. "Ask them."

June picked up a pearl and held it out to Jay. "Look. Fake. From my own collection."

Jay stared at the fake pearl in June's hand and then laughed. "I get it, guys. You were playing a joke on Ray."

Stunned by Ray's mild reaction to the pearls, Cait stared at his back as he walked across the room, thinking what an odd mood he was in.

When Ray reached the tiny coffee corner, he hesitated and glanced over his shoulder, "This new gadget another one of your surprises? Will it blow up if I use it?"

Annoyed Ray hadn't shown appreciation when he saw the new Keurig, Cait opened her mouth to respond, but then her cell phone rang and she walked away, leaving June to explain how the new coffee maker worked. "Sadie?"

"Cait, the black car returned. When they saw Luke in the driveway, they stuck a camera out the window and took his picture before backing around and driving off. Luke got in his car and took off after them."

"That's not good," Cait said. "Did you call Detective Rook?"

"Why bother?" she said. "They're long gone by now. But I'm afraid Luke will do something stupid and get hurt if he catches up with those guys."

"Try calling Luke. Tell him to leave it to the police."

"I did, but it went to voice mail," Sadie said. "Maybe I should drive around looking for Luke's car."

"No! He'll come back." She turned to see Ray and Jay entering the wig and makeup room, June right behind them. "Wait for him, Sadie, and call me when he returns. I'll try to reach Detective Rook." As soon as she hung up, she phoned Rook but got his voice mail and left a message. She wanted to go over to Sadie's, if only for support, but decided her time would be better spent preparing for the actors' arrival.

Niki sat beside Cait, his soft brown eyes watching her. She leaned over and stroked his head. Her cell rang and she recognized Rook's number. "Rook, the black car was back at Sadie's and Luke's place. They took Luke's picture and drove off. Luke did a stupid thing. He went after them. What the hell do you think is going on?"

"Don't know, but the Sloanes need to leave it to the police. It's never good when citizens take it upon themselves to go after the bad guys. Usually ends in disaster."

"I agree, but Luke has a stubborn streak. I thought about driving around to look for him."

"Waste of time. But let's hope Luke doesn't find them." He paused. "Sadie never called to report the car was back."

"She thought it was too late to do anything about it. She

tried calling Luke, but he didn't answer. I'm not sure what to do, except wait to hear back from her when Luke returns." She heard a deep sigh from the other end of the phone.

"That's all you can do. Don't you have a festival to worry about?"

"Yes."

"Then that's your priority. I'll call Sadie. If Luke's back, I'll have a talk with him. He won't like it, but he has a lot at stake."

# *Chapter 5*

Waiting for something to happen was not one of Cait's virtues. She wanted to help Sadie and Luke. She wanted to know who those men in the black car were and what they wanted from the Sloanes or the Harpers. But Detective Rook was right. She had her hands full with a festival to run, hundreds of patrons to greet over the weekend, and a group of college theater students descending upon the Blackfriars Theater. The timing couldn't be worse.

"Still, there has to be something I can do," she muttered to herself. "Like researching the Harpers." She glanced over her shoulder to look for June and spotted her showing Ray the different choices of coffee. "I'll be at the house."

June waved and held up a cup of coffee.

Cait found Marcus in his office pounding on the computer keyboard. "One of these days you're going to break it. Anything wrong?"

"No," he said, without lifting his eyes from the keyboard, "but I wish those kids would make up their minds when they want to use the Blackfriars Theater. First they said this afternoon and then changed to the weekend. I don't think it's a good idea to have them here while *Twelfth Night* is playing in the Elizabethan Theater. Do you?"

"Why not? It wouldn't be any different than if there was another play like there usually is," she said, "but maybe Saturday morning *would* work best. There's supposed to be a staff member with them." She smiled. "I warned Ray he could be inundated with questions from the kids about what it's like to be a stage manager. It's bound to happen. I can't wait to see his reaction to a bunch of college students."

Marcus picked up the receiver. "I'll call and suggest Saturday morning. They'll have plenty of time when the festival ends."

"Fine. I'll be upstairs for a while." She left Niki with Marcus, grabbed a bottle of water from the refrigerator, and headed to the stairs. The first thing she noticed when she reached her bedroom on the top floor was the unmade bed and the indentation in RT's pillow. Her breath caught, remembering the feel of his arms around her. She turned resolutely to the desk and sat down to boot up her laptop. She typed in the name Vincent Harper. Who were the Harpers? Why would they be threatened? Why did they sell their winery after only two years?

She read over the information, from when Vincent received his bachelor's in marine biology at UC Santa Cruz, to how he spent summers working at his uncle's winery in Sonoma, California. He'd held several odd jobs before joining his sister, Pamela, in their adventure of wine making. She clicked on several links but nothing jumped out to suggest a clue as to why anyone would threaten him.

Curiosity propelled Cait toward Facebook and found Vincent had an account. She scrolled down until she came to a picture of Vincent and Pamela raising a bottle of champagne to toast their purchase of Spring Haven Winery. Then she looked for a picture celebrating the sale, but found nothing. In fact, there hadn't been any new activity on Vincent's Facebook in the past couple of months.

Next, Cait typed in Pamela Harper. She'd earned an engineering degree from San Francisco State University and an MS in Viticulture & Enology from UC Davis. Like her brother, Pamela also worked at their uncle's winery in Sonoma when she wasn't in school. She had a Facebook page and posted pictures of their winery but nothing about the sale, which Cait thought interesting. Maybe it was a quick sale because they couldn't pay the mortgage. Other pictures posted had been taken at different winery events throughout California, most with the same man at her side.

Cait slumped back in her seat. She didn't know the Harpers, but if she were still a police officer, she'd find a way to gather their fingerprints and compare them with computerized records stored by the California Department of Justice and the NCIC index, the National Crime Information Center. If a person had been arrested anywhere in the country or served in the military, their fingerprints would be on file. She knew Sadie and Luke were innocent of any wrongdoing, at least not of a criminal nature, which meant the blame for their problems had to fall on the Harpers. Cait shut her laptop, closed her eyes, and thought about RT. *Where is he now? Will he call when he's back home in San Diego and before he leaves for wherever the navy sends him?* It took her a while to realize her cell phone was ringing.

She dug in her pocket, pulled it out, and glanced at the screen. "Hi, Sadie."

"Oh my God," Sadie said, her voice pitched higher than normal. "I'm freaking out. There's a body in the winery—"

Cait jumped up and tripped over a stack of books on her way to the door. "What?" *God, please don't let it be Luke.* "Who?"

"A man. I didn't get close enough to tell anything else."

Cait's heart thumped in her chest. *Thank God. Not Luke.* "You called the police?"

"Luke's back. He called. They'll be here any minute. Cait, what's going on? Why is this happening?"

"I don't know. I'll be there shortly." *Welcome to the English world, Sadie.*

Cait parked her Saab on the street behind two police
cars. Another cruiser and what she assumed was Detective
Rook's unmarked police car were in the driveway. She ran
around to the back of the house toward the winery and immediately spotted Rook, phone to his ear. He saw her and
waved her over. Cait's heart pounded as she looked for
Sadie, but her friend was nowhere in sight. She spotted
Luke and started to go toward him until she heard Rook
calling her. She stopped and waited for the detective to
catch up.

"You heard?" Rook asked.

Cait nodded. "What the hell is going on? Where's the
body? Have you identified him? I knew that threatening
note wouldn't be the end of it. It's only the beginning."

Rook arched his eyebrow. "I don't know what's going
on, the body's in the winery, and since we just arrived we
haven't yet identified him. The techs are on the way. Anything else you'd like to ask?"

She shifted her feet. "Yeah. Is this winery jinxed or are
the Harpers in deep trouble? Luke and Sadie are getting the
backlash of whatever the Harpers were involved in, and I
don't like it."

"I don't blame you," Rook said. He turned at a sudden
fuss behind them. "The techs are here." He walked away,
leaving her wondering how the Sloanes would cope with
this new development.

Luke looked forlorn, his shoulders slumped. Cait went
over to him as Sadie ran out the back door of the house.
"Luke, I'm so sorry. I wish I knew how to help."

"I'm going to crucify whoever's responsible for this," he
said.

Sadie shook her head. "No, Luke, that's not the way—"

He held his hands up. "Don't! I know what you're going
to say. Everything's *not* always in God's hands, Sadie."

"You don't have to be Amish to trust in God, Luke," Sadie bristled. "I was going to say it would make you no better than the person who *is* responsible for all this if you took matters into your own hands. Like when you chased those men in that car."

Cait felt their frustration and wished she had insight into why they were being targeted.

"Sadie, I'm sorry." Luke wrapped his arms around her. "You're right."

"Cait," Detective Rook called, "come with me." His brow furrowed as he directed her to the winery building where the techs were drawing a chalk outline around the body and setting out small evidence markers at strategic places. He pointed. "What do you make of this?"

She covered her nose with her hand at the nauseous smell and stared at the body—from a dark ponytail to pockmarked face, a distended stomach, the dirt under broken fingernails, and partially exposed underwear where cargo jeans had slipped down. *Poor Sadie. If only she hadn't had to see this.* "Hard to say. A personal vendetta?"

"That was my first guess."

She nodded. "Who is he?"

"No ID yet," Rook said.

"How long has he been dead?" She was no expert on estimating time of death.

"Two days at the most."

"Oh, great," she muttered.

While Luke was in Santa Cruz preparing their house for sale, Sadie had been home alone with a dead person in their winery. A chill ran down her back as she glanced around at the crush pad that held the wine fermentation and storage tanks. Stacked wine barrels dominated one side of the large airy room. She'd had a brief tour when her friends first moved in and remembered an intimate tasting room at the far end of the building.

Rook's phone beeped. He checked the screen but didn't answer the call.

"Did the killer encounter his victim here," Cait asked, "or was he murdered elsewhere and then brought here to lay blame on the Sloanes? I mean, wouldn't there be more blood or signs of a struggle?"

He motioned her away from the body and pointed to the floor near a stack of crates. "Those bloody drag marks are all we've found so far. Officers Perough and Vanicheque are checking around outside."

Cait heard footsteps and glanced up to see the officers approaching. *They're fast becoming my new best friends,* she thought. Only last month they had investigated an attempted break-in at the Bening Estate. She smiled. "Looks like we're destined to work together again," she said.

Rook cleared his throat. "Best you remember you're no longer a cop, no matter your friendship with the Sloanes."

Cait rolled her eyes. "Yeah, yeah."

The officers grinned at her. "Nice to see you again, Cait," Perough said. "What's your interest here?"

"Sadie and Luke are my friends," she said as she ran her fingers through her curly hair. "I won't interfere with your investigation, but I know they're innocent of this whole affair, and I intend to help them any way I can, preferably without stepping on anyone's toes."

Perough and Vanicheque exchanged looks. Vanicheque smiled. "I don't see what a little cooperation on all of our parts would hurt, do you, Detective Rook?"

Rook cocked his eyebrow. "Find anything outside?" he asked the officers.

"As a matter of fact, we did," Vanicheque said. He held up a clear baggy. "Want to bet this turns blue when tested?"

Cait knew that meant only one thing.

# Chapter 6

Cait's instinct was to grab the bag of white powder and test it herself. Instead, she asked, "Where did you find it?"

"Outside," Perough answered, "in plain sight. Fortunate a cat or dog didn't find it first. If it's cocaine, as I suspect, the stuff could kill an animal." He held a cell phone up. "Also found a burner."

*Makes sense—inexpensive, simple, and can't be traced by a SIM card.*

"I think we found where the vic was stabbed," Vanicheque said.

"Show me," Rook said.

Happy to escape the smell inside the winery, Cait followed the officers out of the building and around to the side where a patch of grass was flattened and splattered with a dark brown substance.

Rook stooped and studied the grass. "Get a sample and have it tested for a match against our vic's blood."

Cait glanced at dozens of crates stacked against the winery walls, strange machinery, pumps, oak barrels, and more. A smaller storage building was across the way, she remembered, and held cases of wine. Maybe one day when Sadie and Luke's current problem was resolved, Luke would give her an extended tour and demonstrate the whole wine making process. "Why move the body inside?" she asked as she stared at the stained grass. "Doesn't make sense."

"I agree," Rook said. "Unless, the vic was able to stagger inside and then collapsed."

*Beep beep beep.*

Cait reached in her pocket for her cell and glanced at the screen. Warmth spread through her body. "RT." She turned her back to the officers and walked a short distance away. "Where are you?"

"Rest stop," he said. "Cait…"

"Yes?"

"Uh…nothing. Any news about Sadie and Luke's situation?"

She sighed. It bothered her whenever RT would start to speak and then change his mind. It was like he wanted to tell her something, but then decided against it. "I'm at their winery now, along with Detective Rook and his officers. You won't believe what's happened. Luke found a body in the building. It appears the man was stabbed. Oh, and a baggy of a white substance, possibly cocaine, was found. Sadie and Luke are shaken up."

"I'm not surprised," RT said. "I'm sorry I'm not there to help."

Cait sensed his frustration. "Me too, but you have a job to do, RT, a very important job—protecting the US. Livermore PD is on this, and I'm confident they will find who is responsible." She hesitated. "But I'm not sure what this will do to Sadie and Luke. They might want to sell and get the heck out of here."

"Who could blame them?" he said. "You have to be careful too, Cait. Those guys know where you live. I should be there for you."

Cait bristled. She'd been a cop and could protect herself. Her cell beeped once, letting her know she had a call waiting. She ignored it. "RT, I'll be fine."

"Ask Rook to post an officer at your place."

She turned at the commotion behind her and saw Luke and Sadie talking to Detective Rook. Sadie looked white as chalk as she stared at the rusty grass. "I have my Glock."

"Carry it at all times, and make sure your cell is charged."

"RT—I will. Heard any more about where you'll be sent?"

"Not sure, but I might get back sooner than expected. When the first call came, I got the feeling the stint is in the States."

Excitement rose in Cait's chest. *And I wouldn't worry about you as much.* "Great. Maybe you could bring Mindy with you when you come back to Livermore. I'd love to see her again."

He gave a soft chuckle. "I'll think about it. I better get back on the road. I'll be in touch."

RT had never before said he'd be in touch. He'd show up when least expected. But this time she'd sensed a change in his voice. *Maybe he misses me as much as I miss him.*

She checked her voice mail. Her friend Samantha, an ER doctor in Columbus, wanted her to call. But Cait hesitated. Luke Sloane and Sam were cousins. She would be devastated to learn what's happened at his winery. Cait tucked her phone in her jeans pocket and joined Rook and her friends.

"How soon until the body can be removed?" Sadie asked.

"Shouldn't be long," Rook said. "Why don't you wait in the house?"

Sadie groaned. "And do what? Watch out the window?" Stray wisps of red hair had escaped from the bun at the nape of her neck and fell over her face. She blew them away. "Detective, have you been able to locate the Harpers? Or talk with our realtor?"

Rook shook his head. "The Harpers' mortgage lender hasn't returned my call, but from what I've learned so far is it was a clean sale, nothing for you to worry about." He frowned. "I do wonder why they chose to do a 'quick sale,' where the property is sold below what is due on a mortgage loan."

"Is that unusual?" Sadie asked.

"No, and it can be useful in certain circumstances," Rook said. "But after what's happened here, I'd like to know why they had to sell so quickly."

"I should have asked our realtor," Luke said. "Maybe they were running away from someone. Nevertheless, we should have been told if it would affect us and the winery." He glanced at Sadie. "We couldn't have afforded to buy this place if not for a trust fund left to me by my grandmother."

Rook smiled. "You answered one of my questions."

Luke nodded. "What's the other one?"

"I was curious how Sadie and Cait met."

"She mentored me at college and then introduced me to Luke." Sadie reached for Luke's hand. "The happiest day of my life."

Rook nodded. "Cait's full of surprises."

Cait cleared her throat and changed the subject. "I looked the Harpers up on the Web." She noticed the question in Rook's eyes but chose to ignore it. "Both of them worked at their uncle's winery in Sonoma. Both have been to college. They posted pictures on Facebook when they bought the winery, but there are no posts about selling it or what they're doing now."

Sadie frowned. "Our realtor thought Pamela was depressed over selling the winery. Maybe it was sibling rivalry, like one wanted to sell and the other didn't. Or maybe they didn't agree on how to run the business. Whatever it was, it must have to do with the dead man inside there." She pointed to the winery.

"Certainly worth investigating," Rook said. He turned at a rumbling noise coming from the front of the winery. "I think the coroner's here." He hurried off.

"See you around, Cait," Officer Perough said. He raised his hand as he and Vanicheque walked away.

Cait watched the officers as they headed inside the winery building and then turned to her friends. "Luke, Samantha called while I was on the phone with RT. Do you want to call and tell her what's happened or should I when I call her back?"

"Oh, hell, I don't know," he said. "She might hop on the next plane out here. You know how she is about family and friends. Thinks she can fix everything and everyone. Don't get me wrong, I love her for it."

"Kind of like you, Cait," Sadie said, "taking care of everyone else first."

Cait smiled. "Yeah, we're two of a kind. I catch the bad guys, Sam heals their hurts. So what do you want to do, Luke?"

"Luke?" Rook yelled as he came into view.

Everyone turned to see Rook running toward them, his tie flapping against his shirt.

"The white Fiat in your driveway is on fire," he said.

# Chapter 7

I called Dispatch. Where's your hose?" Rook asked.

"Christ!" Luke ran toward the front of the house, Sadie and Cait right behind him, followed by the other officers.

The sight of the Fiat engulfed in flames made Cait's skin crawl. *Luke loves that car. He could have been in it.*

Luke opened the garage, dragged out a hose, and turned it on the burning car. The black ragtop had burned to ashes, leaving only the frame with bits of fabric dangling from it. The leather seats and the body of the car had a few scorch marks but otherwise appeared okay. The fire truck arrived but the fire was out, thanks to Rook's quick action before the fire could get the upper hand.

Sadie sank to her knees. "Oh, Luke. Your car," she sobbed.

Anger tightened Cait's throat as she draped her arm over Sadie's shoulder. "We'll get to the bottom of this. I promise." She glanced at Rook and knew by the set of his jaw he felt the same. She went over to him. "The sooner you identify the body in the winery, the sooner you'll learn what's going on around here. Will you call and let me know who he is?"

Rook glanced over at Sadie, with her head buried in her

hands, and nodded. "And if there's anything your friends haven't told me, I'll expect you to call me." Cait started to protest, but Rook raised his hand. "I'm not accusing them of anything."

"Okay." She turned to watch the firemen gather their gear and prepare to leave. "I'll say goodbye to Sadie and Luke and then I have to go as soon as I can move my car. It's blocked by the fire truck." She joined Sadie and helped her to her feet. "We'll figure this out, Sadie."

"I'm not waiting for the police to talk to our realtor," Sadie said, wiping away tears. "I'm going to call and explain what we're going through here. She must have a contact number for the Harpers. What's happened to Luke and me is their fault, not ours." Her voice grew stronger with determination. "I will not sit and wait for something else to happen."

Cait nodded. "I understand." She hesitated. "You met the Harpers, right? Did they say anything? I mean like their reason for selling?"

"No. They were leaving as we arrived to tour the winery. I think our realtor may have talked to them after introductions were made, but we went on ahead of her, excited to check the property."

"You didn't see the Harpers at the closing?"

Sadie shook her head.

Cait turned at the sound of an engine and saw the fire truck pulling out. "I have to go. Will you call and let me know what your realtor says about the Harpers?"

"Of course," Sadie said. "Thanks again for coming over." She turned and headed toward Luke and Detective Rook.

Sadie's dejected look tore at Cait's heart. She watched them briefly and then got in her car and drove off.

∽∾∽

Cait arrived back at the estate amid an animated conversation in the garage between Ray Stoltz, Marcus, and half a dozen young adults she assumed were from Las Positas College. They all stepped out of her way to allow room to park her car in the middle slot.

"Hi," she said as she stepped out of her Saab. "Are you all from the college?"

Heads bobbed up and down. One thirty-ish woman held out a hand to shake. "Hi, I'm Grace Bishop, theater instructor. You're Cait Pepper?"

"That's me," Cait said, as she admired the tall blonde. "I thought you were coming Saturday."

Marcus quickly spoke up. "They wanted to see the theater. I didn't see why they couldn't come this afternoon if it was okay with Ray."

Ray shrugged. "No problem for me. Can't think of a better use for the Blackfriars since we don't have a play scheduled there, can you, Cait?"

Momentarily stunned by Ray's agreeable manner, Cait shook her head. Ray's snarly disposition had disappeared overnight. She wasn't sure if she knew this new Ray.

"We wanted to have a look at the theater before Saturday," Grace said, "so we'd know how to prepare and what to bring."

"Oh, sure," Cait said. "Have you seen the theater yet?"

"No, we just got here," Grace said. "We were hoping to meet you before we left. By the way, these guys are Lucky, Krista, Joanna, Owen, and Brett," she said, tapping each student on a shoulder. "A few more will be in and out over time."

Cait tucked her keys in her jeans pocket. "Then let's head on over to the theater." She glanced around. "Where's Niki?" she asked Marcus.

"In the house. I guess I should let him out to see everyone since they'll be around for a while." He turned to leave. "We'll catch up with you."

Cait smiled. "Niki's my chocolate lab, six months old and playful."

"I had a yellow lab," Lucky said, shoulders slumped as they walked toward the theater.

Cait looked at Lucky and wondered if he was a reluctant actor or appeared unhappy because he'd lost his dog.

When they reached the gate to the theater complex, Ray cleared his throat, "June and Jim are at the Elizabethan theater if you need them. Jay and I shouldn't be much longer. I'll let you know when we're leaving so you can lock up."

"Thanks, Ray," Cait said.

Ray hesitated before turning to Grace. "I'll be around from now through Sunday. If you need anything, ask."

"That's so nice of you," Grace said. "We'll try to keep to ourselves and not disturb you or your actors."

Cait stared at Ray's back as he walked away. *What on earth has happened to the old Ray?*

Marcus and Niki joined them as Cait unlocked the Blackfriars Theater and turned on the lights. Niki searched Cait's hands, as if expecting a treat. Cait reached into her pocket and gave him one. "This is Niki. I'll try to keep him out of your way while you're rehearsing."

Tall, lean Lucky kneeled and wrapped his arms around the dog's neck. "Don't worry. He won't be a problem. I can tell he's a good boy."

Cait watched Lucky stroke Niki's head and was touched by the lost look in his eyes. Had his dog died recently?

"Cait," Marcus said. "Detective Rook's at the house. He says it's important."

She hesitated as she glanced at Grace and the young actors, their voices raised in excitement as they made their way toward the stage.

"Go," Marcus said, "I'll stay here and show them around."

"All right. Thanks. I wonder what Rook wants."

"If the expression on his face means anything, I'd say it's not good news."

Cait's heart raced and she left the theater. *If anything's happened to Sadie or Luke…*

# Chapter 8

Cait found Detective Rook in the meditation garden, a grim look on his face, his cell to his ear as she approached. When he saw her, he tucked the phone in his shirt pocket.

"Marcus said it was important," Cait said.

"Sorry to pull you away," he said. "It's about the dead guy at the winery."

"You've identified him?"

"The officers found his wallet in his pants pocket. Either it was overlooked or the killer was searching for something else."

"Like drugs."

"Yeah. The guy's a cop. Or was. He's a PI, as of late."

Cait's jaw dropped. Speechless, she stared at Rook. "I hate when that happens."

"You and me both," he said. "Tends to complicate an investigation."

"His credentials were in his wallet?" she asked.

"Yes, along with a lot of money."

"What about a gun?"

"No gun has turned up yet. Hopefully he's not a good cop gone bad, but Vanicheque's doing a background check. We'll see where that goes. Hopefully, it will give us some clue about what the guy was doing at the Sloanes' winery."

"Those men in that black car killed him or know who did," Cait said.

Rook shuffled his feet. "Which is why you need to take precautions since they know where you live."

"I can't stop thinking about that. I've now got half a dozen college students and their instructor to worry about. They'll be here on and off to use the Blackfriars Theater for their own rehearsals. I've no idea how long that'll last, but I wonder if it's safe to have them here. What do you think?"

"I don't see a problem," he said. "You'll probably never see those men again, but if they're stupid enough to come, officers will be here during the play and until everyone has left."

"The college guys will be here Saturday morning, not in the evening. They didn't mention anything about Friday or Sunday so I better pin them down to a schedule. They're only here now to look over the theater." She drew a deep breath and slowly let it out. "I never anticipated a problem when I agreed to let them use it."

He nodded. "I better get going."

Cait walked with him to the front of the house. "By the way, what's the name of the dead PI?"

Rook stopped in his tracks. "Why?"

She stared at him. "Geez, Rook. I don't know. Maybe because his name might come up during this investigation?"

Rook smiled. "Regan Alex Thornton."

"Cute. RAT. He didn't look like a cop."

"Maybe he was in disguise." He pulled his keys from his slacks pocket as he frowned at her. "Talk to you later."

She watched him drive off then turned and looked up at the three-story yellow Victorian she'd inherited. *You're a pretty lady, but I've had more than my share of problems since moving in.*

❧❧❧

Cait returned to the Blackfriars Theater where Grace and her students were standing on the small stage.

Grace saw her, smiled, jumped down, and came toward her. "This theater is so perfect. These kids can't believe their luck. Thanks so much for giving us permission to use it."

"I'm happy it'll work for you," Cait said. "What play will you be rehearsing?"

"*The Comedy of Errors*. If you like slapstick humor, this is the one for you."

"I've never seen it," Cait admitted.

Grace smiled. "It's one of Shakespeare's early plays. The kids are having a lot of fun with it."

"*Twelfth Night* is playing this weekend at the Elizabethan theater," Cait said. "If you come early Saturday, you might catch the actors rehearsing."

"They wouldn't mind?" Grace asked.

Cait laughed. "I don't see why they would. I met a couple of the actors who were here last month. They were all friendly. If you'd like, I can introduce you sometime."

"I'd love that. *Twelfth Night* is one of my favorite plays."

Laughter from the stage caught their attention. Cait looked over and saw Lucky with the girl she thought was Krista.

"Lucky has the role of Dromio of Syracuse, a bumbling comical slave," Grace said. "Krista plays Adriana, a fierce and jealous woman. They're both serious about continuing their education in theater and attending the American Conservatory Theater in San Francisco. It's one of the best acting schools in the country."

"So I've heard. I wish them luck," Cait said.

"They're naturals. They'll do great. We should go. Thanks for letting us inside to see the theater."

"You're welcome. Can you give me a schedule for when you expect to use it? So someone is here to let you in." *And to avoid possible trouble from men in a black car.*

"Oh, sure," Grace said. "A couple of these kids have

jobs, so I'll have to check with them, and then I'll let you know."

"Great. Thanks."

Marcus and Niki walked up the aisle, followed by the five students. "Ready to go?" he asked Cait.

"I think so," Cait said "Maybe you could escort everyone back to their car while I head over to the Elizabethan. I need to catch up with Ray and the Harts."

When everyone was outside, Cait secured the theater. She stood and watched the group until they'd passed through the gate. Memories from her happy college days flashed across her mind until she shook off her nostalgia and turned away.

She entered the Elizabethan Theater by the side door and found the Harts in the green room relaxing on one of the leather sofas. June nursed a bottle of water while Jim drank what smelled like freshly brewed coffee. Cait's stomach ached from hunger. She'd forgotten to eat lunch again, and now it was closer to dinnertime.

June grinned when she saw Cait. "I don't know what's happened, but Ray's been bouncing around all over the place, happy as a lamb. Do you think it's the college kids who turned him into mister nice guy?"

Cait sat next to June. "Hard to tell. Could be he sees them as an opportunity to share his experience as a stage manager."

June cocked her head. "'If our virtues did not go forth of us, 'twere all alike as if we had them not.'" She smiled. "From *Measure for Measure*."

"You're a walking book of Shakespearean quotes, June. I don't know how you do it."

"From years of reading the bard and a good memory, thank the Lord, or I'd be a dance hall gal instead an actor." She rose and tapped a few steps to prove she could dance.

Cait laughed. "Have I told you lately how happy I am that you and Jim decided to move your RV here?"

"Often," June said.

"What's all the racket?" Ray asked as he walked across the room, brushing his hands along the sides of his jeans.

"Racket?" June asked. "I'll have you know—never mind. Are you and Jay ready to leave so Cait can lock up?"

Cait glanced around the green room. "Where *is* Jay? And Jim?" she added, noticing that he was suddenly missing.

"Jay took stuff to the truck," Ray said, "that I don't want to be stolen. I'm not Jim's keeper."

Cait frowned. "Stolen?"

"It wouldn't be the first time something's gone missing," Ray said. "If you remember."

Cait shook her head. Same old Ray. "Whatever. Let's go. I'm hungry." Outside the theater, she asked Ray, "What time should I expect the actors to arrive tomorrow?"

"The usual. Nine o'clock," he said. "It's a good group of actors. You're going to like them, all highly professional. I'll introduce you when they get here."

"It will be nice to see Toni Behren and Betsy Ryder again," she said, as she remembered both actors from when they were there last month.

Cait and June said goodbye to Ray as he turned toward the parking lot where he'd parked his truck.

"Now tell me," June said, "what happened at your friends' winery?"

Cait briefly closed her eyes. "There was a dead PI in the winery and Luke's car was set on fire."

June grabbed Cait's arm. "Oh, my God. Are Sadie and Luke okay?"

Cait nodded. "Fortunately." *For now, anyway.*

# Chapter 9

Cait's cell phone rang as soon as she walked into the house. Surprised to see RT's number on the screen, she answered with, "Are you in San Diego?"

"Yeah, got home about an hour ago. You doing okay?"

She leaned against the kitchen counter. "I'm fine. The college students left and I'm thinking about fixing something to eat."

"Any news from Rook?"

She started to say no and then remembered RT didn't know about Luke's car fire or who the dead guy in the winery was. "Yes. They've identified the body. He's an ex-cop turned PI. The police found his wallet in his pocket."

"A PI working undercover?" RT said. "He shouldn't have been carrying any official ID. On the other hand, he could have been killed for an uncollected drug debt. Being a PI doesn't mean he wasn't on the take."

"True, there is that. I hate the possibility of a cop gone bad. It changes my perspective on life. A burn phone was found but no weapon that I know of," she said. "I hope Rook keeps me in the info loop."

He chuckled. "He will, if he knows what's good for him. You'd be all over his back, considering the Sloanes are your friends."

Cait stooped and wrapped an arm around Niki's neck. "There's more bad news. Luke's Fiat was set on fire. He cherishes that car. It was a gift from his dad ten years ago."

A long sigh came over the phone. "They've upped the ante, Cait. Some serious business is going on there."

"It became serious when that body was found in the winery."

After the call ended, Cait sat on the kitchen floor, drew Niki closer, and pulled a treat from her pocket for him as she pondered RT's call. Something was definitely up with him, she thought. Two calls in one day had never happened before.

Her phone beeped.

Shep's number showed on the screen. "Hi," she answered.

"What are you doing next Monday?"

She rose and perched on a stool at the counter. "Uh...I don't know. Recovering after the end of another play. Why?"

"That's when my vacation starts," he said. "'Use it or lose it,' the boss said. If it's not convenient for you, I can always play more golf at Pebble Beach. I've got a couple of friends who will be there."

Happy at the thought of seeing Shep again, she said, "Please come. The play ends Sunday afternoon. After that, I'm free. Unless you want to come sooner to see the matinee."

"Can't. Got stuff to clear up before I leave and my reservations are made. I'll be staying at the Hilton in Livermore. That way your boyfriend won't get any crazy ideas about us."

"RT's not here. He's in San Diego, awaiting orders for his next mission. And FYI, he's a *friend*." *Uh, maybe a tad more.*

"Sure. If you say so. I'll call when I get there. In the meantime, don't do anything I wouldn't do."

She grinned. "That gives me a lot of latitude, Shep."

"You take care now," he said and disconnected the call.

Cait went to the freezer, took out a frozen chicken dinner, set it in the microwave, and grabbed a foil-wrapped chocolate ball from a dish on the counter while she waited. Marcus had recently started bringing chocolates to work and would leave them in plain sight to tempt her. She knew this because he thought she'd lost weight worrying about everyone else instead of herself. Her mindset as a cop was to protect and serve, something she never took lightly to this day.

When her dinner was ready, she peeled back the plastic and tested it with a fork to see if it was cooked through. Satisfied, she grabbed a bottle of water from the fridge, more chocolate and, along with Niki, went upstairs to her bedroom, determined to read up on the viticulture materials she'd temporarily abandoned last month when someone had tried to kill her.

The sun was slipping below the horizon as Cait settled on her chaise to read while she ate. Niki settled on the floor next to books from her class. Admittedly, the vineyard didn't interest Cait as much as the Shakespearean theaters. Although Ohio was home to good grapes and fine wine, and nothing beat a relaxing day exploring Ohio's beautiful countryside dotted with rolling vineyards—and sampling the fruits of their bounties—she had not taken advantage of the tours when she lived there. Never could she have imagined she'd end up owning a vineyard, but now that she did she needed to take classes, join a local vintner group RT had recommended, and immerse herself in whatever it took to produce the best grapes she could. Failure was not an option.

When Cait finished eating, she read over what she'd highlighted during class. Soon the book slipped from her hand as she struggled to stay awake. She lost the battle, but only for a minute when a loud noise jolted her awake. She jumped up to her feet, knocking her book to the floor, the room now in total darkness. She reached out for Niki but couldn't find him. "Niki!"

When he didn't respond, she reached for the lamp next to the chaise and turned it on. Niki stood at the window, his paws on the windowsill, a low growl emanating from him.

"What is it, Niki? What did you hear?" She cupped her hands against the window and tried to see the driveway three stories below. There were no streetlights on the country road and no moon to help her see.

A loud bang erupted.

Niki barked.

Heart pounding, Cait jumped away from the glass, recognizing a gunshot, and how vulnerable she was standing in front of the window.

She kneeled and peered over the windowsill as headlights lit up the driveway.

A lone figure stood in front of a car with a shotgun in his hand. Cait assumed her light had drawn the person's attention when he glanced up at her window. When he turned his back to her, he shot several rounds right into the vineyard, as if he were making a statement for her benefit.

*Good grief! Who is this idiot? Why is he shooting into the vineyard?*

Unsure if the Dispatch Center could receive cell phone calls from outside the city limits, she ran to the desk and used the landline to call nine-one-one.

"Livermore police. What is your emergency?"

"Someone is in my driveway shooting into the vineyard!" She gave her name, location, and what little she knew to the dispatcher.

After she was assured police were on their way, she turned the lamp off and stood at the side of the window. She squinted to see if the car was still there. If it was, the headlights had been turned off, making it nearly impossible for her to see.

"What's he waiting for? Why doesn't he leave?"

Niki looked up at her.

"It's okay. Help is on the way."

Cait thought she heard sirens. She squinted enough to

see the car turn around and quickly disappear into the night. She hurried down the stairs, still in her jeans and T-shirt, and unlocked the privacy door. She cautiously stepped onto the second floor and then continued to the first floor, ready to open the door when the police arrived.

Cait didn't recognize either police officer. She stepped out onto the porch, her hand resting on Niki's back.

"Are you Ms. Pepper?"

"Yes," Cait said. "You just missed him."

She didn't want to go into detail about what had happened at Sadie and Luke's winery or about the men she assumed were responsible for the shooting. She'd rather call Detective Rook in the morning. "My bedroom is up there—" She pointed. "—on the top floor. I heard a loud noise, turned on a light, and looked out the window. The light caught his attention and he looked up at me. That's when he started shooting."

The officer studied Cait, as if waiting for her to explain why anyone would do such a thing. "Did you call the sheriff's department?"

"No. I didn't think about it." *Don't give me any guff about city versus county law enforcement. Been there, done that.*

"We'll have a look around, ma'am, but there's not much we can do at this time."

"I understand. Thanks for coming."

June and Jim Hart ran from around the side of the house, dressed in their street clothes. "We heard sirens. What's going on?" Jim asked.

"Someone decided it would be fun to shoot up the vineyard," Cait said. "You heard the gun shots?"

"No. We heard sirens and then saw flashing lights," June said.

"Damn! I'll bet it's those same men I saw in front of the house," Jim said.

"That's what I'm thinking."

The officers returned. "Your vineyard is off the beaten

path. I think someone intentionally came up here to scare
you. Any idea who that could be?"

A sudden chill coursed through her body in the cool
night air. "It's complicated," she said. "If you don't mind,
I'd rather call Detective Rook in the morning instead of going into detail. He's working on a case that might have bear-
ing on this incident."

The officers nodded. "Understood. You have a good
night."

After the officers left, June frowned. "Cait, why would
you be targeted for something you had nothing to do with?"

Cait shook her head. "Good question."

# Chapter 10

Cait returned to her bedroom, all thoughts of reading her viticulture book gone. Instead, she sat at the desk and opened her laptop. When the original name of Sadie and Luke's winery eluded her, she typed in Turtle Creek, the name they had changed it to after they bought it. As she scrolled down the page, her hopes lifted when she found a link about the winery's history. Scanning the page, she saw Spring Haven Winery, the original name, and clicked on it.

Cait hoped to find a clue as to why the Harpers sold the winery after only two years. Maybe they also inherited a problem when they purchased the winery, perhaps a financial situation that had never been resolved. She skimmed the details about the winery and found the property consisted of seven acres planted in cabernet, chardonnay, and petite sirah grapes; produced 3,000 cases of wine per year; and had a 990 square foot winery building and an 800 square foot storage building. A picture of the 2,200 square foot country-style house reminded Cait of the first time she'd seen Sadie standing on the wrap-around porch. The glow on Sadie's face had been as bright as the morning sun.

Cait continued clicking links, hoping to find a hint of suspicion clouding the winery's history. All she found were praises for the wines, and how every time a bottle was opened, it was a different experience and pleasant surprise. Cait had yet to try any of the Sloanes' wines, but she certainly would now.

She yawned and glanced at the time on the screen: eleven-forty. Tomorrow was Friday. Ray Stoltz would be early, arriving ahead of the actors. She wanted to be ready so she could let him in the theater. However, she wasn't willing to give up the search just yet. She stretched and then sat up straight in her chair. Five more minutes, she promised herself, then I'll go to bed.

Cait tapped a few keys and found Pamela Harper's Facebook page. She wanted another look at the pictures of the siblings celebrating ownership of their winery. As she scrolled, she carefully scrutinized the photos. She remembered there was one man who appeared in most of the pictures. Not Pamela's brother, Vince. Perhaps a friend? Or someone in partnership with the Harpers? Cait's eyelids began to droop. Reluctantly, she closed her laptop. *Questions for another day*, she thought.

☙☞☙

Cait dragged herself out of bed the next morning, feeling less than energetic, but confident a hot shower would shake off the cobwebs. The Shakespeare festival and local college students would need her full attention. She enjoyed being around young adults. She'd been a School Resource Officer at a local high school in Columbus, Ohio, spending lots of time on campus being accessible to students and school administrators. She'd also been a resource within the school district for questions related to juvenile law, substance abuse, and school safety.

She glanced at the clock and decided seven wasn't too early to find Detective Rook at his desk. She wanted to let him know about last night's shooting.

"Good morning, Cait," Rook said. "What's got you up so early?"

Cait sat on the edge of the bed. "A shooting last night." As she explained what had happened, she heard a deep intake of breath from the other end of the line.

"The situation isn't going to go away, is it?" he asked.

"I never thought it would, not after Luke's car was set on fire. That was personal. What are we going to do about it?"

"The *police* will look into it while you run your festival. Did the officers find anything when they were there?"

"No. It was too dark. They assumed I was intentionally targeted," she said. "I told them I'd call you this morning because it involved an ongoing investigation."

"Did you get the officers' names?"

"No. Sorry."

"I'll pull the report and stop by later."

Cait set her cell phone on the bedside table and headed to the bathroom. *Dang it. How can I help Sadie and Luke?* She didn't think they were financially secure enough to recover from a scandal involving their winery.

❦

Cait followed the smell of freshly brewed coffee as she walked into the kitchen. Marcus was sitting at the counter leafing through the *Independent* newspaper, a hot cup of java at hand. "Good morning, Marcus. Aren't you a little early?" She opened the back door to let Niki out.

He glanced up at the big round clock on the wall. "Nope. It's eight. Wasn't sure I'd be on time. I had to stop by the retirement center in Tracy to check on my mom. The staff wants her moved into the assisted living building, but she refuses. They wanted me to convince her it's for her own good."

"I'm sorry. Is her health failing?"

"They think so. She falls. Is more confused as time goes

on. I guess we'll see how it goes. I'll talk to them more about it later." He sighed as if exhausted, folded the paper, and then slowly stood and turned toward his office behind the kitchen. "Those college kids will be here about noon," he said over his shoulder. "Grace Bishop called to ask if it was okay. I don't see why they shouldn't come, do you?"

Cait picked up a clean coffee mug from the table and filled it to the brim. She glanced at Marcus, who was settling into his office chair. "I'm okay with it, but there could be a problem."

Marcus swiveled in his seat and stared at her. "What do you mean?"

"Remember the black car Jim saw in the driveway, with two men inside?"

"Yeah. What about it?"

"Last night, someone thought it would be fun to shoot a gun into the vineyard. What's the possibility it was the same men?"

Marcus frowned and ran his hand through his sun-bleached hair. "You've gotta be kidding. Where were you when this happened?"

She sipped her coffee, found it too hot, and set it on the corner of his desk. "In my bedroom. I can't take the chance of those men returning while Grace and her students are here. I let Detective Rook know what happened. He said he'd come by later."

"That stinks. Why you? Because you're friends with Sadie and Luke?"

"I don't know."

Loud pounding on the back door startled Cait. She looked out the window. "Ray and Jay are here. Let's not mention what happened last night unless we have to. Ray might go ballistic." She opened the door and the brothers walked in.

Ray sniffed and smiled. "Sure smells good in here."

"Don't forget there's a new Keurig in both theaters," Cait said. She pulled her cell phone from her pocket and tapped the screen. "The Elizabethan Theater is now open."

Ray's eyebrows shot up. "I forgot about that new app."

Jay slapped his brother on the back. "You gotta keep with the times, bro. Toss your old phone and get a new one so you can get all the apps you want." He grinned at Cait. "Ray thinks change is as fun as having a tooth extraction."

Cait laughed. "He's not alone. Let me know when the actors arrive." She tested her coffee again—perfect.

On his way out the door, Ray looked back at Cait. "Those college kids coming today?"

Cait glanced at Marcus. "I think so."

Ray nodded and left.

Cait's cell phone buzzed. She glanced down and her heart skipped a beat when she saw RT's private number on the screen. "Hi," she said.

"I had a dream about you last night," he said. "You gave up your inheritance and moved back to Ohio. I called to be sure it was a dream, and you were still in California."

Cait wanted to tell him to come see for himself. Then she'd take him upstairs to prove it. Instead, she said, "I'm not going anywhere, RT."

"I'm still in San Diego. This job involves a lot of wait-ing." He hesitated. "Cait, I've given a lot of thought to us and have come to the conclusion that long distance dating sucks."

*Dating? Is that what we've been doing?*

"And I think our relationship needs to change," he continued. "You like Mindy, right?"

Heart racing, she pulled out a stool and sat down. *What's he saying?* "Of course I do, RT. She's adorable." Cait had only seen six-year old Mindy once, for about fifteen minutes when his parents stopped by on their way to Utah.

"Hang on, Cait," RT said. "My other phone's ringing."

*That could only mean one thing—the call he's been ex-pecting.* While she waited for him to return, she topped off her coffee to calm her nerves. *Was RT going to ask me what I think he was?*

"Cait. I'm sorry. I have to go now," RT said. "I'll be in touch."

Cait stared at the phone in her shaking hand.

Marcus glanced at Cait. "You okay? Is RT coming back?"

She shook her head. "He's on an assignment."

Marcus stepped closer. "You guys are in love, aren't you?"

Surprised he'd ask, she blinked. "Why would you think that?"

"I'm not blind or naïve, Cait. It's obvious. I like RT. For what it's worth, I approve." He grinned. "Go for it."

Marcus never ceased to surprise her. When least expected, he'd toss out a comment that told her he understood exactly what was going on. "Time will tell," she said. "Now, about those college kids. Call Grace Bishop. Tell her it's okay to come over today. There's enough of us here to take care of business and watch out for those kids. I'm not going to let anyone spoil our plans."

"What about the actors?"

"Same goes for them," she said. "When Detective Rook gets here, I'll see if he knows of an officer or two looking for overtime."

June tapped on the back door and then opened it. "Hi. How're you doing today, Cait? Marcus?"

Cait's mood brightened. "We're good. I'm going to grab a bite to eat and then catch up with Ray. Want to come along?"

"Yet bet. Wouldn't miss an opportunity to ruffle Ray's feathers."

"What's Jim doing?"

"Cleaning his gun."

Marcus groaned. "Why?"

"It was part of his routine when he was working security. Retirement hasn't changed that." June grinned. "Can't say things have been dull around here since we parked our RV at the Bening Estate."

"For me either," Cait said. "Everyone in my old department thinks I live the life of leisure. If they only knew." She opened the refrigerator for butter and a bagel. "Oh, by the way. My friend, Shep Church, is coming Monday. He's going to Carmel to play golf with friends, but I expect we'll see him often while he's in the area." She slit the bagel and dropped it in the toaster.

"Shep Church?" June asked. "Your friend I met on Skype?"

"Yep. I can't wait to see him."

Marcus frowned. "Is he the one who sent those mug shots last month for us to hand out?"

"That's him."

"He's a good friend?" Marcus asked.

Cait smiled. "The best. You'll like him." Her bagel popped up. "Anyone want one?" she asked.

"Not me," June and Marcus said in unison.

"Then let's go. I can eat on the way to the theater." She buttered the bagel and then opened the door and stepped outside. Niki lay sprawled on the grass in the sun.

"Cait?"

She turned back to Marcus. "What?"

"What if RT returns when your 'friend' is here?"

She stared at Marcus. So *that's* what was bothering him. "Shep and RT are my friends, Marcus. Shep mentored me when I was a rookie cop. Later, we became partners. There was never anything more to our relationship. It will be fine. You'll see." *Who knows what the future holds for RT and me.*

As Cait and June walked to the Elizabethan Theater, Cait thought about the two men and couldn't help but compare them. She knew how lucky she was to have them in her life. Shep and RT were every female's dream date: tall, handsome, with a wicked sense of humor. Both worked in law enforcement and had a serious side, but at times RT's brooding mood confused her. She tried to keep a leash on her emotions for fear of being hurt again, but couldn't. It only took the brush of his lips on hers, and she'd melt. She'd been married and that hadn't worked out. RT had responsibilities in southern California; she had responsibilities in northern California. Being a navy SEAL kept him on edge most of the time, never knowing when or where he'd be sent next. She had no idea if a serious romantic relationship was possible with RT. Still, there was no questioning the nights they spent together and the embraces they exchanged pulled her in farther and farther.

"Earth to Cait," June said.

Cait's mind snapped back to reality. "Sorry."

"A few of the actors entered the theater. Let's catch up. I know some of them. I'll introduce you."

"Can't wait." Cait took a deep breath. "Let's hope everything goes without a hitch."

# Chapter 11

I never tire of *Twelfth Night*," June said as they reached the Elizabethan Theater, "no matter how many times I was in it. I love the disguises and mistaken identities of the identical twins. Did you know the play got its name from the date of its first performance, twelfth night?"

Cait thought about that. "I vaguely remember my professor saying Twelfth Night was a festival in certain branches of Christianity, marking the coming of the Epiphany, the day when the nativity story tells us about the three wise men visiting the infant Jesus."

June clapped her hands. "Good. But in Western church traditions, the twelfth night concludes the twelve days of Christmas. Not many know or even question the name of the play."

"What's surprising to me is I studied Shakespeare in college and now have my own festival."

"There's a reason for everything, Cait. Remember that as you go through life." June opened the door to the theater. "Let's see who's here."

"It will be fun to see Toni Behren and Betsy Ryder again," Cait said, "in less serious roles this time."

"Speaking of Betsy," June said, pointing to the stage, "there she is, talking to Paula."

Cait looked up at the stage. "Paula?"

"You remember Paula Howard. She played Gertrude, Queen of Denmark and mother of Hamlet last month."

"Of course. I forgot she was returning for *Twelfth Night*."

"She wouldn't miss coming here. She loves being part of the festival. Let's go say hi." June started up the stairs.

*I need to look at the list of actors again before I thoroughly embarrass myself,* Cait thought as she followed June to the stage to greet Paula and Betsy.

Betsy beamed at them. "So fun to see you again. I absolutely adore *Twelfth Night*. No matter how many times I see it or what role I play, it's always a fun experience."

Paula grinned as she fluffed her blonde hair. "It's the promise of mystery, romance, and all the good stuff we associate with dreamy far-off places."

Cait laughed, thoroughly enjoying being with the actors. "I'm always eager for each festival to begin, especially when they're featuring my favorite plays, like this one." The curtain was pulled back and she saw Ray Stoltz in the green room in what appeared to be a serious conversation with a tall, distinguished-looking man.

June must have seen the two men also. "That's Mars DeSanto with Ray," she said. "He's argumentative and opinionated, but a great actor. He's cast as Antonio, the sea captain who protects Sebastian. Would you like to meet him?"

"Don't be too quick to judge Mars, Cait," Betsy warned. "He means well. He's just not diplomatic with his opinions. And, more often than not, he's right."

"I agree," June said. "Trust me, all is forgiven when you're partnered with him in romantic scenes."

Cait swore she saw a special shine in June's eyes. She took a harder look at the man. Tall, distinguished looking and tanned. "Introduce me."

"Be careful you don't fall under his spell," Paula warned. "Many have and lived to regret it."

"Mars," Ray said as Cait and June approached. "I don't believe you've had the pleasure of meeting Cait Pepper, Tasha Bening's niece. Cait owns this place now, so you need to be on your best behavior. She's tough." He winked at Cait then turned and walked away.

Cait stared at Ray's back. *What flattering words Ray spoke.*

Mars took Cait's hand and briefly touched it with his lips. "Pleasure to meet you, Cait. May I call you Cait? I adored Tasha." He turned to June. "I heard you were here, June. I'm delighted to see you again."

Cait noticed he didn't kiss June's hand. He kissed her on the lips. *My my,* she thought, *what would Jim think?*

Apparently flustered, June brushed a couple of stray locks back and tried to tuck them in the hair clip on top of her head. "It's nice to see you again, Mars."

Mars smiled. "No matter what anyone says, Cait, I'm harmless. Right, June?"

June drew her five-foot-three body up straighter, as if to prove she was a match for the much taller Mars. "Hmph."

Apparently, Mars had made lasting impressions on each of the women, Cait thought. His blue eyes gleamed with a mischievousness that would draw many to him.

Mars laughed. "I'll see you ladies around. I want to tour this hill-top paradise where we'll be performing." He walked off, leaving Cait wondering what had happened. *I'll have to keep my eye on Mars and June.*

രാഗ്ര

Four more actors entered the theater and joined Betsy and Paula on stage. Cait watched with interest as the group greeted and hugged each other and immediately fell into shoptalk. When her cell phone rang, she answered.

"Cait," Marcus said. "Detective Rook is here. Do you want him to meet you at the theater?"

"No. I'll be right there." She looked for June and found her in the kitchen corner. "I'm going back to the house. Detective Rook is there. Call if you need anything."

"Okay." June glanced over her shoulder. "Cait, did I make a fool of myself? I mean when Mars...uh, you know...kissed me?"

Cait would have laughed if June hadn't looked so serious. "No, of course not. He is different, isn't he?"

"Ha. Have you ever loved and hated someone at the same time?"

*Oh, dear.* "Well..."

"Never mind. Hate's too strong a word. Go see the good detective. Maybe he can shed light on the shooting incident last night. I'm going to try to make myself useful around here and meet and greet the new arrivals."

"About last night, maybe we could ask Jim to come and keep an eye on everyone," Cait said. "It might be a good idea if he had his gun with him."

"Good idea." She searched the pocket in her slacks for her phone. "Darn, I don't have it with me."

"I'll call Jim. See you later." As Cait walked to the house, she wondered if she should carry her Glock over the weekend.

Detective Rook and Marcus were talking when Cait walked in. "Sorry to drag you away from the theater," Rook said, "but I'm going to look for casings in front. Thought you might want to join me."

"Absolutely," Cait said. She glanced at Marcus. "What time is Grace Bishop coming?"

"About eleven."

"Who's Grace?" Rook asked.

"The acting instructor from Las Positas College," Cait said.

"Oh, yeah. I don't see a problem with those kids being here," Rook said. "For now, anyway." He checked his watch. "I need to get back to the station pretty quick."

Cait opened her cell phone after they were outside.

"Okay. And then I'll call Jim. I want him at the theater in case there's any trouble."

Rook raised his eyebrow. "I've got a couple of officers looking for overtime this weekend. They might be free to come today."

"I don't think that's necessary. Jim and I will be armed, but definitely have the usual contingent during the festival," Cait said.

They'd reached the front of the house. Rook glanced around and then up at the house. "You could see the shooting from the third floor window?"

"A little," she said.

Rook scooped up a few brass shell casings from the driveway and dropped them in his pocket. "It's probably futile trying to get imaging fingerprints from these, but you never know."

Cait heard a car coming up the driveway and turned to see who it was. Relieved to see Kurt Mathew's white pickup, she smiled and waved to the horticulturist. He parked in back of Detective Rook's unmarked Ford.

"Hello," Kurt said as he climbed out of his truck.

"Detective Rook, you may remember meeting Kurt last month." As the men shook hands, Cait said, "I'm still trying to convince Kurt to manage the vineyard full time, but he won't commit."

Kurt looked at Rook. "Should I be concerned you're here?"

Rook and Cait exchanged glances. Rook pointed at the vineyard. "Someone came up here last night and took shots into the vineyard." He removed casings from his pocket and showed them to Kurt. "You're sure to come across more in the vineyard."

"Why the hell would anyone do that?" Kurt asked.

"Don't know," Rook said. "I'd appreciate it if you would keep an eye on the place when you're here and report any disturbance to the police or to Cait."

"I'll bring my gun the next time."

Cait raised her eyebrows. *Seems everybody in California packs heat.*

Rook smiled. "I want the person alive."

Kurt nodded. "I'm here now to walk the rows and examine the grapes, but I'll keep watch for trouble."

"We won't keep you, Kurt," Cait said.

"I'll be on my way," Rook said. "Looks like I don't have to worry about you, Cait. You got a handle on things around here. What time's the play start tomorrow night?"

"Seven."

"Perough and Vanicheque will come at six." He got in his car and drove off.

"Geez, Cait," Kurt said. "You've got more problems than most vintners have with beetles in their vineyards."

"Lucky me. Is that why you won't commit to full time employment?"

"I'm still thinking about it."

Cait recalled there was a problem between Marcus and Kurt, but both refused to talk about it.

The sound of a motor caught Cait's attention. A white van pulled in behind Kurt's pickup. When the doors opened, Grace Bishop jumped out, along with five of her student actors.

"Hi," Grace said. "Is it okay to park here?"

"Sure, it's fine," Cait said. "I'll take you over to the theater and unlock it." She turned to see Kurt smiling as he looked at Grace. "Grace, this is Kurt Mathews. He manages the vineyard for me. Kurt, Grace and her students are from Las Positas College and will be using the Blackfriars Theater for their rehearsals."

He nodded. "Nice to meet you."

"Let's head on over there," Cait said. "See you, Kurt."

Niki bounded around the corner. Lucky, one of the students, stopped to ruffle Niki's fur.

"Come on, guys, let's unload the van," Grace said.

"The parking lot would be closer to the theater. Follow me."

Grace jumped back in the van while the students walked with Cait.

"This is a cool place," Lucky said as they walked, Niki at his heels. "You're lucky to live here and have your own theaters."

Cait looked at Lucky's serious face. "I know."

"I met Tasha once," the student named Joanna said. "She was your aunt?"

"Yes. How did you meet her?"

"She came to our class. She talked to us about following our dreams," Joanna said.

Cait recalled June and Marcus telling her how Tasha wanted to involve students from the college in her theaters. Cait hoped to follow through with the plan.

They reached the parking lot and everyone pitched in to help Grace carry boxes to the theater. Once Grace and her students were ready to rehearse, Cait and Grace exchanged phone numbers, with instructions to let Cait know when they were ready to leave.

Cait stood in the hot courtyard between the Elizabethan and Blackfriars and offered up a prayer that her troubles were over, the play would go on without a hitch, and everyone would remain safe.

Her cell phone rang. Cait stared at the screen, then took a deep breath and answered.

"Everything okay, Sadie?"

"Is this a good time for you to come over?"

"Yes. What's going on?"

"Pamela and Vince Harper are here."

# Chapter 12

Impatient to meet the Harpers, Cait felt the drive to Sadie's house was longer than the usual five minutes. She wanted answers to the questions whirling around in her head, answers that would relieve her friends of the stress they'd been under since finding a body at their winery.

Cait didn't recognize the Subaru or Lexus she parked behind in front of Turtle Creek Winery. She assumed one belonged to the Harpers. She glanced at Luke's burned car in the driveway as she approached the house and renewed her promise to find out who was behind her friends' tribulations.

"Cait!" Sadie waved to her from the porch. "Thanks for coming." She took Cait's hand and turned to the couple standing at the porch railing with Luke. "Pamela, Vince, this is Cait Pepper, a dear friend of mine. Cait has a vineyard not far from here."

Cait studied the siblings as she shook Pamela's hand. *They look like movie stars.* Blond, blue eyes, tall, tanned, late thirties or early forties. Pamela wore white jeans and a pink sleeveless blouse. Vince was dressed in tight jeans and a white sports shirt. He wore a pair of ear buds, the wires disappearing in his collar.

"I don't shake hands," Vince said, a hard line of arrogance evident behind a lazy smile.

"And this is Holly Gardner, our realtor," Sadie added.

*So that's who the other car belongs to*, Cait thought.

"Let's sit on the porch," Luke said, "if that's okay. Cait, help yourself to the iced tea Sadie prepared."

Cait didn't want tea. She wanted to get on with the situation at hand, but she poured herself a glass when she saw the others already had theirs.

When she was seated, Luke leaned forward. "To catch you up, we explained to Holly and the Harpers what's happened since we bought the winery. Vince and Pamela deny knowing anything about it or who the dead guy found in the winery might be. That's as far as we got before you arrived."

Cait wished Detective Rook was there. She'd prefer to sit back and observe while the Harpers explained their part, if any, in the situation her friends found themselves in. "Is Detective Rook coming?"

"I left a voice mail," Luke said. "Haven't heard back from him yet."

Cait nodded. She sipped her tea, set the glass on the table next to her, and then turned to the Harpers. "This is a lovely winery. I'm curious why you sold it."

The siblings glanced at each other. "Vince and I bought the winery with the intention of the family taking over the business one day," Pamela said. "One generation passing the torch to the other. Like our Uncle Calvin did." She hesitated. "Selling was a difficult decision. We love Livermore. It's a great place to grow grapes, raise a family, but it's a lot of work to keep up a vineyard and my brother gets bored easily. Isn't that right, Vince?"

He adjusted his ear bud. "Yeah, I get restless when I'm tied down to any one place for too long. It was time to move on, at least for me."

Cait thought he sounded like a spoiled brat. Thinking of the dead PI, she wondered if Vince was capable of murder.

"I get that, but when you have a passion for something, the work can be fun. That's what my dad always told me."

"I guess," Vince said.

"How about you, Pamela. Are you the restless type?"

Pamela pursed her lips and frowned. "No, but Vince and I entered this venture together. Something new to try."

Cait watched her closely. "I thought you and your brother grew up helping your uncle with *his* vineyard."

The siblings stared at Cait. Vince tugged on his shirt collar. "How did you know?"

"The web's available to anyone who has an interest in searching it." *Let them figure out what else I might know.*

"I don't understand," Pamela said. "Why the interest in us?"

Cait glanced at Holly, who'd kept silent so far. "Sadie and Luke are my friends. I care about them, and I'll do whatever I can to help clear up what's going on here. I'm sure you would do the same for your friends."

"We're sorry for their problems," Pamela said, "but they bought the winery and what happened later has nothing to do with us. I'm not even sure why Holly tracked us down and asked us to come here today, but if you or anyone else try to blame us, think again." She stood.

*Or what*, Cait thought. *You'd sue?*

"Pamela," Holly said. "Please sit down. This needs to be sorted out. Sadie and Luke bought this winery in good faith, and no one is blaming you for anything, but I'm sure if you were in their shoes you'd want to know what's going on." She moved to the edge of her seat. "What about enemies? Any reason why someone would come after you, like for unpaid debts and finding the Sloane's instead?"

*Bravo, Holly Gardner*, Cait thought.

"No!" Pamela refilled her glass and took a long drink.

Cait noticed Pamela's hand shaking and her eyes watering, as if she were about to cry. She felt sorry for her, but Cait's dad had always told her to listen to her instincts. Pamela knew something, but was afraid to talk about it.

What could it be? Then Cait remembered the other man in those celebration photos on Pamela's Facebook page and wondered who he was.

"We should go," Vince said and started to stand.

Cait wasn't ready to let them go. She still had questions that needed to be answered and this could be her only chance to ask. "Pamela, were you and Vince the only owners of this winery?"

Pamela glared at Cait. "What do you mean?"

Cait smiled to lighten her question. "I was nosy and looked at your Facebook page. One man appeared in many of the pictures posted celebrating your ownership of the winery. I wondered if he'd also bought into the winery, like a partner."

"Oh. No. He's…a friend."

Cait forced a smile. "I haven't been in Livermore long, and it's my intention to meet as many of the vintners as I can. I'm sorry you left before I had a chance to get to know you. Do you mind if I ask what your plans are now? Will you stay in Livermore?"

Again, the siblings exchanged glances.

"We haven't decided," Pamela said.

*This is going nowhere.* "If the police need to contact you, where can they reach you? It would be helpful if you left your phone numbers with Sadie and Luke. Sadie, do you have a pad and pen?"

"Sure. I'll get them."

"Use mine," Holly offered, as she pulled a pen and pad from her purse.

Vince jumped up. "The police? I knew we shouldn't have come here today."

The hard look Pamela gave Vince didn't escape Cait. When Pamela finished writing, she returned the pad and pen to Holly.

"Our cell numbers are on there." Pamela stood. "There's nothing more to say."

Cait also rose, thinking hard how to detain them longer.

"The friend on your Facebook looks familiar. Would you mind telling me his name?"

"You wouldn't know him. He's not from around here. Let's go, Vince."

Cait, Sadie, Luke, and Holly leaned against the porch railing and watched Vince and Pamela climb into the Subaru and tear down the lane.

"I'm sorry," Holly said. "I'd hoped the Harpers would be more forthcoming and offer a suggestion as to why you're being targeted."

"It's okay, Holly," Sadie said. "At least we have their cell phone numbers. We'll pass them on to Detective Rook."

"It's not okay, Sadie," Cait said. "They were nervous because they're hiding something. Have you searched the house or the winery to see if they accidentally left anything behind?"

Sadie shook her head. "I've only done general cleaning."

"What exactly should we be looking for?" Luke asked.

Cait shrugged. "Papers, anything with a name on it we could track down."

"You're still thinking about that man on her Facebook page," Luke said.

"Guilty." Cait said. "It's a long shot, but worth checking, because it was obvious she didn't want to talk about him."

"Oh," Sadie said. "There is a toy rabbit."

Cait raised her eyebrows. "Do you still have it?"

"Yes. I didn't know what to do with it. I'll be right back." She hurried into the house.

"She didn't tell me about any rabbit," Luke said.

Sadie came back out. "Here it is." She opened a plastic bag, pulled out the rabbit, and handed it to Cait. "I found it in the space beneath the stairs when I put our luggage away."

Cait briefly examined the rabbit, noticed one chewed ear, and then returned it to Sadie.

"I should have asked Pamela if she wanted it back," Sadie said.

"You can ask the next time you talk to her." Cait reached into her pocket for her keys. "I should go. Try calling Detective Rook again if he doesn't get back to you soon."

"Thanks for coming," Luke said. "We'll try not to bother you again, unless the winery goes up in flames."

"Please, no more drama. I'm glad you asked me to come. It was interesting." She waved and hurried down the driveway.

∽∾∽

The tension Cait had felt the whole time she was at Sadie's slowly drained away when she returned home. Niki met her in front of the garage, tail wagging, and waited while Cait pulled her car inside. As soon as she stepped out of the car, Niki jumped up on her. Cait gave the dog a big hug, and they walked together around to the back of the house.

Inside, Marcus was cleaning the coffee pot. "You were gone awhile. Learn anything new?"

Cait sank down on one of the stools at the counter, exhausted. "I don't know. The Harpers were reluctant to talk, but they know more than they were willing to tell. Are you leaving?"

He nodded. "I have to stop by my mom's. The group from the college left, but they'll be back in the morning. Ray, the actors, and June and Jim, are still at the Elizabethan. I think Ray was looking for you."

Cait nodded. She didn't know what she would do if it were not for Marcus. They'd come a long way in a short time in understanding each other. His devotion to Tasha had been rock solid. When Cait came along, he'd been reluctant to change. "Have I told you lately how much I appreciate what you do around here?"

His lip hitched up a little in a half smile. "It's my job."

"It's more than a job to me, Marcus."

Someone knocked on the door. Marcus opened it, letting Ray and the Harts in on his way out.

"The wanderer has returned," Ray said.

"Sorry I had to run out like that," Cait said. "Everything okay?"

Ray wiped his brow with his sleeve. "Surprisingly, yes. You can lock up. We'll return tomorrow. What about those kids? Are they coming back?"

"In the morning, I think," Cait said. "I'd like to introduce Grace Bishop to a couple of the actors."

Ray shuffled his feet, a flustered look on his face. "Sure. Why not? What do you know about Lucky?"

*Ah. So Ray already knows one of their names.* "I know Lucky is serious about acting as a profession. And he loves dogs. Why?"

"Seems like a good kid. I gotta go. See you tomorrow."

"Ray likes those kids," Jim said as soon as Ray was out the door.

June grinned. "That's a side of Ray most people never see. Told you he was a softy at heart." She headed for the door and then turned back. "Oh, Marcus said you rushed out of here to meet the people Sadie and Luke bought their winery from. Did you learn anything that might be helpful in solving the mystery behind the dead guy?"

"They denied knowing anything about him or anything else, but they're lying." Cait told them how uptight Vince and Pamela appeared to be and their reaction to her questions. "I had more questions, but didn't want to come on too strong and scare them off. They didn't stay long as it was."

Jim smiled. "I bet you were a great interrogator when you were a cop."

"I'd like to think so. I probably won't sleep tonight thinking about what I should have asked while I had the chance."

"Don't lose sleep over it, Cait," June said. "'We are such

stuff as dreams are made on, and our little life is rounded with a sleep.'" She smiled. "Shakespeare was not of an age, but for all time."

# Chapter 13

Cait was in bed by ten, but try as she might, sleep wouldn't come. What June had said about Shakespeare being not of a particular age but for all time swirled around in Cait's head. She'd read those words of praise for Shakespeare before, but couldn't remember who'd said them. The central themes in most of his plays were universal: lust, greed, ambition, jealousy, and other basic human emotions. Cait stared at the ceiling and thought about the attitude of birthright in the modern day compared to Shakespeare's day. Then she thought of Sadie's strict upbringing in her Amish community and the pressure on her to always be perfect.

Sadie's father, a buggy and harness maker in Sugarcreek, Ohio, shunned his daughter, as had the rest of their community, after she left them for what the Amish call the English world to continue her education. She'd gotten her degree in psychology and then met and married the man of her dreams, Luke Sloane. Twelve years later, Sadie and Luke were living Luke's dream of owning a winery—until turmoil disrupted their lives.

Cait rolled over and bumped into the familiar weight of Niki, who often slept on the other side of the bed. The comfort of having the dog next to her helped relieve the loneliness she often felt during RT's absences. Comforted, she finally slept.

కించి

Marcus walked in the back door at eight-fifteen Saturday morning as Cait and Niki entered the kitchen. He also had an app on his cell phone to open the house and the theaters. Then Niki raced outside as the door was closing. "Accident on the Altamont," Marcus said. "A semi jack-knifed and almost went over the rail trying to avoid slamming into another truck. I'm thinking of getting a motorcycle. At least then I can maneuver on the lane lines."

Cait smiled as she tried to visualize Marcus in leather, balancing a bike on a narrow strip between other vehicles, but couldn't. A helmet would muss his hair. She plugged in the coffee pot. "Maybe you should reconsider."

He stopped at his office door and looked at her. "Why?"

"They're dangerous."

"So is walking across the street."

She knew he was right, but she'd had a boyfriend who'd been killed on a motorcycle, so always looked askance at their value as transportation.

Her cell phone rang. She checked the screen and saw Detective Rook's name. "Good morning, Detective."

"Morning, Cait. What did you think of Vince and Pamela Harper?"

She set out a mug for her coffee. "They're guilty of something, but probably not murder."

"Why do you say that?"

"They're scared," she said. "I'm surprised you weren't there."

"Unavoidable. I did talk to Luke this morning, and he told me you're a good interrogator. *That* I wish I'd seen. No wonder they were scared."

"Aren't you funny this morning? They left before I barely got started with the questions." She poured coffee into her cup and sipped. "Vince nearly jumped out of his boots when I mentioned the police. You might check if he has a record. Anyway, Holly Gardner, the Sloane's realtor, has their cell numbers. You should call them before they leave town for good."

"Now why didn't I think of that?" he said.

Cait loved telling Rook the obvious. She always got the expected answer. "So, what now? Sit and wait to see if anything else happens? I've got a busy day ahead. The college kids will be here this morning, and then the actors. If you've never seen *Twelfth Night*, I'll let you in for free tonight. Policeman's special."

"Is that a fact?"

Cait smiled when she saw Marcus standing in the doorway rolling his eyes.

"Seriously, Rook, what are your plans for my friends? Their winery is tucked away at the end of the lane with only one neighbor. Shouldn't they have protection? What if those men in the black car decide to pay them another visit and shoot their way in?"

"I can't leave an officer standing guard at their winery *in case* something happens," he said. "I trust Luke to call nine-one-one if things get out of hand. Do you know if he has a gun?"

"God, it seems like everyone in California carries a weapon. No, I don't know, and I hope he doesn't."

"In the US, guns are used eighty times more often to protect a life than to take one."

"I'm familiar with the statistics, Rook, but they're my friends. There was a dead body in their winery, and Luke's car was set on fire. How much more can they take? If Luke has a gun, he could accidentally shoot someone to protect what's his. I'd hate to see that happen."

"That's a possibility the police will try to keep from happening," Rook said, "but we need something to follow up on. You should understand that."

She did. "Will you call the Harpers and talk to them?"

"Sure. I know Holly Gardner, the Sloanes' realtor. I'll get the phone numbers from her. Enjoy your festival. I'll be in touch."

Cait's coffee had gone tepid, so she topped it off. "Was I too tough on Detective Rook?" she asked Marcus.

He pointed his finger at himself. "You're asking *me*? My association with the police has been prickly at best, you know."

Cait grinned. "You're reformed, Marcus. You wouldn't dare cause trouble while working for me. And Detective Rook admires how you've turned your life around. No need to fear him or any of the officers that come here."

"Whatever." He walked back to his office.

Ray's face appeared in the window as he tapped on the back door. When Cait opened it, he said, "Top of the morning to you, Caitie!"

"Goodness, what's gotten into you, Ray?" she said. "Makes me suspicious."

"That's because you were once a cop," he said. "Cops are suspicious people. The sun is hotly shining, the hills are golden, the birds are tweeting their heads off, and another festival is upon us. What's not to like?"

*Whoa, now I am seriously worried.* "How poetic, Ray." She glanced at his brother Jay, who'd followed him in. "Is he sick?"

Jay tucked his hands into the pockets of his coveralls. "Nah, he'll settle down before the play starts tonight, back to his usual grouchy self. Can you open the Elizabethan Theater for us? I have to mend a few costumes."

Cait smiled, thinking of big Jay sewing on the ancient machine in the theater's loft. "Should I replace that relic of a sewing machine?"

He shook his head. "It still works."

Cait picked up her smart phone and tapped the screen a couple of times. "The theater's open. If you need anything, let me know." She glanced at the wall clock and then at

Ray. "I expect the college kids will be here soon, but they won't bother you or get in your way."

"I could teach them a thing or two, you know, about staging," he said. "Lucky seemed interested."

"I think he's interested in everything having to do with the theater," Cait said.

Ray's cell phone rang. He dug it out of his shirt pocket, glanced at the screen, and then answered it. "It's open. I'm with Cait. Be there shortly." He slipped his phone back in his pocket. "Actors are too impatient. Let's go, Jay."

June came in the door as Ray walked out. She carried a dish. "Saved you a pork chop from last night."

"Thanks." Cait was hungry enough to eat it for breakfast, but put it in the refrigerator for later and dropped a bagel into the toaster instead. "Ray's chipper this morning. I'm thinking of inviting the students here every month there's a play if it would help improve his attitude."

June laughed. "Maybe he wants to teach those kids the tricks of the trade of managing theaters." She hesitated. "Cait, Jim will be over in a little while. Not that we expect trouble, but in case those men in that suspicious car turn up again he'll be prepared to confront them. He felt bad he didn't get their license plate the first time."

"Why would they come back here?" Cait asked.

"Why did they set fire to Luke's car or murder that guy in the winery?" June countered.

"I intend to find out." Cait's bagel popped up. "Want one? Coffee?"

June removed the clip that kept her hair up in a knot on top of her head and shook her hair out. "No thanks. I thought I'd open the gift shop and take inventory. If business is brisk this evening, we may need to reorder for next month." She rewound her hair, tucking in loose strands, and reclipped it at the nape of her neck.

"The key's under the wine barrel by the door," Cait said. "Fumié and Ilia are coming over this morning. I think Ilia's going to handle sales before the play while Fumié entertains our guests. She'll stroll around as she sings and plays the guitar, like she did last month."

Cait hadn't seen Fumié Ondo for a couple of weeks while she attended to her mother. A graduate of the University of California at Davis, her dream of becoming a park ranger had been on hold during her mother's bout with cancer.

"We'll miss Fumié when she goes to Santa Rosa to the park ranger school," June said.

"So will Ilia." Ilia Kubiak, a local professional photographer, and Fumié had become inseparable, and Cait loved watching the slow progression of their relationship.

"'Love looks not with the eyes, but with the mind, and therefore is winged Cupid painted blind.'" June smiled. "*Midsummer Night's Dream.*"

"I don't believe that's entirely true," Cait said. "Most of us are interested in appearance. That's infatuation. True love is in the heart, the mind, and the soul." *Is that what I feel for RT?*

"Then why is Cupid painted blind?" June asked.

"Okay. Maybe it's partly true."

"That I can agree with," June said. "I have to go. Can I borrow your electronic notebook for the inventory?"

"Sure. I left it on the counter in the gift shop."

June nodded. "I'll run over to the Elizabethan Theater after I finish the inventory."

Cait let Niki in while she ate her bagel and downed another cup of coffee. She'd forgotten about Marcus until she heard him in his office pounding on the keyboard at his computer. "What are you doing?" she asked from the doorway.

He stopped typing. "Answering emails. Did you know the remaining plays for this season are sold out?"

"Honestly, I haven't given it much thought. We've always had a full house. I hope it continues to sell out."

"Would you consider scheduling a play for the middle of the week to accommodate more people?"

She leaned against the doorframe. "I don't think so, Marcus. One weekend a month is as much as I can handle. I'm not a pro at this, you know. I inherited this business. And don't forget the vineyard or the viticulture classes I need to attend. I have to understand how to cultivate grapes if I'm going to keep the vineyard producing. There's only me. I don't have a partner."

Marcus stared at Cait with a raised eyebrow.

*Oh, dear. I forgot to follow up after I asked him if he was interested in learning about the vineyard.* She stepped into the office and stood beside his desk. "Marcus, would you like to share vineyard responsibilities with Kurt Mathews? You could learn a lot from him and also take viticulture classes at Las Positas College."

Red crept up his neck. "That's not possible."

"Why not?"

"He knows about my prison record."

"So? What's that got to do with growing grapes?" she asked.

"He doesn't trust me."

She smiled. "I do, and I'm the boss."

He shook his head. "It wouldn't work."

She leaned closer. "Will you think about it?"

"I've *been* thinking about it."

"Good. It's a start. We'll talk about it later. I'm going to the theater. If you see Grace Bishop, unlock the Blackfriars Theater for them."

She gathered her cell phone and left the house, with Niki at her side. She'd gone as far as the gate to the theater compound when she heard her name called.

"Cait, wait up."

She turned to see Jim heading toward her. "If you're looking for June, she's at the gift shop."

"I wanted to see you. I'm carrying." He raised the back of his T-shirt enough to expose his gun. "I doubt anything will happen, but I'm prepared."

Cait hadn't planned on carrying her gun until she dressed for the play, but, seeing Jim's gun, she reconsidered. *Better safe than sorry.*

Laughter caught their attention. Cait turned to see Grace and her students coming toward her.

"Those students are another reason to be armed," Jim said. "You're responsible for their safety while they're on your property."

She nodded. "I know. What is it about this festival that attracts the wrong kind of attention?" She took out her cell phone and unlocked the Blackfriars Theater.

"Hi, Cait," Grace said as she approached.

Cait smiled. "Hi. The theater's unlocked. Let me know when you're ready to leave so I can lock it back up."

"I will. Thanks."

"Grace, I haven't forgotten about introducing you to the actors," Cait said. "I'll let them know you'd like to meet them."

"I don't want to interfere, but that would be great."

"It's a good thing you're doing," Jim said after the students entered the theater, "allowing them to use the theater."

"What good's an empty theater? Anyway, I like being around students. I learn from them." Cait started across the courtyard as her phone rang. She hoped it was Detective Rook calling to let her know he'd talked with Pamela or Vince Harper. Instead, it was RT.

Her heart skipped a beat as she sat on the low wall surrounding the courtyard. "RT, hi."

"Hey. I think I can come up next week if it's okay with you."

*More than okay.* "Of course it is."

"How's everything with Sadie and Luke?"

"They're managing," she said. "I met Pamela and Vince Harper. They sold the winery to Sadie and Luke." She told him about the meeting and how reluctant the Harpers were to talk about the sale. She briefly mentioned the toy rabbit.

"At least they were willing to meet. I called to let you

know there's a chance I can come up. I'll try to call later.
Gotta go."

Excitement raced through her body. *RT's coming next
week!* Then she remembered Shep. *He'll be here Monday.
RT and Shep are bound to cross paths.*

# Chapter 14

When Cait entered the Elizabethan Theater, she heard loud voices and instruments being tuned. She hesitated, not wanting to interrupt, but Ray caught sight of her and motioned her up to the stage.

"Where's a professional handyman when you need one?" Ray said as Cait climbed the stairs. He had a string of cords draped over one shoulder while trying to untangle two others. "Who the hell left these cords in this mess?"

She wanted to laugh at Ray and the mess of wires, but thought it might provoke him further. "Probably your own guys, Ray," Cait said. "What seems to be the problem?"

"Safety! A huge issue when the actors have to walk over cords strung all over the floor to reach an outlet."

Cait glanced around looking for a technician. "What happened to the guys who usually work with you?"

"Damned if I know," he said.

Cait pulled her phone from her pocket. "I'll call Jim. I'm sure he can help straighten the cords out." After she'd explained the problem to Jim, she turned back to Ray. "Jim will be here in a minute, but don't yell at him like you did me."

"I don't yell," Ray snarled.

The door to the theater opened and Jim slipped inside.

He smiled at Ray when he reached the stage. "Looks like you're in a bit of a bind."

"Hmph. Help me sort this mess out and then see why the electrical outlet behind the curtain doesn't work."

Cait backed away and left them on their own. She knew Jim could calm Ray's blustery manner.

Betsy Ryder walked over and laid her hand on Cait's arm. "How familiar are you with *Twelfth Night*?"

"Oh, it's one of my favorite plays," Cait said. "Rich in poetry and music. I'm excited to see it tonight, particularly since this will be the first time we'll have musicians in the orchestra pit."

Betsy smiled. "I don't know if you know this, but Tasha saw *Twelfth Night* at the Lake Tahoe Shakespeare Festival about eight years ago and was inspired enough to duplicate that version of the play for her own festival. Many of us saw it and loved it. This particular production begins with the famous quote, 'If music be the food of love, play on,' and ends with Feste singing 'For the Rain, it Raineth Everyday.' The music choices were carefully chosen for each scene, most likely different from what you've probably heard before."

"Now you've got my attention. I can't wait to see it," Cait said.

"I need to go," Betsy said, "but let's talk later. I'd like your opinion of the play." She slipped away to join a small group of people on the other side of the stage.

Jim came up to Cait. "That was an easy fix. Ray's more impatient than the actors."

Relieved there wasn't a last minute major crisis, Cait looked across the stage at Ray on his knees holding a roll of duct tape. Curious, she asked, "What was the problem with the outlet? Hadn't he plugged the cord in the right way?"

"Something like that—"

A sudden burst of music filled the outdoor theater. Startled, Cait moved to the side of the stage and out of the way of the actors.

Jim laughed. "Wow that was great. Even I recognized the music from Eleanor Rigby."

"Betsy Ryder warned me the music would be different," Cait said. "I think I'm going to love this new version."

The music slowed and then went into a short version of the Beatles' "Fool on the Hill." Cait watched and listened as it segued from one song to another, building her anticipation to an even higher level. Immersed in the moment, Cait was unaware June had joined them until she spoke.

"What do you think, Cait?" June asked. "Isn't the music fun and exciting? Tasha knew what she was doing when she suggested this version of *Twelfth Night* for her own festival."

"You knew? Why didn't you tell me?"

June rested her hand on Cait's shoulder. "Because I wanted you to be surprised."

"I was," Cait said. "Betsy explained a little, but I had no idea it would be so powerful."

"What's different, from what you'll see here and what's played in Lake Tahoe, is a few of the actors sat on the side of the stage and mimed a string quartet performance on two-dimensional cutouts of musical instruments."

"You saw the play at Lake Tahoe?"

June laughed. "Of course. Most of us have."

"Cait?" a soft voice called to her.

She turned to see Sadie standing at the foot of the stairs. Afraid another incident had happened at Turtle Creek Winery, Cait rushed down the stairs. "Sadie, what's wrong?"

Sadie smiled. "Nothing. I wanted out of the house for a bit. Luke is so distressed over his Fiat I decided to give him space to vent his anger. I hope I'm not interrupting."

Relieved, Cait smiled. "No, of course not."

"Okay if I watch? I heard a little of the music when I came in. Luke and I are looking forward to the play tonight."

"Let's sit over here," Cait said, as she led Sadie a couple of rows back.

They talked softly as they watched the actors on stage.

"What's it like running your own Shakespeare festival?" Sadie asked.

"I imagine it's much like owning your own winery. Not all fun and games. There's the business end of it, but so far I've left most of that up to Marcus. My aunt Tasha had a three-year plan and scheduled the actors and plays. If she hadn't done that, there wouldn't be a festival. I don't know what will happen at the end of three years."

Sadie was quiet for a few minutes. "I don't know what will happen if Luke and I lose the winery," she said, finally. "He isn't as worried as I am, but I'm afraid the other wineries around here will shun us if they think we're involved in a murder investigation. Our reputation is at stake."

Never one to be overly concerned about what neighbors thought, as long as she knew she'd done nothing wrong, Cait tried to put herself in Sadie's place, where quilting and baking were the only creative avenues open for women in the Amish community. Shunned by her people, Sadie persevered until she'd accomplished her goal—getting a degree. If she could leave her family, her church, her humble upbringing, she could survive the threat to the winery. Cait wasn't sure she could have done as well herself.

"Detective Rook called before I left to come here. He wanted us to know he met with Pamela and Vince at the police station," Sadie said. "He didn't say much about how it went, except he agreed with you—they know more than they're letting on."

"I'll give him a call. Maybe I can get more information. At least, the Harpers haven't left town yet. If they were running, they'd be gone by now."

"That's what I thought," Sadie said. "Luke wasn't so sure. He doesn't trust them."

Cait and Sadie spent a few minutes watching the actors until Cait remembered Grace and her students were at the Blackfriars Theater. "Sadie, I need to have a word with a couple of the actors. I won't be long."

Cait ran into June backstage. "Grace wants to meet the actors. Do you think Betsy and Paula would mind if I brought her over?"

June grinned. "Are you kidding? They'd be happy to talk to her. I'll tell them while you get Grace."

"Great. Thanks." Cait rushed back to Sadie. "Come with me."

Sadie rose from her seat. "Where are we going?"

"I'll explain on the way."

Sadie and Cait were met with laughter as soon as they stepped inside the Blackfriars Theater. Lucky and Krista were on stage while Grace watched them from a few rows back. She turned when the door opened and waved to Cait.

"That's Grace, the acting instructor," Cait said. "I hope this is a good time for her to take a break."

"Hi," Grace said as she came up the aisle to meet them.

Cait introduced Sadie and then asked Grace if she could take a few minutes to meet a couple of the actors.

"Yes! We're about finished here for the day anyway. Give me a second to tell the kids." It wasn't long before she was back with Cait and Sadie and on their way to the other theater.

June, Betsy, and Paula were waiting backstage. Cait made introductions. "Grace and her students are from the local college and are rehearsing *Comedy of Errors* in the Blackfriars Theater."

Cait was impressed with Betsy and Paula's enthusiasm as they talked with Grace. She and Sadie left them alone until it was time for the actors to go back on stage.

"That was so cool," Grace said. "They were open to answering my questions about acting. Now I wish I could see them on stage tonight, but I have another commitment."

"Betsy and Paula are committed for a couple more plays, so there will be another opportunity for you to see them."

"I hope so. I better get back to the students," Grace said. "Thanks again."

"I should leave too," Sadie said, "or Luke will come

looking for me." Then she gasped. "Oh, no, he can't. His car—"

"It's okay. I'll walk you to your car," Cait said.

When they came around to the front of the house, Cait noticed the back end of a black car turning down the driveway. She grabbed Sadie's arm.

"What's wrong?" Sadie asked.

"Stay here." Cait ran part way down the driveway, hoping the curves would slow the driver enough for her to see the license plate. But it didn't. "Damn!" She hiked back up and rejoined Sadie.

"It was the same car that had been at our house, wasn't it?" Sadie asked, her voice trembling.

Cait reached in her pocket for her cell phone. "I don't know. I'm calling Rook." She punched in a number.

"I was about to call you," Rook answered. "I talked t—"

She didn't give him time to finish speaking. "I bet the black car from the Sloanes' winery is the same as the one that just left my house! The police need to keep an eye on their winery tonight while they're here watching the play." Cait took a deep breath. "Afterward, an officer should follow them home to make sure they're safe. I'm going to do the same for Sadie right now. We'll catch up later," she said and disconnected the call.

# Chapter 15

"Why would those men follow Sadie here and then sit out front in their car?" June asked when Cait returned to the outdoor theater. "Obviously, they weren't being too sneaky. Do they want to be seen?"

"Apparently, considering everything they've done so far," Cait said. "Maybe they came to my door, rang the bell, and when no one answered, decided to wait and see what would happen next. They probably recognized Sadie's car. I'm grasping at straws with that dumber than dumb scenario, but I've never run into anyone so blatantly obvious with their intentions. I assume they wanted to see who lives in the house."

"It's my fault," Jim said. "If I'd been patrolling the grounds as planned, I might have at least gotten the plate number and maybe a description of the men."

Alarm swept over Cait. "No way, Jim. Who knows what they wanted, or if they were armed! Better you were helping Ray with the mess of cords."

"Stop blaming yourselves," June said. "Cait, those lugheads dared to come back here after shooting up your vineyard the other night. That tells you how stupid they are. Stupid people do stupid things, and one day the police will catch the bastards."

Jim and Cait stared at June.

"What?" June asked. "I've given this situation a lot of thought and here's how I see it. Cait, what's your connection to Turtle Creek Winery? Sadie and Luke, of course. And their connection to the winery? Pamela and Vince Harper. So what's the Harpers' connection to Sadie and Luke's troubles?" She shrugged. "Something is missing from this puzzle, but I'm working on it."

Cait glanced up at the denim blue sky. A bird flew past in pursuit of another bird. After several seconds, she said, "Maybe the missing link is a business partner. Possibly the man on Pamela's Facebook page."

"Who?" Jim asked.

Cait shook her head. "I don't know who he is. Pamela wouldn't say, but he could be important." She smiled. "Nothing like a falling out between business partners to create a motive for murder."

"Exactly," June said. "Do you think one of those men could be the Harpers' partner?"

Cait shook her head. "No. He'd know I have nothing to do with the winery or the Harpers. It has to be something else." She glanced at the stage, now a whirlwind of purposeful commotion. The number of actors seemed to have multiplied. "Let's set that aside for now. We have work to do. I haven't met most of those actors."

"We'll have to remedy that," June said. "You've met Mars DeSanto. He plays Orsino, Duke of Illyria and its ruler. Harrison York, the one in the wild print shirt, is Feste the jester. Paula is Lady Olivia, the rich countess, and Betsy Ryder is Viola, full of wit and charm. Avery Harman plays Sebastian, Viola's twin brother. He's the cute young guy wearing a tartan tam hat. Avery's from Scotland. We can visit backstage later so you can meet the rest of the cast."

"Mars fits the role of Orsino perfectly," Cait said, watching for June's reaction.

June rolled her eyes. "You've pegged him right. He's a lady's man."

"Cait!"

Cait turned to see Ray motioning to her. "Looks like damage control is needed again." She crossed the stage and walked to the green room where Ray stood in the entry, waiting with his arms crossed.

"Jay wants you up there," Ray said, pointing to the loft.

"Yes, master," she muttered before carefully climbing the laddered stairs. She found Jay going through a rack of costumes. "What's up?"

Jay leaned over to avoid hitting his head on the rafters. "These are Tasha's old costumes. I could use bits and pieces from them to repair torn and abused ones." He grunted. "Actors can be unbelievably hard on their costumes, and then they'll turn them over to me to repair. Instead of letting Tasha's dresses collect dust, I could put them to better use. With your permission, of course."

Cait rifled through the rack. Many of the dresses came from the wardrobe in her bedroom. When she'd moved into the house four months ago, she'd cleared out Tasha's clothes to make room for her own and had hung some of her costumes on the rack in the loft. Others were stored in clothes bags downstairs in the dressing room. Cait thought Tasha would like having her old costumes recycled.

"You may use them however you want," she said.

"I was hoping you'd say that." He dug into a pocket of his coveralls and pulled out a tissue to blow his nose. "One more thing. Ray wondered if you'd be willing to donate a couple outfits to the theater department at the local college. He says colleges never have enough funds to buy costumes and rely a lot on donations."

*Ray said that? Interesting.* "Sure. You decide which ones to donate and, after the festival, I'll see that Grace gets them."

Jay smiled and thanked her.

Cait left Jay and returned downstairs as her cell vibrated in her pocket. She checked the screen—Shep.

"You haven't changed your mind about coming, have you?" she asked.

"No. I'm just leaving the office and wanted to see if there's anything you'd left behind when you took off for California. I could bring whatever it is with me."

Memories of her old office made Cait a little lightheaded. She leaned against the stair railing and closed her eyes to visualize the corner office that was now Shep's. Had she overlooked anything when she left? Then she remembered. Early in her marriage, her now deceased ex-husband had once sent her a small-framed picture of himself as a baby with a note saying their baby would look like his baby picture. Problem was, Cait hadn't been able to get pregnant and he blamed her. For a police chaplain, with a degree in sociology and church ministry, he could be maliciously spiteful. Cait had tossed the note out and slipped the picture into a bottom desk drawer. She'd forgotten about it. Until now. The reminder still chilled her.

Shep had been in her office when she opened the package and had seen how upset she'd been. "I'm sorry, Cait," he said. "It was thoughtless of me to bring it up. I needed to be sure you didn't want it."

"I don't."

"How about the stuffed giraffe you left sitting in my chair?"

Cait smiled. "No! That was my gift to you when you took over my office."

He chuckled. "Just kidding. I'll see you soon. Bye, Cait."

"What are you smiling about?" Ray said after Cait slipped her phone back into her pocket.

"A friend is coming to visit next week."

He raised his eyebrow. "RT's back already?"

"No, an old friend from Ohio. Shep Church is a detective in the department where I worked."

Ray crossed his arms over his broad chest and stared hard at her. "You two-timing RT?"

She sighed. *How many times do I have to explain?* "No,

Ray. Shep was my mentor when I was a rookie cop. He's one of my best friends, but not in the way RT and I are friends."

"I guess it's okay."

She raised an eyebrow. "I didn't realize I needed your permission." She turned to walk away and then stopped and looked back. "I told Jay to pick a couple costumes to donate to the Las Positas College art department."

Ray gave her thumbs up.

Cait ran into Fumié and Ilia on her way to the house. Fumié's black tresses flowed down her back. Her dark eyes danced as she and Ilia walked hand-in-hand.

"Hey! Ready for tonight?" Cait asked.

Fumié nodded. "Ilia's got a new camera he's dying to use."

Cait glanced at the camera dangling around Ilia's neck. "Another one?"

"You sound like my mom," he said. "Professional photographers need different cameras for different venues. I got this with my royalty check from book sales."

Cait remembered the large coffee table book he'd published. She leaned over to take a closer look at his camera. "It has more bells and whistles than I'd know what to do with. Can it drive your car for you?"

He grinned. "No, but it's a powerhouse Canon. I'm still working my way up the ladder with my choice of cameras." He glanced toward the Blackfriars Theater. "Are the students from the college still here? I'd like to take their picture."

"Sorry, they've left, but they might come back in the morning before the matinee."

"Good. I'll be here," he said. "Fumié and I will nose around a little and then we'll see you tonight."

"Is six early enough?" Fumié asked.

"Should be," Cait said.

"Are Sadie and Luke coming?"

Cait smiled. "Yes. They're looking forward to it."

"Great. I'll look for them."

Cait watched the young and talented couple cross the courtyard toward the Elizabethan and almost came to tears. A sense of loneliness swept over her. She breathed deeply and then stumbled around behind the Blackfriars Theater, her favorite place to meditate. She sat on the ground, brought her knees to her chest, and rested her forehead against them. Only once before had she lost control and sobbed uncontrollably—when the plane her parents were on went down at sea five years ago.

Cait started when something cold brushed against her neck. She looked up to see Niki sitting beside her. She wrapped her arms around the dog and buried her head in his warm brown fur. Partially shaded from the hot sun, she looked toward majestic Mount Diablo, but her thoughts were on why she'd broken down in tears when she had so much to look forward to. Was it about the play? Concern Sadie and Luke might be followed to the theater tonight? Or was she nervous Shep and RT would meet and not get along? That didn't make any sense because she cared for both of them in different ways, but whatever was troubling her, she needed to pull herself together because it was getting late and she had to prepare for an evening of entertainment. It was no time to worry about the Harpers or the men in a black car.

# Chapter 16

Dressed in a long black and white striped cotton T-shirt dress and white wedge sandals, Cait swung around in front of the mirror in her bedroom for a last look before heading downstairs. With no place to hide her Glock in her outfit, she'd have to count on the police officers to deflect trouble. Not that she expected any, but the safety of the actors and the people attending was her responsibility and always on her mind.

She checked the time on the nightstand—five-forty-five—then slipped her cell phone inside a small beaded shoulder bag, and reached for a sweater. Downstairs she found Marcus spruced up in black slacks and a short-sleeved powder blue shirt opened at the neck to show off a thin gold chain. His sun-streaked blond hair appeared relaxed without the mousse he often used.

Cait smiled. "You look great, Marcus. I appreciate your coming tonight to help with the gift shop. What a relief to have it out of the house and into the delightful building you and Fumié designed and built."

"It was fun," he said. He looked Cait up and down. "Lookin' good, yourself. Guess you're not armed. It would spoil your dress and how it fits—" His face turned red.

She glanced at the wall clock to alleviate his embarrassment. "Goodness. Where did the time go? Fumié and Ilia will be here soon. Do you have your cell phone so you can go in and out of the house when you want?"

He reached in his pocket and showed it to her. "Those two officers are here."

"Perough and Vanicheque?"

"Yeah. They're in street clothes. Said others would be coming soon and probably Detective Rook, too."

Someone tapped on the back door. Cait opened it when she saw June and Jim through the window.

"Show time," June said. "I get excited no matter how many times I see Shakespeare's plays." Her blonde hair sparkled from the diamond-studded combs she'd used to hold it in place.

"You'd think she was the one going on stage," Jim said. He shoved the right side of his jacket aside, displaying his gun. "Let's hope I won't need this."

"You and me both," Cait said. "Obviously, I can't carry mine. Shall we head on over to the theater?"

"Should we put Niki in the house?" Marcus asked.

"No, he'll be fine outside," she said.

Two uniformed officers approached as they stepped outside. "Either of you Cait Pepper?"

"That would be me," Cait said. She read the officer's nametag: B. Saylor.

"Wanted to let you know we're here and Detective Rook will arrive soon," the officer said.

"Thanks." She introduced the Harts and Marcus. "And this is Niki. He shouldn't be any bother. Just don't shoot him."

The officer leaned over and ruffled Niki's fur. "Not a chance. Enjoy the evening."

"I can help Marcus with sales before I go back stage," June said on their walk over to the theater complex. "Where will you be?"

"In an aisle seat seven rows back on the right," Cait said. "I reserved the aisle seat in front of me for you."

June grinned. "Thanks."

"You can't see the play if you're hanging out back stage."

"No, but...thank you."

"Ilia and Fumié have seats, too. Marcus preferred to stay at the gift shop."

"I better head on over there," Marcus said as he pulled his cell phone out of his pocket. "Catch you later."

"Oh, there's Fumié and Ilia," June said as she waved to them.

Fumié wore a yellow sundress and sandals. Her black hair was pulled into a ponytail.

"She's adorable," June said. "Her guitar's almost as big as she is."

"A lot of talent in a small package," Cait said. "No wonder she caught Ilia's attention." She glanced across the grounds as small groups emerged from the parking lot. "I worry about the weather in the open theater. It's hot during the day but down right chilly at night. I hope everyone brought a sweater." Her own black sweater was draped through her purse strap.

"Nothing you can do about the weather," Jim said. "I'll leave you two now. I'm going to stroll around and try to look like I'm part of the crowd."

Cait and June settled on the brick wall surrounding the courtyard for a few minutes and watched as people began to stream in. A few fanned themselves at picnic tables beneath the oak trees, while others were drawn to the tiny gift shop where Marcus stood by the open doorway. Fumié strolled in and out of the courtyard, strumming on her guitar and singing. She went from poignant tunes to more upbeat ones, and at least one Cait recognized as a Beatles' song.

"I'm going to have a word with Marcus," June said as she rose, "then head back stage to see if there's anything I can do to help. I'll see you later."

Left on her own, Cait crossed to the theater and picked up one of the programs the volunteer was handing out. As she leafed through it, she checked her watch. *Twenty minutes to show time. All looks peaceful now. If only it stays that way.*

Her cell phone beeped. She opened her purse and glanced at the screen. She recognized RT's number. She turned her back on the theater and wandered off to talk privately.

"Hey. How's it going?" she asked.

"I'd rather be there with you," RT said. "Nervous about the play?"

"I'm always nervous until a new play starts." She noticed Sadie and Luke hurrying toward the theater. Seeing them reminded her of all the recent incidents that she hadn't told RT about, but now wasn't the time or place to get into it. "The play starts soon."

"I know. That's why I'm calling—to tell you to relax and enjoy it."

"I'll do my best. Any idea when you can come? Or if you'll bring Mindy?"

"Not sure exactly when I'll get there. Whether Mindy comes with me depends on my folks. They want to take her to Disneyland." He chuckled. "They're afraid once she's in school she'll have other priorities."

Three soft beeps, followed by a male's voice, announced over the speaker, "Show starts in ten minutes. Please take your seats."

People hurried into the theater.

"I heard that," RT said. "I'll let you go. We have unfinished business to take care of when I get there." He disconnected the call before she could respond.

*Unfinished business? What does that mean?* Cait put her phone on vibrate, looked for Sadie and Luke, and then entered the theater when she didn't see them.

❦❦❦

The curtain rose as Cait settled into her seat. June's seat

in front of hers remained empty. Musicians entered the stage playing melancholy music. The opening scene began with Orsino, the Duke of Illyria's famous first line, "If music be the food of love, play on!"

As Cait watched and listened to the background music, she decided Mars DeSanto fit the role of passionate Orsino perfectly.

Although Cait knew the play by heart, having seen it many times, the music was different from what she'd heard before. When it switched to a song based on the Beatles' "Fool On the Hill," Betsy Ryder appeared as Viola, along with Antonio, a sea captain. Cait looked forward to seeing how Betsy disguised herself later as the young boy Cesario.

Other venues larger than Cait's had a lot more actors than hers, but, as she watched her, heart swelled with pride at what took place in her own theater. Apparently, the audience loved it too, judging by their laughter.

Cait was startled when she felt a tap on her shoulder. She turned to see Detective Rook crouching beside her.

"Come with me," he whispered as he stood.

Cait gave one last glance at the stage and then, reluctantly, rose and followed Rook down the aisle. Outside, she asked, "What's happened?"

"The officers have detained a man at the house. I want you to tell me if you recognize him from the shooting at your vineyard the other night."

"How could I? It was dark and my bedroom is on the third floor."

"I know. I'd still like you to take a look."

She frowned. "Why is he being detained? Was he trying to break in the house?"

"The officers heard Niki growl and then noticed a man on the porch with his hand on the doorknob. He offered a weak explanation, said he's a realtor interested in the property."

"Poor excuse," she said. "Let's go see this so-called realtor."

"He's driving a black SUV," Rook said as they walked.

Cait stopped in her tracks. "Then it's him!"

"Maybe."

"Arrest him and end this disaster."

"You know I can't do that, Cait, not without proof he's responsible for setting Luke's car on fire or shooting up your vineyard. If you can positively identify him, then I'll arrest him."

"Don't forget the dead body at Sadie's winery." She shook her head in despair and continued walking. "I should have brought my Glock."

Rook glanced at her long T-shirt dress. "You don't need it. That's what the officers are here for."

She shrugged. "Habit, I guess. By the way, how'd you know where to find me?"

Rook smiled. "It took a while. I asked Jim and he called June."

They walked around to the front of the house. Cait memorized the license plate on the black Escalade in the driveway before stepping up onto the porch. She stared hard at the tall, dark skinned man dressed all in black, his black hair combed neatly back to his shirt collar. Black beady eyes stared back at her. He didn't show any recognition in his gaze. She glanced at Detective Rook and shook her head. She didn't recognize him.

Cait held her hand out. "I hear you're a realtor. I'd like to see your business card." When he didn't respond, she said, "Okay, so *why* are you here?"

"I heard this property was for sale."

"You heard wrong. Do you usually conduct business at night? Or shoot up a vineyard?" She had nothing to lose by asking about the vineyard.

"I don't know what you're talking about."

She assumed the officers had already checked his ID, but she couldn't resist asking questions. "What's your name?"

After a brief hesitation, he shifted his feet and said, "Miguel."

"Last name?"

When he didn't answer, she said, "I can have you arrested for trespassing or you can make it easy and give me your full name. Your choice."

"Quintero. You can't prove I've done anything wrong."

"Maybe, maybe not." Cait wasn't finished with him yet. "Where's your partner?"

He laughed. "I've got no partner."

She wanted to slap the smile off his face, almost certain he and his buddy had sat inside the same black car now in her driveway and watched as she and RT ate dinner outside the Ale House the other evening. She glanced at Jim because he had seen a similar car pull up in front of her house a few days ago. At least now she had a license plate.

"Can I go now? You've got no reason to hold me," Quintero said.

Cait looked at Rook.

Rook nodded. "But if she sees you around here again, you will be arrested."

"Si." Quintero grinned at Cait as his eyes slid from her head to her toe. He then sauntered down the steps, climbed in his car, and drove off without a backward glance.

Cait hugged Niki and ruffled his fur. "Good boy." She looked at Detective Rook. "I wish you could've arrested the jerk, if only for disrupting me while I was enjoying the play." She checked the time on her cell phone: eight-thirty. "It's intermission."

"If he's our guy, we'll get him. I'll walk you back to the theater."

"I'm grateful the officers are here. Who knows what might have happened if they hadn't caught him trying to get inside."

He smiled. "It's how we earn our big bucks."

She lightly punched his arm. "Yeah, sure. Thanks anyway."

When they reached the Elizabethan Theater, Rook patted her shoulder. "Enjoy the rest of the play."

e/oe/o

The crowd was beginning to filter back into the theater. Before Cait went in, she checked on Marcus at the gift shop. "How's it going?"

"I think you need to restock," he said. "June stopped by, but I had everything under control. I thought I saw you walk out of the theater with Detective Rook. What was that about?"

"A guy was here posing as a realtor. He's gone now, but I'm sure he's responsible for what's been going on at Sadie and Luke's house and mine." Then it dawned on Cait— maybe Miguel Quintero had followed her friends here. She needed to warn them before they went home.

"What's wrong?" he asked.

"I need to find Sadie and Luke. See you later." She hurried back to the theater for the start of the second half of *Twelfth Night*. Instead of taking her seat, she walked to the rear of the theater to search for Sadie and Luke. When she couldn't spot them right away, she tried to be inconspicuous and not disturb anyone, but her nerves were twitching and the night air chilled her. She slipped her sweater on and continued to look for her friends while she watched the play.

Feste the jester stumbled onto the stage and joined a group in singing "O, mistress mine, where are you roaming?...then come kiss me sweet and twenty."

Cait couldn't help be drawn into the music when she recognized "O Mistress Mine." It had been modeled after the Beatles' "When I'm Sixty-Four." From there, it segued into "Hold Thou Peace Thy Knave," based on Bob Dylan's "Rainy Day Women."

She finally spotted Sadie and Luke half way down in middle seats and relaxed enough to be drawn into the next song. "Come Away Death," a song about unrequited love, had been fashioned after the Beatles' "Fool On the Hill."

Before Cait knew it, the play was almost over. Feste was joined on stage by all of the actors to sing "For the Rain it Raineth Everyday."

The lights went on, and the audience were on their feet clapping for more. Cait's heart filled with pride and joy, knowing she was partly responsible for keeping the festival going. She started down the side aisle, keeping an eye out for her friends. She glanced up at the night sky. The full moon all but obscured the stars, but what she thought was a star quickly shot across the sky. She made a wish.

*Chapter 17*

Immediately after the play ended, Cait called Detective Rook and suggested he have a couple of his officers follow Sadie and Luke home. Before she went to bed, she repeated her wish from the previous night—to keep her friends safe. She slept better knowing nothing else had happened to them, at least not that she knew of.

Saturday morning RT called while Cait was on her second cup of coffee and second slice of toast. "I'm sorry, Cait, but it doesn't look like I'll make it after all. A situation's come up," he said.

Cait set her coffee down and glanced out the window. The sun appeared to have lost its sparkle, the birds were silent, and her heart ached from disappointment. "What happened?"

"A rescue operation is all I can say."

"That could take a while."

"Yeah, it could, but it could also be a quick in and out situation. Not anything we can predict." He hesitated. "This life would be hard on a marriage."

*Did RT use the M word?*

"Yes, I suppose it would be," she said. "Especially with children."

"So far Mindy understands I have to be away for long

periods of time. I'm fortunate my folks can care for her while I'm gone."

Silence opened up between them. Cait was at a loss for words.

"Can you hang in there, see where our relationship takes us?" he asked.

Her heart leaped with joy. "I'd like that. I understand how important your work is."

"That's a relief. I think we have a special relationship. I'm not sure what exactly, but I do know I don't want to lose it. I...care about you."

Cait cuddled her phone to her ear. "Same here."

As soon as the call ended, she wished she'd said more encouraging words to RT, but she was still hesitant. Once bitten, twice shy.

Distance tore many relationships apart, but what she felt for RT was strong and she hoped, with time, she'd be able to express her feelings without fear.

Sadie called five minutes later. "Cait, Pamela Harper wants to come over and pick up the toy rabbit."

Cait set her coffee down. "Hmm. That's interesting."

"She sounded nervous, but she's coming around eleven to pick it up."

Cait glanced at the wall clock: Ten. She had a funny feeling about Pamela, but didn't want to worry Sadie unnecessarily. Still, she wondered why Pamela hadn't mentioned the rabbit when she and her brother met at Sadie's house.

"I took the rabbit out for another look. It smells funny, but maybe that's because it was stored in a plastic bag." She hesitated. "Something's off about it though."

*I knew it. It bothered me too.* "How do you mean, Sadie?"

"You know how sometimes sand is used to hold something upright, maybe to set it on the edge of a shelf? That's what it feels like. Not cotton, as I assumed."

Cait scrambled off her stool. "Can you delay her coming,

say you have an appointment? I want another look at that rabbit before she gets there, and I don't want to wait until after the matinee."

"I could try."

"Okay. We've got an hour. I'd call Detective Rook to let him know, but it's Sunday. If I can't reach him, I'll try calling Officers Perough and Vanicheque at the police station, see if they can come."

"Cait, you're scaring me."

"I hope I'm wrong about my suspicions. See you soon." She hung up.

As Cait made her way upstairs for her purse and keys, Officer Vanicheque called and confirmed he, Officer Perough, and another officer would be there by one o'clock for the matinee.

"We may have a problem at the Sloanes' winery." She explained the urgency to get to Sadie's house before Pamela Harper got there.

"Worth checking out," Vanicheque said, "considering the baggy of cocaine we found at the murder scene. We'll see you there."

Relief spread through Cait. "Thanks."

She called June on her way out of the house to tell her where she was going and why. "This shouldn't take long, but it's what I have to do."

"Of course you do," June said. "Don't worry. Everything's good here."

Cait was thankful Pamela's car wasn't there when she arrived at Sadie's.

Sadie and Luke were on the porch when she drove up. "That was fast," Sadie said. "I couldn't get hold of Pamela. I was afraid she might come early. We're sorry to drag you away from your festival, but I didn't know what else to do."

Cait went up the stairs to the porch. "You did the right thing by calling. Where's the rabbit?"

"Inside," Luke said. "I'll get it."

"Two police officers are on their way," Cait said. She

turned at the sound of a car coming down the lane, and was relieved it wasn't Pamela's.

Officer Vanicheque parked the unmarked car at the end of the road, and then he and Officer Perough walked up to meet Cait and the Sloanes.

Luke opened the screen door. "Come on in."

Luke handed the rabbit to Officer Vanicheque. "I wanted to slit the thing open to see what's inside, but Sadie wouldn't let me."

"I'm glad you didn't." Vanicheque set the bag on a hall table and removed the rabbit. He squeezed its body and extremities, and then pulled a Leatherman from his pocket.

"Wait!" Sadie said.

"I need to slit it open," the officer said.

"I know, but how do I explain to Pamela?"

"You don't," he said. "You won't need to if she comes while we're here." He made a cut large enough to expose and puncture a small bag of white substance, similar to the one found outside the winery building where the PI had been killed.

Eyes wide, Sadie leaned over. "I don't suppose that's flour."

Cait smiled.

The corner of Perough's lip turned up in a half grin as he pulled the baggy out and set it on the table. He withdrew a small testing kit from his pocket. He placed a tiny amount of the suspected white powder into one of the vials containing a pink liquid. The liquid mixed with the white powder. He then went through a similar process with the next vial. A chemical reaction occurred, changing the liquid from pink to blue. He raised his eyebrow at Cait and then broke the last vial. The liquid separated, pink on top and blue on the bottom.

"Cocaine," Cait said. The sight sent a jolt through her body, and a frisson of fear for her friends.

"*Presumptively* cocaine," Vanicheque said. "If Pamela comes, we can arrest her."

"Oh, God," Sadie said as she slumped into a chair.

"Look at it this way. At least we kept it from hitting the streets," Perough said to Sadie. "Thank you for following up on your suspicions and calling Cait."

"How much would it be worth on the street?" Luke asked.

"Depends on whom you ask. This looks to be about quarter of a kilo, approximately half a pound. It will have to be sent to the crime lab for testing."

"I'm afraid to ask," Luke said, "but do you think the Harpers used this winery as a front for drug trafficking? If that's the case, it would explain the dead body I found inside the winery."

"For your sake, I hope not," Vanicheque said. "It would make matters worse." He glanced at his watch and then out the window. "Pamela may get spooked by the cars out front and decide to leave. We'll take this rabbit with us when we go, but if she does come, act innocent and tell her we stopped by to have a look around, saw the rabbit, and took it with us when we left." He handed Luke his card. "Give her my card. Tell her I'd like to talk to her. If she creates a problem, call nine-one-one."

"Can one of you stay here for a little while in case Pamela does come?" Cait asked.

Perough smiled. "We have to work your festival."

"I have a gun and a license to carry," Luke said as he pointed to a small table.

Perough raised his eyebrow. "You should call the police instead." He glanced at his watch again. "It's after eleven, but we could hang out a little longer in case she shows."

"Good," Cait said. "I was hoping it wasn't drugs, but Sadie, you recognized a problem and acted upon it. I have a feeling Pamela had second thoughts about coming." She leaned over and hugged Sadie. "I have to go, but it's going to be okay."

Cait backed out of the driveway, grateful she was there to help her friends solve the mystery at their winery. She hadn't been so lucky when she moved to the Bening Estate and encountered her own mystery. Until she met Royal Tanner.

*e/ɔe/ɔ*

Jim and June were in front of the garage when Cait returned. "I was beginning to wonder if you were going to be late for your own party," Jim said.

Cait glanced at her watch. "There's plenty of time."

"So what happened?" June asked. "Did Pamela take the rabbit and leave happy?"

"She didn't show when I was there, but the police stayed behind for a while." Cait sighed and shook her head. "That rabbit was stuffed with cocaine."

"Good grief!" June said. "Poor Sadie. Poor Luke. They must have been scared to death the cops would take them to jail."

"Not going to happen, but I'd like to get my hands on both Harpers and wring the truth out of them." Cait glanced over at her own vineyard. "I hope there aren't any more drugs found at their winery." *The cocaine in the rabbit doesn't seem to be enough to keep those men in the black SUV hanging around.*

"Let's hope not. 'Truth will come to light—in the end truth will out,'" June said.

"I'm too tired to think where that came from," Cait said.

"*Merchant of Venice*," June said. "Let's go in. You should eat before people start coming. Marcus is already here."

Marcus sat at the kitchen counter, eating grapes and flipping through a magazine about motorcycles. He looked up when Cait walked in. "Good, you're here. Ray's at the theater."

Cait slumped down on a stool. "I hope he doesn't need me because I'm too tired to cope with him."

"Nope. He's good." Marcus stared at Cait. "Want a sandwich?"

She smiled. "Thanks, that'd be great."

"Peanut butter and jelly, a Dr. Pepper, and potato chips coming up," Marcus said, getting up. "I'll have the same." He pushed a bowl of grapes toward her. "Help yourself to these while I make sandwiches."

"I like your friends, Cait," June said, "and I wouldn't wish their troubles on anyone, but you can only do so much to help them and then leave the rest up to the police. This week should be fun for you. Shep comes tomorrow and RT will follow soon."

"RT can't come. He's on a rescue operation."

Marcus had his back to them, but Cait knew he was listening. He wasn't happy about Shep's visit because he considered RT a friend. He didn't understand Cait's relationship with Shep.

"Oh, too bad," June said, "You were looking forward to seeing him."

"Yeah."

"Does he know about Shep?"

"No. It's tricky. RT knows Shep and I are close."

"That's good, isn't it?"

"They should know each other. They're both important to me."

"Then make sure you explain to RT," Jim said. "Men hate games when it comes to affairs of the heart."

Cait smiled. "You're full of wisdom."

There was scratching at the door.

"Niki," Cait said and got up to open the door.

"We've got to go," June said. "I want to talk with Ray, and Jim's going to do whatever he wants. See you later."

Niki raced into the kitchen, ignoring Cait in favor of his bowl of food.

Marcus set Cait's lunch in front of her. "I'll take mine with me. I'm going to open the gift shop in case people come early."

Cait smiled at Marcus. "Thanks."

Marcus left, leaving Cait and Niki alone. While she'd been at Sadie's, she'd remembered she'd not returned Samantha's phone call. Talking to her friend was the best medicine she could have right now. She pulled her phone from her pocket and called her number. Sam, an ER doctor, was also Luke's cousin, and deserved to know what was going on at his winery.

"Hey, Cait! How are things going?" Sam asked.

"Sam, have you heard from Luke?"

"No, why?"

"Then you don't know about his and Sadie's problems at the winery."

"No. That doesn't sound good."

Cait hated to be the bearer of bad news. "Sam, a man's been murdered in their winery. Luke found the body."

"*What*? How did *that* happen? What do the police say about it?"

"They're investigating, but that's not all." She took a deep breath. "Luke's car was set on fire."

"His Fiat? His pride and joy?"

"Afraid so. The ragtop burned, and there were a couple of scorch marks on the body of the car. Otherwise, it's okay."

"Unbelievable. Why would anyone do that to him?"

"I don't know. There are a few leads." Cait figured she'd given Sam enough bad news for one day. The cocaine situation could wait.

"Wait until Shep gets there. He'll find out what's going on."

Sam had known Shep about as long as Cait had, and he was one of Sam and her husband's best friends. In Sam's eyes, he was perfect.

Cait sighed. "He'll be on vacation, spending most of his time golfing with friends. He doesn't need to get involved with my problems."

"Ha. He knows Sadie and Luke. He'll want to help them."

Cait laughed. "I'm not going to ask."

"Where's RT?"

"On a mission."

"Too bad," Sam said. "RT and Shep should meet. Do you know how lucky you are to have those two hot guys care about you?"

"To clarify, Sam, my feelings for them are completely different." She checked the time on her cell phone. "I'll let you go. The matinee starts at two."

"Okay. I'm working the late shift tonight, but keep me in the loop about Luke. I'll call him soon."

"Okay, Sam. Bye."

Cait finished eating and then hurried upstairs to change her clothes before heading to the theater. People arrived early for the Sunday matinees so they could picnic at the tables under the oak trees before the play. That had been her intention all along in getting these tables set up, and she was happy to see how much they were appreciated. Fumié provided music before the play. Ilia photographed people arriving at the theater and would use those pictures to help promote the festival.

Cait wanted to see *Twelfth Night* without interruption, even though her mind dwelled on her friends and their safety. Minutes before two o'clock, she checked in with the three police officers. She wore her T-shirt dress again, leaving everyone's safety in the hands of the police. She put her phone on vibrate, slipped it into her clutch purse, and entered the theater.

# Chapter 18

The hot sun in the open-air theater hadn't deterred the audience's appreciation for the poetry, music, or the actors. The many plots and subplots of *Twelfth Night* had been woven together with skill and formed a perfect tapestry.

Cait left the theater in a melancholy mood, humming the final song, "For the Rain it Raineth Every Day." Tempted to check her phone for messages, she parted from the crowd and opened her purse, but changed her mind when Marcus motioned to her from the gift shop.

"Hey," he said as she approached. "I'll hang here awhile and then close up as soon as everyone has left."

"The actors will be out soon to talk with people," she said, "but there won't be enough sales for you to stay. Why don't you go? I'll watch the shop."

"I'll stay." He looked over her shoulder. "There's Detective Rook."

Cait turned, surprised to see the detective.

Rook, dressed in tan slacks and a navy sports shirt, frowned as he walked toward Cait. "The play over?" he asked.

"Yes."

"Good. We need to talk about the rabbit."

She stared at him. "Okay."

"What rabbit?" Marcus asked.

Cait hadn't had a chance to tell Marcus about the stuffed rabbit at the Sloanes' winery and what its contents were. "I'll explain later, Marcus."

Rook turned away. "Let's walk."

She looked at Marcus and shrugged then followed Rook. "What's going on?"

He glanced at her. "I should have swept the winery and the house after the murdered PI was found and that bag of cocaine located. I should have suspected there would be more."

"Is that what you wanted to talk about? To warn me you're going to do a full sweep of the Sloanes' property?"

He nodded. "Tomorrow morning." He swiped his brow with a handkerchief. "Must be a hundred today."

Anger rolled across her chest. "Do they know about the sweep, or are you going to surprise them?"

He stopped walking and turned to her. "Of course they know. I wouldn't have given them advance notice if they weren't your friends and not suspects. I'm giving you the opportunity to be there."

Her anger eased a little. "Thank you. I'll be there. What time?"

Rook nodded. "I'll let you know." He hesitated. "Heard from RT?"

Rook and RT had become friends when Rook's brother and RT were on a mission together. Rook's brother later died on a similar operation RT had led.

"He's on a mission," she said. "But Shep Church will be here tomorrow. You'll finally have a chance to meet him." Rook and Shep had talked on the phone last month after both of their departments became involved in the same murder investigation involving Cait when her life was at stake.

"Why's he coming?"

She laughed. "Can't the guy take a vacation?"

"Sure, but the timing is odd. You're involved in another murder investigation. Or maybe he's coming to offer help."

"I didn't invite him, if that's what you're wondering. It so happens he has to take vacation or lose it. You should know how that works, Rook." She glanced back at the courtyard outside the theater where people were gathering. "I need to talk with our guests and the actors before they pack up and leave. Let me know when the sweep goes down."

Rook grinned and raised his eyebrow. "Anything going on between you and Detective Church?"

*Geez.* "We're best friends. Nothing more."

Ilia and Fumié ran up to Cait. "Oh my gosh," Fumié gushed, "that was the best Shakespeare play ever. I couldn't stop laughing. I loved Feste the clown best of all, and the music."

"I loved Viola when she disguised herself as a boy," Ilia said. "Cait, a couple of the actors were looking for you."

Cait noticed Detective Rook had slipped away. "Okay. Thanks to both of you for the music and photography. You round out the whole festival with your talents. For that I'm grateful."

"Aw shucks, ma'am," Ilia said, faking a southern accent. "My pleasure."

Cait and Fumié laughed.

Ilia glanced over Cait's shoulder. "I think those cops are looking for you."

Cait turned to see Vanicheque and Perough approaching.

"I meant to tell you Pamela Harper was a no show," Vanicheque said.

"She probably saw our cars and then left," Cait said.

"What's going on with Sadie and Luke?" Ilia asked.

The band ran onto the courtyard and sprang into music from the play. The actors clapped and joined in the singing. "I'll explain later, Ilia," Cait said. She glanced over and saw Marcus swaying to the music. "Too bad there isn't music for all the plays."

Ray joined Cait. "Now that's what I call a success. Everyone's happy and saying how much they loved the play." He glanced at the darkened Blackfriars Theater. "Too bad those college kids didn't see it. Might inspire them to greater heights beyond college. I'm going to hang around for another day to talk to them."

Surprised, Cait stared at him. "Why would you do that?"

"I like those kids, particularly Lucky. He shows promise, but he looks like he's carrying a burden on his shoulders. Any idea why?"

Cait thought about Lucky and that he'd lost his dog. "A lot on his mind, probably. Plus, I don't think his parents encourage his interest in the theater."

"Yeah. I get that," Ray said. "Like Tasha. It's why she left home to fulfill her dream of becoming an actor."

Cait felt uneasy discussing Tasha in front of the police officers, but Ilia and Fumié had known Tasha and why she devoted so much of her time to the festival. Cait had freely opened the Blackfriars for the use of the arts department at Las Positas College because it had been Tasha's wish.

"So you don't mind if I hang around another day?" Ray asked.

"Of course not, Ray. I think it's wonderful. I'm sure Grace will appreciate anything you do to encourage her students."

Ray's face lit up. "It'll be fun."

"Cait," Officer Vanicheque said. "We'll be on our way as soon as the place empties out."

She nodded. "Thanks for being here. Hope it wasn't too boring for you."

Vanicheque chucked. "We could use more assignments like this."

"We could too," Ray said before he walked off.

Cait and June made the rounds of the actors before they packed up to leave. Betsy and Paula would return next month for the August festival, along with debonair Mars DeSanto. The more Cait saw of Betsy and Paula, the more comfortable she became among each group of actors. She couldn't imagine what she'd do with her time after the last festival in September.

Everyone had cleared out by seven o'clock and Cait was alone in the house with Niki when Detective Rook called.

"Ten o'clock in the morning," he said. "I don't think the sweep will take long unless we find a load of crack."

"Don't joke about it," she said. "I'm sure Sadie and Luke are already freaked out, worrying what their neighbors will think when they see all those police units."

"I don't remember another house on their street," he said.

"There's only one and it's as you turn into the lane," Cait said. "It's set back behind a small vineyard."

"I'll pay more attention next time. See you at ten," he said.

After they hung up, she considered calling Sadie and Luke, but decided nothing she said would ease her friends' anxieties. She prepared a tray of snacks and took it upstairs to the second floor to watch TV, something she hadn't done since she'd moved into the house. With the tray on her lap and her feet on the ottoman, she flipped through channels to find a reality show to watch. Niki curled up at her side and soon was snoring.

Later, the landline next to the sofa woke Cait from a senseless dream. The old TV crackled with static as the screen filled with gibberish. She jerked upright and caught the tray before it fell to the floor and reached for the phone.

"Hello," she answered.

A long silence and then a hang-up.

It rang again.

"Hello?"

Silence.

Cait slammed the receiver down and rose. "Come on, Niki." She took the dog up to the third floor bedroom, stripped out of her clothes and into a pair of old shorts and T-shirt, covered her head with a sheet, and fell fast asleep.

# Chapter 19

Diffused light from the stained glass windows lent a rose-and-gold glow to the bedroom walls. Cait luxuriated in the pillows, happy the festival had ended on a positive note, and leaving the day open with nothing better to do than eat a leisurely breakfast and read the paper. Until she remembered—

The sweep at Sadie and Luke's winery.

She tossed the sheet back and glanced at the clock on the nightstand: eight-oh-five. She climbed out of bed and hurried into the bathroom. The hot shower helped unclog her foggy brain. Not such a lazy day after all. As soon as she finished dressing in shorts and a T-shirt and towel-dried her curly hair, she went down to the kitchen. She perched on a stool at the counter with her first cup of coffee and a chocolate croissant, courtesy of Marcus.

"Ray's here," Marcus said.

Something else she'd forgotten. "What about Grace and her students?"

"They're here, too." He raised his eyebrow. "Why hasn't Ray left with the rest of his crew?"

Cait set her coffee mug down. "He's taken a liking to Lucky and his interest in the theater. I'll run down to the theater to watch the kids rehearse for a while." She checked the wall clock: eight-fifty. "The police are doing a sweep of Sadie and Luke's winery at ten and I need to be there."

He stared at her. "Why? Because a dead guy was murdered in their winery?"

"Because drugs were found inside the house and more could be on their property."

His jaw dropped. "*What*? No way!"

"Not their drugs, Marcus. They found cocaine in a stuffed rabbit left behind when the Harpers moved out."

He pulled a stool from under the counter and sat down. "That sucks. What do you think about the sweep?"

Cait wrapped her hands around her coffee mug. "Terrible. I hope they don't get discouraged and decide to take a loss and sell."

"How will the sweep go down?"

She rose and refilled her coffee. "The point is to discover evidence of a crime. The police will inspect every inch of the property. And probably have a police dog to sniff out drugs."

"Sounds like an intrusion of privacy to me. Can the police search their property without a warrant?" Marcus asked.

"Sadie and Luke gave their permission. The police have reasonable suspicion to search since cocaine was found in the rabbit. And then there's the bag of cocaine where the murder had taken place."

"They won't be arrested will they?"

Cait smiled. "No."

"Well then, if it proves they're innocent..."

"Right. I want to make a quick stop at the Blackfriars Theater before I go."

"Is that friend of yours still coming?"

"Yes. His name is Shep Church." She rinsed her dishes and then put them in the dishwasher. "He's a good guy, Marcus. Give him a chance."

"Never said I wouldn't." He went into his office.

⌘⌘⌘

Cait quietly entered the darkened Blackfriars Theater to the sound of laughter.

As Lucky and Joanna circled each other on stage, Cait remembered she hadn't seen *Comedy of Errors*, the play they were rehearsing, and wished she had the time to sit down and watch.

Ray turned and motioned to her from a front row seat. When she tapped her wrist to indicate she didn't have time, he rose and walked up the aisle. "What's up?"

Ray didn't know about the drugs or the sweep and there was no reason to tell him. "I have to go to Sadie's. How long will you be here?"

He shrugged. "Hard to say. No matter what his folks say, Lucky plans to make the theater his life's work. I think he'll succeed. I'd like to help. I'm a stage manager, not an actor, but I think all actors should learn about different areas in this business. Since I don't have a kid of my own, I invited Lucky to Oregon for the Ashland festival. He seemed interested."

Cait smiled. "With Fumié off to Santa Rosa ranger school soon, I could use his help around here next season. Do you think he'd be interested?"

Ray smiled. "You'd do that?"

"I'm not the shrew you seem to think I am."

"Hey, I never called you a shrew. But if I did, it was in fun."

"Maybe I stretched it a little. Look, I have to go, but if Grace needs anything, tell Marcus." She reached for the door handle. "Maybe I'll be back in time to see you before you leave." She left, restraining the door so it wouldn't slam shut behind her.

Cait had forgotten to tell June Hart she was leaving until she was in her car. She called her after she backed out of the garage. "I'm on my way to Sadie and Luke's winery. The police are doing a full sweep of the place for drugs. I don't know how long I'll be, but you can call if you need to."

"It's not fair," June said. "They should be having fun

with their new venture in the wine business. Do you want me to come with you?"

"I would, but Ray's still here at the Blackfriars Theater with Grace and her students. I bet they'd love a pro like you to watch them rehearse, maybe even offer a little advice."

June laughed. "I'll go over now. Give my best to Sadie and Luke."

Cait drove down the steep hill and onto Tesla Road. Five minutes later, she pulled onto Post Lane and was relieved she'd arrived before the police. She ran up onto the porch and knocked on the door.

"Thank God, you're here," Sadie said as she opened the door for Cait.

Cait stepped inside. "What's wrong?"

"Luke. He's fit to be tied. He wishes we hadn't given permission for the sweep."

"Sadie, they don't need your permission. They have reason to search. You know that. Doesn't he want to be cleared of any illegal activities?"

"Of course. But I've never seen him this upset."

"Where is he? I'll talk to him."

"I'm here," Luke said, coming in from another room. He walked over to Sadie and pulled her into his arms. "I'm sorry, sweets. It's you I worry about." His voice cracked. "You were shunned and excommunicated from the only life you've ever known, all because you wanted to further your education. And then along I came. You married me, an Englisher. Now look what's happened." He kissed the top of her head.

Dismayed over Luke's anguish, Cait was about to say something when she heard the sound of car doors in front of the house. "The police are here."

Sadie and Luke broke their hold and opened the door.

Cait counted four cars when she stepped out onto the porch. Detective Rook's was the first car and the only unmarked one. *At least they didn't arrive with sirens blaring.*

"Morning," Detective Rook said as he walked up the

stairs. "We should be in and out of here in no time. We'll start in the house."

A slightly calmer Luke shrugged. "Whatever."

An officer exited the last car with a dog. He held the leash as the dog tried to pull ahead, and, in his other hand, he held a small white towel. "This is Finn," the dog handler said as he neared the house. "As you can see, he's ready to get started. Stay back from him and he'll be fine."

Cait watched the German shepherd with interest as the officers filed into the house. Finn covered the house quickly, in a tenth of the time it would take human officers to search the same area.

Once outside, Cait and her friends followed Finn and the officers into the winery, but stood back out of the way. From her years as a cop, Cait assumed the towel had cocaine on it or the smell of it when the dog handler held it under Finn's nose. The dog and officer circled the building until Finn stopped and began pawing the floor, apparently going after the scent.

Cait froze. *Oh, God. It can't be.*

# Chapter 20

The dog then stopped at a shrink-wrapped stack of pallets loaded with boxes. "What's he doing?" Luke asked.

"He's alerting me to the spot where he smells drugs," the handler said.

Luke dragged his hands through his hair and groaned. "You're saying there are drugs in those wine bottles?"

"Let's have a look," Detective Rook said. "Got a knife? And a ladder?"

Officer Perough pulled his Leatherman from his pocket. "I'll have a go at it."

"I'll get a ladder," Luke said.

"I can't watch this," Sadie said, "but I can't *not* watch either. Are sniffer dogs ever wrong?"

"I don't know about other dogs," Finn's handler said, "but this guy here has never missed."

Luke returned with a ladder and opened it in front of the pallets. "Just so you know, these pallets of bottles were already here when we bought the winery." He stepped aside, making room for the officer to mount the ladder.

Cait counted six pallets, but from where she stood she couldn't begin to guess how many cases were on each one. She inhaled deeply. *Drugs could be hidden anywhere in this shipment.* She hated what drugs did to people—destroying their wills and draining their self-respect.

As Officer Perough cut through and tore away part of the shrink-wrap, the name on the case boxes became clear—Spring Haven Winery.

"It's not the name of your winery now, is it?" Perough asked.

"No!" Luke and Sadie said in unison.

"We changed it to Turtle Creek Winery, and we didn't order those glass bottles," Luke said. "Now will you believe we're innocent?"

Detective Rook rubbed his chin. "Never said you weren't."

"You didn't have to," Luke said. "Why else the sweep?"

Rook frowned. "To make sure there were no more drugs on your property. Would you rather I had you arrested?"

"Luke," Sadie said. "They're just doing their job."

Cait watched the officer pull sealed bags from between cases of wine bottles and knew he'd found drugs. The other officers in the building gathered around the ladder.

"Looks like Finn's perfect record is still intact," Officer Perough said, as he handed down what Cait assumed were bags of cocaine. "There's plenty more where that came from. We need to take this whole shipment apart."

*✺✺✺*

It was past noon when the officers and Finn left with a garbage bag of cocaine found between the cases and the bottles. Detective Rook stayed to talk to Sadie and Luke. Cait knew how exhausted her friends must be, because she felt the same way. Drained from all the commotion, her friends appeared somewhat relieved the sweep had ended and the drugs found. Yet Cait knew they had to be worried someone would come looking for the cocaine. She thought it remarkable how well Sadie held up during this crisis while Luke had nearly fallen to his knees in despair.

They sat around the kitchen table, untouched glasses of sun tea in front of them, while Detective Rook scanned the bill of lading that had been taped to the shrink-wrap.

"The glass bottles were shipped from the American Canyon warehouse here in California two months ago," Rook read. He glanced up. "Mid-May. The glass originally came from Vitro Packaging De Mexico."

"Mexico?" Luke said. "That explains it! How does this even happen? I mean, don't investigators check shipments at the border?"

"Sure they do," Rook said, "but it's not possible to open all the boxes, and smugglers hide drugs between boxes containing legitimate goods. There are methods to detect hidden drugs at the border, but it's difficult to keep pace with the imaginative ideas of smugglers." Rook took a long drink of his sun tea and then set the glass back down. "The Mexican drug trade is everywhere in the United States. Cartel operations range from traditional drug running to using a horse ranch as a front for laundering drug money. You are not the first victim."

"What happens now?" Luke asked.

Sadie looked at Rook as she wrapped her hands around her glass of tea. "What about the dead PI in our winery? How's he involved? And those men in that black car?"

"And why was my car set on fire?" Luke asked.

The longer Cait listened, the more she began to see a pattern. "Those men who followed you are here to collect the drugs, and they won't stop until they do. They're probably only couriers, but the kingpins need them to get their illegal drugs onto the street."

"Cait's right," Rook said. "They're messengers. They scare people, like when they set your car on fire, Luke." He scratched his head. "There's a reason those drugs came here. Someone's responsible and then bolted and left Pamela and Vince Harper to bear the brunt of drug trafficking from this winery."

*Maybe the man on Pamela's Facebook page*, Cait thought. *I'd bet my new Saab he brought all this havoc upon the winery.*

# Chapter 21

"Why haven't you arrested Pamela and Vince?" Luke asked. "Force them to tell you who's responsible. They must have some idea. Hell, what more do you need?"

Rook's impatience was beginning to show as he tapped his pen on the bill of lading. "This receipt shows a truck load of glass bottles sent to this address. It does not specifically name the Harpers."

"Semantics." Luke jumped up and paced the room.

"Bring them in for questioning," Cait suggested. "From the little time I had with them, I knew by the way they looked at each other before answering each question that I'd hit a sensitive spot."

"Now, why didn't I think of that?" Rook said sarcastically. "Listen, my officers are looking for them as we speak."

Eyes wide, Sadie swallowed hard. "They're missing?"

"Hope not," Rook said.

Luke sat back down. "Don't forget the stuffed rabbit. If you ask me, *that* cocaine is Vince Harper's."

"Haven't forgotten about that either," Rook said.

"So what do we do now?" Luke demanded. "Go about business as usual? Whatever that means, considering we only moved here six weeks ago."

Sadie reached across the table and clasped Luke's hand. "Luke, we'll continue with our plans for an open house. We haven't done anything wrong."

Cait smiled at Sadie's efforts to calm Luke. "Good idea." She stood. "Shep's coming today." She opened her purse, checked her cell phone, and saw she hadn't missed any messages from him. "He said he'd call for directions once he got here, but it wouldn't surprise me if he came ahead anyway."

Detective Rook tucked his pen in his shirt pocket, picked up the bill of lading, and rose. "I should go, too." He reached over and shook Luke's hand. "We'll get to the bottom of this."

Sadie and Luke followed the detective and Cait outside onto the porch. "I hope you'll let us know about any progress," Luke said.

Rook nodded. "Of course."

"How much is all that cocaine worth?" Sadie asked,

Rook shrugged. "Prices fluctuate."

Sadie frowned. "I counted six pallets. There must be hundreds of cases of glass bottles in that shipment. Twelve in a case adds up to thousands of bottles. This winery was small and prosperous when we bought it, but that's a lot of bottles. Are you sure you got all the cocaine? Maybe there's more *inside* the bottles."

"Not only is she a mathematical whiz, she's thorough," Luke said.

"Good point, Sadie," Rook said, "but the officers dismantled the shipment and found only the duct-taped bags of cocaine."

Cait hugged Sadie. "I'll bring Shep over to see you."

"I'd like that."

Cait followed Rook down the driveway. When they reached her car, she asked, "Learned anything about the dead PI?"

"We're still looking into it."

"It'd be interesting to know who hired him," Cait said.

"What about Miguel Quintero, the guy from outside my house? Are you going to bring him in for questioning?"

Rook slipped his sunglasses on. "We don't know where he is, but I doubt we've seen the last of him or his buddy. If he's here for the cocaine, he's not going anywhere soon."

Cait sighed. "In other words, you have nothing."

"I didn't say that." He glanced back at the Sloanes who were still standing on the porch, concern etched on his face.

"In the meantime, Sadie and Luke sit on their haunches and hope for the best."

Rook removed his sunglasses and looked hard at Cait. "You're too close to the situation. I understand your concern for your friends, but you know the process. We can't rush to arrest anyone without evidence. If we do, we'll lose them. We have to build our case and that takes time. Trust that we know what we're doing."

"Are you saying I can't be objective where Sadie and Luke are concerned?"

He reached in his pocket for his keys. "I'm asking you to think like the cop you used to be." He climbed into his car, turned the engine on, and backed down the lane.

Cait looked back at her friends standing on the porch, waved, and got into her car. *And I'll act like a cop should the need arise.*

⋐⋑⋐⋑

Cait pulled around the last curve in her driveway and saw a red Toyota rental in front of the house.

*Shep!*

She slammed the car into park in front of the garage and ran around to the back of the house. She heard Shep's familiar bray of laughter even before she opened the door. Inside, Marcus and Shep sat at the kitchen counter. Niki was sprawled on the floor by Shep's feet.

Cait grinned. "Hey! What'd I miss?"

Shep stood and pulled her into a bear hug. "Guy stuff."
He towered over her as he held her at arms' length. "Beautiful as ever. And, according to Marcus, too smart for your
own good."

Cait relaxed in Shep's embrace. Her world had tilted on
its axis after she moved from Ohio to California. She'd left
family, friends, and her job when she accepted her inheritance from someone she'd never heard of. Seeing Shep,
righted everything. His sun-streaked light brown hair appeared a little longer than she remembered, his khaki Dockers and light blue sport shirt were a little travel-wrinkled.
Winning over Marcus so quickly didn't surprise her. Shep's
warm, confident manner had always drawn people to him.

"I dropped my bag off at the hotel and then hauled right
over here without calling ahead," Shep said. "Hope that was
okay. Marcus has been most hospitable."

Cait laughed. "It's fine. Are you staying at the Hilton
where you told me you would?"

"Yes." Shep sat on the edge of his stool. "I heard about
Sadie and Luke's troubles. Marcus told me. Want to talk
about it?"

"Now? You're on vacation."

"Eh, you know I'm not a vacation kind of guy. I get
bored easily. One day of golf with my buds will be enough.
Sadie and Luke are my friends, too."

Cait raised her eyebrow at Marcus.

"Hey, he asked," Marcus said.

She turned back to Shep. "Want to look around? See
what I left Ohio for?"

Shep grinned. "Of course. I can walk and talk at the
same time."

"Go ahead," Marcus said. "I have computer work to
catch up on before I leave."

Shep held his hand out to Marcus. "Thanks for keeping
me company. See you tomorrow?"

Marcus shook Shep's hand. "I'm here most days."

"Okay, then," Cait said. She tucked her cell phone in her

pocket, leaving her purse on the counter. "Let's go."

Outside, she said, "You have to meet June and Jim Hart. I told you about them. They live in their RV. I can tell them about the sweep at Sadie and Luke's winery, too."

He took his sunglasses from his shirt pocket and slipped them on. "Oh yeah. I remember her. We met on Skype."

She led Shep around the house to the front. "That's right. She's a retired Shakespearean actor, one of Tasha's friends. Jim's retired. He was co-owner of an art recovery business, but now he's a silent partner. I offered to pay them for helping me with the festival, but they refused."

Shep slowed and gripped Cait's arm. "I didn't want to ask in front of Marcus, but where's your SEAL buddy? If he's the jealous type, I'll make myself scarce."

She hadn't thought about RT all day because she was worried about Sadie and Luke and the sweep. "He's on a mission, but I hope he'll show up in time to meet you. Come on, the Harts are down this way." She pulled away and through the cypress trees where the Fleetwood Fiesta RV was parked. June and Jim were lounging beneath an awning. They stood when they saw Cait and Shep.

"I recognize you. Hi, Shep," June said. "We met on Skype."

Shep smiled. "We sure did. Nice to see you again."

"This is Jim," Cait said.

As Jim and Shep shook hands, Jim gestured toward two empty chairs. "Have a seat. Can we get anyone a cold drink? Beer, iced tea?"

"Iced tea for me," Cait said.

"Same here," Shep said. He waited for Cait to sit before he pulled a chair next to hers and sat down. "This is quite a setup you got here."

"Retirement's been good to us," June said. "Stay here, Jim. I'll get the drinks."

"Cait keeps asking if we're happy here," Jim said. "She's afraid we'll get bored and hit the road. Not going to happen unless she kicks us out."

"Not a chance," Cait said.

June returned with the drinks and a basket of chocolate chip cookies and passed them out. "Would it be impolite to ask about the sweep? I'm dying to know if Sadie and Luke are okay." She sat in a chair next to Jim.

Shep laughed. "Cait refused to talk about it until we were all together." He turned to Cait. "Ready to tell us now?"

Cait took a long drink before she set her glass down on the little metal table next to her. "Okay. This morning, Finn, the police dog, sniffed out cocaine inside the winery."

June and Jim gasped. Shep raised his eyebrows.

Cait took a deep breath. "The bags of coke were hidden among cases of wine bottles. According to the bill of lading, the shipment originated in Mexico. Somewhere between there and American Canyon, California, smugglers managed to hide the cocaine among legitimate goods. I was pretty surprised. I had hoped the cocaine inside the rabbit was all there was."

"Oh, God!" June leaned forward. "Were Sadie and Luke arrested?"

"No," Cait said. "That shipment arrived there before they bought the winery."

"What rabbit?" Shep asked.

"Oh, I didn't tell you." Cait filled him in about the cocaine found in the toy rabbit, which Pamela Harper was supposed to pick up. She reached for her iced tea. "That's all I know right now."

Shep smiled and relaxed in his seat. "Everyone in your old department thinks you're living the life of leisure, basking in the sun, drinking wine, and hanging out with the actors. Wait until I tell them you're still playing cops and robbers."

"I'm not playing. It's serious," Cait said.

"I know. I'm teasing you," Shep said.

Everyone quietly munched on cookies and drank their beverage until Jim turned to Shep, "Worked much with drug trafficking and cartels?"

"Enough to know the cartels have a turnover of billions of dollars. It's mind-boggling. Cocaine has been smuggled in every way imaginable—statues, wine, rum, baseball caps, globes, and even in bodies and packed into condoms."

"Wow," June said.

Shep turned to Cait. "I'm available to help if Detective Rook's interested. You might let him know the next time you talk to him."

"I will. Sadie and Luke would like that too." Cait moved to the edge of her seat. "Ready for the rest of the tour?"

Shep stood. "Absolutely. Thanks for the tea and cookies, folks. Maybe we can all go out for dinner while I'm here."

"Love to," June said. "I'm glad you're here, Shep. Cait's looking happier already."

Cait rolled her eyes. "Let's get out of here before they embarrass me."

# Chapter 22

I want to show you Tasha's Meditation Garden," Cait told Shep as they walked back to the house. She led him along the footpaths between the blue-red lupine, fragrant lime thyme, and the peach colored Peace roses. "I try to have coffee here as often as I can in the morning." When she reached the marble dolphin perched on a pedestal, she slowly dragged her fingertips over it, reveling in the smooth texture. "One day I'm going to write about Tasha. I'll chronicle what I've learned about her. June and Tasha practically started together in the acting business." She smiled. "The same goes for RT's mom. The three of them have known each other forever and should be a huge help to me."

"You've met his mother?"

"Briefly, when his folks stopped by on their way to Utah a couple of months ago. She even gave me a picture of Tasha."

He grinned and wiggled his eyebrows. "Is that a fact? Getting close to the family, are you?" He glanced down. "Hey, who's this little guy?"

Cait picked up the white cat and cuddled it in her arms. "This is Velcro. You should feel honored. She doesn't come out of hiding unless she trusts you."

Shep stroked the cat. "Her eyes are as blue as the sky."

Cait reluctantly set the cat back down and watched as she scampered off. "Ready to see the theaters?"

"Lead on."

As they walked, Cait enjoyed the chirps, trills, and whistles of the birds in the trees and bushes. She realized what she'd been missing was the comfort of being in the presence of a friend she'd known a long time. She hadn't reached that point yet with RT but, admittedly, the circumstances were different. Shep was more like the brother she'd never had, while RT aroused emotions so deep within her soul that it frightened her.

"Who's that?" Shep asked as they reached the garden gate into the theater courtyard.

Jarred from her thoughts, Cait squinted into the sun as she looked to where Shep pointed. "That is Ray Stoltz. I forgot he stayed over a day to watch the college students rehearse. And his brother Jay." She waved. "Ray! Jay!"

Ray turned. "There you are. We were just leaving." He looked at Shep.

"This is Shep Church," she said. "He's visiting from Ohio. Shep, meet Ray and Jay. I may have mentioned Ray, the stage manager, who mistook me for the hired help."

Shep laughed as he shook hands with the brothers. "Oh, yeah. I heard about you."

"Oh, hell," Ray groaned. He stood a little taller than six-two Shep. One corner of his mouth turned up. "Cait and I manage to get along as long as it's her way."

Cait placed her hands on her hips. "Excuse me? I give in to you all the time because you know more than I do about theaters and actors." Then she realized he was teasing.

Ray shifted his feet. "Huh."

"I don't suppose Grace and her students are still here," Cait said. "I'm going to show Shep the theaters."

"They left," Ray said. "See you next month, Cait." He walked away.

"Nice meeting you, Ray," Shep said.

Ray nodded. "You, too. Stay out of trouble, Cait."

Cait watched him go. "He's taken an interest in Lucky, one of the student actors. He sees promise in his acting abilities."

"Seems like a nice enough guy."

"A little gruff, but he means well. Let's see the theaters."

ᥱᢣᥱᢣᥱᢣ

"Wow," Shep said, after they left the Elizabethan Theater. "More impressive than I imagined. I'll never be able to lure you back to Columbus. You've got a gold mine here."

"Strange how life happens," she said. "A professor of mine suggested I take classes in Shakespeare to round out my portfolio."

"We all need guiding lights in our life, people to help us find the way."

She looked up at him. "Like you, my mentor after the police academy."

"Cait!"

She turned to see Detective Rook walking toward her. *This can't be good*, she thought.

"Marcus said I'd find you back here," Rook said. He looked at Shep. "You must be Detective Church." He shook hands with Shep. "I'm Detective Rook. We talked on the phone last month. I knew you were coming so I took a chance you might be here."

"What's up?" Cait asked.

Rook pulled his cell phone from his jacket pocket. He found what he was looking for and then handed the phone to her. "Have a look at this."

She stared at the picture on Rook's phone. "A hummingbird? Whose tattoo?"

"It's on the dead PI's shoulder blade. Recognize it?"

"No. Should I?" She showed the tattoo to Shep.

"Are you referring to the dead PI found in the Sloanes' winery?" Shep asked.

"The same," Rook said. "Cait told you about it?"

Shep nodded. "And the cocaine. This could be a drug cartel symbol."

Even the hot sun couldn't stop the sudden chill that crept into Cait's body. "So the PI's not a PI, but a drug dealer?"

"No, he was legit," Rook said. "He could have a drug history. Got an officer looking into it."

"Like I've said before, find out who hired him and you'll be half way home," Cait said.

The detectives exchanged glances.

"What?"

"Once a cop, always a cop," Rook and Shep said in unison.

She groaned and returned Rook's cell phone. "Give me a break."

"One more thing," Rook said. "Sadie wanted to know the value of the cocaine in the shipment of bottles. In the San Francisco Bay Area, it's worth twenty to twenty-seven thousand dollars per kilogram. That's about two pounds per kilo. There were seven bags of cocaine stashed in that shipment."

Cait's jaw dropped as she did the math. "I assume the DEA will get involved."

Rook nodded. "I'm giving them a heads up about what we found, mostly to see if they already have an investigation going on with the Sloanes' winery. We'd normally handle it ourselves, but Homeland Security might also be brought into the mix since the cocaine could be traced back across the border."

"This is so unfair to Sadie and Luke," she said.

"I agree."

"I'm here for a few days," Shep said. "Let me know if I can help. Sadie and Luke are my friends too."

Rook smiled. "Thanks. I appreciate the offer."

As he walked away, Cait called to him. "Rook? Thanks for keeping me in the loop on their situation."

Rook raised his hand in acknowledgment.

"Nice guy," Shep said.

"Yeah, he is." *Hmmm. I wonder if the Livermore PD is hiring. I spend more time working crimes than I do with my own Shakespeare Festival.*

# Chapter 23

Niki ran over and jumped up on Cait, begging for attention. Cait stooped and wrapped her arms around the lab's neck. "There you are. Where'd you disappear to?"

Shep leaned over and reached for the dog's paw. "Shake?"

Cait's eyes widened when Niki offered his right paw. "I didn't know he could do that."

Shep looked over at her and grinned. "He's the gift from your SEAL buddy?"

Cait stood. "From his daughter, Mindy."

"A dog's a good idea. You'd be all alone up here without June and Jim. It's nice you have people, and a canine companion, looking out for you."

"I'm very lucky, Shep."

Cait's phone rang.

She took it from her pocket and glanced at the "unknown caller" screen. "Hello."

Silence.

She waited, then disconnected. "Another hang-up."

The phone rang again.

She checked the screen. "Sadie?"

"Cait! Two men are hanging around the winery in back.

What should I do? I can't get hold of Detective Rook."

Cait's heart jolted. "Call nine-one-one. Where's Luke?"

"Running errands."

"Okay. Shep's here. Lock your doors. We'll be there shortly."

"Sadie's in trouble," she told Shep.

"What happened?"

"Two men are in her backyard. Probably the same two we've seen before. I can guess what they're looking for."

"Yeah, cocaine."

"My keys and purse are in my bedroom. Can we take your rental?"

"Sure."

"Oh, wait. I should put Niki inside." She unlocked the door for the dog and then left, securing the house behind her.

They raced around to the front of the house. Cait quickly climbed into the Toyota and fastened her seat belt.

Shep got behind the wheel, pulled around the driveway, and drove down the hill. "How far?"

"Five minutes. Turn right at the bottom of the driveway."

When they reached Post Lane, Cait said, "Turn left. They're at the end." She expected to see a black Escalade, but there were no cars parked on the road or in the Sloanes' driveway. Disappointed, she sighed. "I was looking forward to confronting those bastards. Could they have left already?"

Shep pulled off to the side in front of Sadie's house and shut the engine off. "Maybe they left their car on the street we came down." he said as he got out.

Cait jumped out of the car and slammed the door shut. "There's no parking there."

Sadie came out the front door and down the driveway to meet them. "They're gone!"

Cait glanced around, as if expecting to see the men lurking behind a tree. "Already?"

"I scared them off." Sadie reached up and gave Shep a

hug. "It's been a long time, Shep. I'm so happy to see you."

Shep smiled. "I'm glad to see you too, Sadie. I'm sorry about all this. What did you do to scare those men off?"

Her eyes sparkled. "I used Luke's gun."

Cait gasped. "Oh, Sadie, you should have stayed inside. You could have been hurt!"

"Do you know how to use a gun?" Shep asked.

The sun glistened on Sadie's red hair. She'd pulled it back in a bun and tied a pink ribbon around it. "No. The Amish are taught a gun is for hunting wild game and any other use is a sin. That's why they reject the use of violence, even in self-defense." She tilted her head to one side, mischief in her eyes. "Those men were fair game because they were on our property."

Shep laughed. "Can't argue with that."

The more Cait saw Sadie, the more she was amused at how she rationalized her behavior. *What happened to the quiet, shy, Amish girl I'd mentored in college?* When she recovered from the image of Sadie with a gun, she asked, "Where'd those men disappear to so fast?"

"That's the thing," Sadie said. "There wasn't a car. They must have cut through the field behind us. There's a road back there. At least that's the direction they ran."

Shep looked at the house and the grounds. "Nice spread you have here. Why don't I have a look around to make sure they're gone?"

Sadie nodded. "I would appreciate it. When you're done, come in for a cold beverage."

"Okay," he said as he turned toward the vineyard.

"Come on in, Cait. Iced tea?"

"Iced tea would be great."

Inside, Cait noticed Sadie had hung a patchwork quilt in the Amish colors of deep green, red, blue, and purple on the wall above the fireplace. "What a beautiful quilt, Sadie."

"Thanks. We hung it this morning, but it will eventually go in the wine-tasting room, along with others I've made. Be right back."

Sadie disappeared into the kitchen. While she was gone, the landline rang.

Shep returned while Sadie was still in the kitchen. "What's the name of their winery?"

"Turtle Creek," Cait said. "There's a shallow creek along the side of the house that inspired Sadie to want to change the name."

"The last time I saw Sadie and Luke was before they moved to Ashland, Oregon. I hope they'll be happy here once this mess is resolved."

Cait sauntered round the room, admiring the simple furnishings and colorful pillows. "Me too. They're selling their house in Santa Cruz and hope to start a family here."

Sadie returned with a tray of beverages. "Sorry it took so long. The realtor called. Okay if we sit outside?"

"Sounds good," Shep said. "There's no one out there now, Sadie. As you said, they must have cut through the back."

"Thanks for checking." Sadie led them through the dining room, out the French doors, and onto the porch. When they were seated in the gazebo, Sadie handed them their drinks. "Would you please not tell Luke about the gun when he comes home?"

"Don't you think he should know?" Cait asked.

Sadie glanced off into the distance. "I suppose he has to know about that. This whole situation has him so upset. He feels responsible."

"That's because he's protective of you. You need to tell him about those men before Detective Rook does," Cait said. "You did leave Rook a message, didn't you?"

Sadie nodded. "Yes."

"Maybe Luke could take you to the shooting range and teach you the basics about a gun," Cait suggested.

"I agree," Shep said. "Those men won't give up until they find what they're looking for. You need to be prepared."

"Prepared for what?" Luke asked as he came around the side of the house.

Shep jumped up and held his hand out. "Hey, Luke."

Luke smiled and shook Shep's hand. "Heard you were coming here on vacation."

"I was forced to use it or lose it," Shep said.

Luke set a shopping bag on the table and sat down. "What were you talking about? Who should be prepared for what?"

Cait noticed Sadie's reddened cheeks and waited for her to tell Luke about the men who had been there snooping around the winery.

Sadie took a sip of her iced tea and then set it on the table. "We had visitors." After she explained, omitting her use of the gun, Luke jumped up and hurried into the house.

When he returned, he stood over Sadie with concern in his eyes.

Cait thought he looked tearful.

"Sadie, did you use my gun to threaten those men?"

Sadie looked up at Luke. "What do you mean?"

"My gun is always in the right-hand drawer. I found it in the left drawer. What did you do?"

"Nothing. Except to let them know I had a gun. They fled through the field."

Luke crouched in front of Sadie and took her hand. "Never do that again. If anything ever happened to you, I wouldn't want to live."

Now Cait wanted to cry or sneak out and leave Sadie and Luke alone.

Shep cleared his throat. "Maybe we should leave. You both need to talk and figure this out. Detective Rook knows I'm here and that I'm willing to help."

Cait stood.

Luke rose. "Sadie should go to Santa Cruz until this is over."

Sadie jumped up. "I'm not leaving you here alone."

"Not a bad idea," Cait said. "I've never been to Santa Cruz. I could visit you."

"There you go," Luke said. "It's settled."

Sadie set her hands on her hips. "Nothing's settled, Luke. However, I will go for one day only to get my sewing machine and boxes of fabrics. I want to make quilts and pillows to decorate the wine tasting room."

"I'll go with you," Cait said and then turned to Shep. "Do you want to come?"

Shep shook his head. "You go, stick your toe in the ocean. Detective Rook and I can hook up and work on the mystery at the winery."

"If you're sure. Santa Cruz is only an hour's drive."

"I'm sure," Shep said. "There's nothing to keep you from going. Your festival is over. You've got June and Jim to watch your place and take care of Niki."

"How about tomorrow?" Sadie asked Cait.

Cait nodded. "Sure. Looks like we're going to Santa Cruz."

# Chapter 24

Cait and Sadie were on the road by nine o'clock the next morning. Sadie's BMW purred in and out of traffic on southbound I-680. The open sunroof tossed their hair and warmed their faces. Cait had never felt freer, but also a little guilty for leaving Shep so soon after his arrival.

"Any bites on selling your house?" Cait asked.

Sadie changed lanes. "Several, but at ridiculous offers. We're not willing to give it away. It's a block off the ocean and in a desirable neighborhood."

Cait remembered that Sadie and Luke bought their winery with money from a trust fund Luke's grandmother had left him. Apparently, having two mortgages wasn't a problem for them.

"We may decide to rent it," Sadie continued. "We'd need the rental income to make the repairs and upgrades to the winery and the Livermore house. I'd like to expand the tasting room so I can hang my quilts."

More comfortable behind the wheel than in the passenger seat, Cait cringed as Sadie took winding Highway 17 through the mountains. She relaxed only when they exited onto the coast Highway 1.

"Won't be long now," Sadie said.

Fifteen minutes later they pulled into the driveway of a
two-story natural wood-and-stone contemporary house—not
at all the small, modest dwelling Cait had expected to see.

"Welcome to Santa Cruz," Sadie said. She sighed. "I
loved being here. Artists, surfers, students from the university, families, and visitors. Such an interesting town. We
shouldn't have a problem renting the house. Let's go inside."

"Wow, Sadie," Cait said when she stepped into the en-
tryway with a soaring ceiling and balcony overlooking a
great room. "I had no idea this would be so beautiful. No
wonder you don't want to leave it." Like the outside, there
was lots of wood, but Cait saw nothing to resemble the simple lifestyle Sadie had grown up in.

"I do love it, but it's not me," Sadie said. "The house has
been in Luke's family for eons and gone through remodel-
ing over the years." She walked into the great room and
pivoted as if seeing the room for the first time. "There's no
denying it's got everything one could wish for. I've enjoyed
living here, particularly being so near the ocean, but I would
never tell Luke how uncomfortable I've been here. I'm used
to a simpler style."

"Can you sell it since it's been in Luke's family for such
a long time?"

"Yes. Only his parents are left now, and they seldom
come to visit. They have a nice place in Napa where their
winery is. We can't afford to keep up two places. Want a
look around? Then we'll walk down to the beach." She
grinned. "Shep told you to stick your toe in the ocean."

"I'd love to."

Sadie took Cait upstairs. The master bedroom balcony
looked out over the ocean. Cait sighed with envy as they
stood at the railing. "I don't know, Sadie. I'd find this hard
to give up."

Sadie smiled. "Henry David Thoreau wrote 'A man is
rich in proportion to the number of things which he can afford to let alone.' A life uncluttered by most of the things

people fill their lives with leaves space for what truly matters. That's how I was raised. I wake up early so I have quiet time for what's important to me: reading, writing in my
journal, and meditating." She turned and leaned her back
against the railing. "Don't get me wrong, Cait. As much as I
miss my family, I don't want to go back to the Amish lifestyle. The pressure to always be perfect is difficult, and
women have no voice in family matters. Luke loves my
quilts, pillows, and faceless dolls, and thinks I can sell them
along with the wine. What do you think? Would people buy
my quilts?"

"Sadie, of course people will buy your beautiful quilts.
There's nothing like them in Livermore that I know of."

Sadie grinned. "Good, because I'm giving you one to
hang on a wall in your new house. Let's have a look so you
can choose the one that's right for you." She walked back
into the bedroom and down the hall to another room where
she opened chest drawers filled with quilts and other Amish
handiwork. She laid several on the bed. "Pick one while I
gather my sewing machine and boxes of material. We'll
take it all back with us."

Cait had a difficult time deciding on a quilt as they were
all beautiful, but finally narrowed her pick down to a quilt
with a tan background and multi-colored prints of plum,
reds, yellows, blues, and greens. "This will be perfect for
the room I plan to turn into a dining room."

Sadie smiled. "Good choice. The pattern is called Trailing Stars. Let's take everything downstairs and then we'll
be ready for a walk on the beach."

෨෧෨

They spent an hour walking along the beach, their sandals in hand, before settling on a place for lunch. They
chose a restaurant across from the Boardwalk and sat at an
outside table where they could watch tourists board the Santa Cruz Big Trees & Pacific train.

"This has been fun," Cait said. "I'm not ready to go back."

When Cait's cell phone buzzed, she was reluctant to answer because she didn't want anything negative to interfere with how much she was enjoying Santa Cruz. She slowly reached into her handbag, saw Shep's number, and knew he wouldn't call if there weren't a problem.

"Hey."

"Been in the water yet?" he asked

"Of course, as you told me to. And you would love it here."

"Then you won't mind staying another day," he said.

Cait sat up straight in her chair. "Why? What's happened?"

"Encountered a couple guys snooping around your vineyard. I came by to talk to June and Jim to make sure nothing was happening during your absence."

"I appreciate that, Shep. Was one of them Hispanic, driving a black Escalade?"

"You got it."

Cait rolled her eyes. "Damn. Why would they think I have anything to do with drugs?"

"Don't know, but I think you've seen the last of them."

Cait smiled. "What did you do, Shep?"

"Persuaded them you had nothing they were after."

Shep had a way with his eyes, facial expression, and tone of voice that could scare the hair off of a squirrel without laying a hand on it. "Thank you." She looked at Sadie. "How soon can we leave?"

Sadie glanced at her watch. "It's two-thirty. If we leave by three, we'll avoid traffic going back."

"I heard that," Shep said. "I still think you should stay at least another day."

"One day won't make a difference," Cait said. "I'll see you soon."

Sadie rubbed her fingers up and down her glass of iced tea. "Still trying to convince us to stay here longer?"

"Yes. I don't know why those men came back to my place. None of this makes sense. But one thing I do know." She drained her tea. "We're going to have another talk with Pamela and Vince Harper. And then we're going to look deeper into who their other partner is. I'm betting that's where we'll find answers to your troubles."

# Chapter 25

The drive back to Livermore was quiet, each woman deep in thought. Cait had seldom questioned Sadie about why she'd left Sugarcreek, besides her need for higher education. Sadie had never talked about her obedience to her community and God or submission to the Ordnung, the set of rules for Amish living. Cait had been to Sugarcreek, nestled at the foot of Appalachia, several times before she'd met Sadie. She'd seen the farms, the buggies, the simpler lifestyle, and the serenity. She wondered what went on in Sadie's mind as she tried to understand the chaos at the winery. Cait doubted the years away from Sugarcreek could erase all Sadie had been brought up to believe in.

"If you'd like," Sadie said, "you could go back to Santa Cruz with us when we pack the rest of our belongings. We could spend more time at the ocean."

Drawn from her thoughts, Cait turned in her seat to face Sadie. "I would love to. And I'd like to buy a couple of your beautiful quilts for my Shakespeare theaters."

Sadie smiled. "That can be arranged."

Twenty minutes later, Sadie dropped Cait off at her house with a promise to call.

The sound of the car door closing had Niki racing around the side of the house to greet her. He jumped around Cait as if she'd been gone for days. Right behind him came Shep.

"You're back," Shep said. He glanced at her sandaled feet. "How was the water?"

"Cold." She removed her sunglasses and stroked Niki.

"Hope you don't mind my hanging out here. You've got a good thing going with June and Jim and Marcus. I can't see you ever leaving."

"Nope. I'm here to stay, as far as I know anyway." She tilted her head. "By the way, how *did* you get those men to leave?"

Shep draped his arm across her shoulder. "Since you asked, let's go inside, and I'll tell you."

Marcus was in the kitchen when they walked in the back door. "Hey, you missed a little excitement while you were gone."

"So I hear. I'm waiting for details," Cait said.

"I didn't lay a finger on either of those snakes," Shep said. "But I did reach in their car and grab the keys. Their Escalade couldn't be hot-wired, so they had no choice but to have it towed. I understood their Spanish, but it was too dirty for your ears."

Marcus laughed. "The expressions on their faces were priceless. And June and Jim almost didn't keep it together when they saw the SUV being loaded onto the tow truck, and how those guys had to ride up front with the driver. Is that even legal?"

Cait laughed. "Don't know and don't care. Shep, you could stay here tonight in case they return."

He hesitated. "They can't come back unless they have another car. But keep your gun handy just in case. And call nine-one-one and then me. I let Detective Rook know what happened."

"Good, glad you called him," she said. "Want to go downtown for dinner?"

"I'd like that." He turned to Marcus. "Join us?"

"Thanks, but I want to finish up here before I leave. And then I need to stop by to see my mom on my way home."

"I'll ask June and Jim if they want to go with us," Cait said. She opened the door to leave and found the Harts on the doorstep.

"Shep said you'd be back by now," June said. "Have a good time?"

"Perfect. I'm glad we went," Cait said. "Shep and I are going downtown for dinner. Would you like to join us?"

"Love to," June said, "but I've got a roast in the oven. You heard what happened when those men came and started snooping around?"

Cait smiled. "Oh, yeah. Classic Shep." She turned to him. "By the way, what did you do with their keys?"

Shep shook his pants pocket. "I almost tossed them into the vineyard, but it would be too easy for them to find."

Jim chuckled. "While you're at dinner, I'll walk around the property, make sure those guys haven't been stupid enough to return."

"I'd appreciate it." Cait glanced at the clock on the wall: five o'clock. "Shep, okay if we leave by five-thirty? We can stroll through downtown and decide where to eat."

He shrugged. "Whatever."

"Good. Come upstairs and I'll show you my apartment."

"And I'll check on our dinner," June said. "Enjoy your evening."

Marcus headed to his office.

Cait led the way upstairs, with Niki following behind them. On the second floor, she said, "I never seem to have enough time to spend on this floor, but there is a small TV, tiny kitchen, and guest bedroom. And tons of books."

Shep walked around, flipped through pages of an art book on the coffee table, and nodded. "Nice." He tested the leather sofa. "Real nice."

"You could change your mind and stay here instead of at the hotel. Upstairs is my bedroom." She unlocked the door to her bedroom. "RT installed this lock so no one could come up. With the gift shop on the first floor, people would start to wander up here."

Shep and Niki followed Cait up the stairs. "I like your SEAL already."

Cait smiled. *Me too.*

"Cool," Shep said as he walked over to the bay window and looked out. Next, he strolled over to her desk where her laptop lay.

"Like living in a tree house." The sun streamed through top panels of the stained glass, spreading multiple colors across walls and the chaise lounges.

Niki located a sunny place and sprawled out on the rug.

"This is nice, Cait. Now I can visualize where you are when we're on Skype." He turned toward the stairs. "Why don't I wait downstairs on that comfy sofa while you get ready?"

"Okay. I won't be long," she said. "Don't get too comfortable or you won't want to go out for dinner."

"Not a chance," he said as he headed down the stairs.

Niki watched him go, but didn't move from his place in the sun.

Cait changed into white jeans, a long-sleeved blue shirt, and sandals. She grabbed a pink sweater from the back of the desk chair, and soon was back downstairs with Niki where she found Shep leafing through another coffee table book. She sat next to him on the sofa. Shep set the book aside.

"How are things in my old department?" Cait asked.

"The same wisecrackers, couple of new officers, and too many homicides to keep up with." He settled into a corner of the sofa, one leg over the other, and launched into a story about a rookie.

Cait was laughing at Shep's story when she thought she heard footsteps on the stairs. Even Niki rose with a low growl. She turned, expecting to see Marcus.

RT stood on the second floor landing, an uncertain look on his face.

Startled, Cait jumped up. "RT! Why didn't you let me know you were coming?" Her heart raced with excitement at seeing him. She went over and took his hand. "Come, meet Shep. You've heard me mention my mentor at the Columbus PD." She turned to Shep. "Shep, this is Royal Tanner."

Shep stood, walked over and held his hand out to RT. "I've heard about you too. Nice to finally meet you."

RT shook Shep's hand. "Yeah, you too."

Cait stared at both men, disappointed at the coolness radiating from RT and the frown lines etched in his brow. *Is he angry Shep is here? Or jealous?*

"RT, did you drive up or fly?" she asked, anxious to get a conversation rolling.

"Brought the silver bomb," he said, meaning his silver Airstream trailer. "Parked it in the large lot."

"You came at the perfect time because we were about to go downtown for dinner. Now we can all go." *And give you and Shep a better chance to know each other.*

"Not tonight," RT said. "Maybe tomorrow."

Frustrated by his attitude, she said, "Then how about we all have breakfast here? I'll ask June and Jim to join us. And Marcus."

"Hey," Shep said, "why don't we skip dinner, Cait, and you and RT enjoy the evening together. I'll get something to eat and then go back to the hotel. I'll come for breakfast, if that's okay."

Always a gentleman, Shep found a way out of an awkward situation, Cait thought. "I'm starved. So who is going to dinner with me?"

"Don't change your plans for me. Have dinner with Shep," RT said. "Mindy and I stopped to eat before we got here."

Cait gasped. "Mindy's here?"

RT smiled for the first time. "Yeah, and she's eager to see you, but she's asleep in the trailer. We'll see you in the morning for breakfast." He patted Niki on the head. "Mindy's excited to see you, too." He nodded to Shep and then turned to the stairs.

Cait, Shep, and Niki followed RT downstairs. The kitchen door closed behind RT without another word.

Disappointed RT hadn't hugged her or kissed her before he left, Cait turned to Shep. "I could use a margarita."

# Chapter 26

Livermore's First Street pedestrian walkway was lined with hanging baskets of trailing flowers. People sat at outside tables, laughing and talking. It was almost seven by the time Cait and Shep decided on dinner at the First Street Alehouse, the same place where she and RT had recently eaten. They sat at an outside table. Cait kept looking at the street, expecting to see a black Escalade with two men inside.

"If you don't focus on what you're drinking, you'll be guzzling down that bottle of vinegar instead of your wine," Shep said.

Cait shuddered at the thought as she picked up her glass of chardonnay. "RT and I were sitting out here when we first noticed the same Escalade and the two men inside watching us." She sipped her wine and then set it down and started on her beer-battered fried shrimp. "It's silly, but I almost wish those men would show up so I could have them arrested for harassment."

"Let's talk about a more pleasant subject, like Royal Tanner." He grinned. "A jealous son of a gun, isn't he?"

Cait grinned back. "You noticed, huh?"

"Oh, yeah. Cut him some slack. After all, he's been busy serving our country, then when he comes back he finds his gal sitting cozily on a sofa and laughing with another man. I know how I'd feel." He picked up his club sandwich and began to eat. "As much as I appreciate the offer to stay in your apartment, I don't think that's such a good idea with Royal Tanner here."

Cait used her fork to stab another shrimp. "I hadn't thought of it that way. Our relationship confuses me. RT runs hot and cold."

Shep laughed. "That's what men are supposed to do, Cait, confuse women."

She stared at him and bit into her shrimp. "I'm not ready for a serious relationship."

"Sure you are. You just don't know it yet." He took a long drink of his beer and set the glass back on the table. "Mindy is the little girl who wanted you to have Niki for protection?"

Cait's face lit up. "Yes. Wait until you see her. She's adorable."

Shep raised his eyebrow. "You'd make a great step-mom."

"I'm too selfish."

"Nah. You're one of the most giving people I know." He glanced at the tables around them and then leaned in closer. "When you were with our department, you gave your time and your own money to protect children from abusive parents. And you almost adopted a baby girl to keep her from going into the system. But then that ass of a husband of yours put his foot down and denied you the opportunity of having a child."

Cait looked at her plate and decided she wasn't hungry any more. She pushed it away and finished her wine. "He wanted his own child, not someone else's."

Cait knew Shep would make a fantastic dad, but he hadn't allowed himself to get seriously involved with another woman after his fiancé died from a brain tumor five years ago. Instead, he worked long hours, and, when he wasn't working, he biked, ran races, played tennis, and swam at a club near his house. Women fell all over themselves whenever Shep walked into a room, vying for his attention. He was one of those men who seemed to get better looking with age—the graying tips of hair at his temples, the crinkly smile lines at his eyes. She prayed he would meet someone to love again and raise a family. *What a pair we are. Both unlucky in love.*

"His loss." Shep nodded at her empty glass. "Another one?"

"No thanks."

"Then let's get out of here." He motioned to a waiter for the check. "I'll drive you back and then turn in myself after I make a few phone calls."

Cait raised her eyebrow. "You're on vacation, remember?"

He pulled out his wallet and removed a credit card to pay the bill. "Got a difficult homicide I should check on."

"Have you set a golf date with your friends at Pebble Beach?"

"Wednesday, but that's subject to change."

"Why?"

"You never know." After he signed the bill, he tucked his wallet away. "Ready?"

Cait pushed her chair back and rose. She knew he was on vacation, but she also knew he couldn't turn his back on a friend in trouble, and Sadie and Luke were his friends.

They worked their way around the tables and out onto the street where they'd lucked out with a parking space in front.

"Sadie and Luke's situation at their winery intrigues me," he said. "If I can help, it's what I want to do."

Cait wrapped her arms around herself against the chilly night air.

When they were in the car, she gave him a speculative glance and measured the unflinching intelligence radiating in his eyes. "I'm so glad you're my friend and not my enemy."

c/෨c/෨

The next morning, Mindy timidly entered the kitchen door with RT. Her eyes lit up when she saw Cait and Niki. She dropped to her knees, wrapped her arms around the dog's neck, and looked up at Cait. "Isn't he the best dog ever?"

"You bet," Cait said. She set the spatula down and smiled at Mindy. "And he's the most thoughtful gift anyone's ever given me."

Marcus entered the kitchen from his office. "Hey, RT." He looked at Mindy. "I didn't know your daughter was with you when I saw you last night."

"She was asleep in the trailer," RT said. "I didn't want to wake her to bring her inside. Where's your friend?" he asked Cait, his voice cool.

"Shep will be here," Cait said. "He had business to tend to. Sit down and I'll pour you a cup of coffee. Mindy, how about a glass of orange juice?"

Mindy nodded, her blonde curls bobbing up and down.

RT picked Mindy up and set her on a stool at the counter. "Smells like Cait's fixing bacon, one of your favorite foods for breakfast. I wonder how she knew."

"Daddy, *everyone* likes bacon."

The doorbell rang.

"I'll get it," Marcus said. When he returned, Shep was with him.

Shep smiled. "Morning, everyone. Smells good in here."

Cait looked at the three men in her life and hoped they would all get along. She smiled. "Hi, Shep. Pull out a stool. Breakfast is ready—waffles, sliced strawberries, and bacon. Juice and coffee, too."

"I'll get the coffee," Marcus said. "I've eaten, but I'll snatch a strip of bacon."

"Thanks, Marcus," Cait said. She set the food on the counter, poured orange juice for Mindy, and then sat down to eat. "I never thought this would happen, all of us together like this. That includes you, too, Marcus."

After Marcus filled everyone's coffee cup, Shep held his out. "A toast to Cait from her ex-fellow officers. As much as the Columbus PD would like to have you back, I don't see that happening. All of us wish the best for you."

Caught off guard, tears flooded Cait's eyes. At a loss for words, she cut her waffle and mumbled thanks.

Shep, sitting next to Cait, smiled. "Hey, don't cry. When I leave, you'll be happy to see me go."

*Not a chance*, Cait thought.

"Cait, my daddy will make you feel better," Mindy said.

*He definitely could if he'd allow himself to*, Cait thought. She smiled at Mindy. "Shep, I forgot to introduce you to RT's daughter, Mindy."

Shep set his coffee cup down and smiled at the little girl. "I've heard nice things about you, Mindy. How old are you?"

"Six. I'll be in first grade."

"You'll have lots of fun in school," Shep said.

"That's what my daddy said. Do you have a kid?"

Shep smiled. "No, but I'd like to."

"Why don't you?"

"Mindy," RT said. "Eat your breakfast."

Cait said, "Shep and I had dinner last night at the Ale-house, where you and I ate."

RT looked at her. "See any black Escalades?"

Cait shook her head. Thinking about Mindy sitting there taking everything in, she said, "Later, Shep can tell you the latest about that car and the men inside." She exchanged looks with Shep who nodded.

There was a knock on the back door.

When Marcus opened it, Grace Bishop stood on the doorstep.

"Hi," Grace said. "Oh, sorry. Looks like I'm interrupting. We're here for another rehearsal, if that's still okay."

Cait slid off her stool. "Come in, Grace. Of course it's

okay. I forgot, that's all." She picked up her cell phone from where she'd left it on the counter and punched a few buttons to unlock the Blackfriars Theater. "Done. Let me or Marcus know when you're leaving."

"I will, thanks," Grace said and left.

Cait shut the door and explained to Shep and RT that Grace and her students were from Las Positas College and needed a place to rehearse their upcoming play.

As Cait started clearing the dishes, her cell phone rang. She glanced at the screen. "Hi, Sadie."

"Cait, there are a couple men here from the DEA and one from Homeland Security," Sadie said. "I called Detective Rook and he's coming, but I thought you might want to come too."

"I do. I expected they'd get involved. Shep and RT are here. We'll see you shortly." She disconnected and looked at her friends as they stood at the counter watching her. "It didn't take long for the DEA to show up at Sadie and Luke's winery, along with Homeland Security. Detective Rook will be there too. I assume you both want to go with me."

"Absolutely," Shep said.

"Sure," RT said. "Do you think June and Jim would look after Mindy while we're gone?"

"They would love to," Cait said and smiled at Mindy.

Mindy stared at her dad, a bewildered look on her face. "Who's June and Jim?"

"Honey, June gave you freshly baked chocolate chip cookies the last time we were here," RT said. "I'll walk you over to their RV. Niki can come, too. Okay?"

Mindy grinned. "I remember. Maybe she'll have more cookies."

"June always has cookies," Cait said. "Niki's outside, RT. We'll meet you in front."

"After RT and Mindy left, Shep said, "We can take my rental."

She slipped her cell phone into her jeans pocket and hoped there wouldn't be any trouble at Luke and Sadie's.

# Chapter 27

Unfamiliar cars were parked in front of Sadie and Luke's house when Cait, Shep, and RT arrived. Another car pulled in behind theirs and Cait recognized it as the unmarked Ford Detective Rook usually drove.

"Lots of law enforcement agencies here," Shep said.

Cait nodded as she ticked off the ones she knew were there: LPD, CPD, DEA, Homeland Security, and US Navy.

Rook shook hands with RT and Shep. "Never expected this, the four of us together. When did you get here, RT?"

"Got here last night," RT said.

"Good to have you back. So let's get this over with." Rook started up the driveway.

Voices could be heard from around back, so he headed in that direction. It took Cait two seconds to spot the DEA agents standing in front of the winery building talking to Luke. The bulge beneath their suit jackets made it clear the agents were carrying. Standing apart from them was a third man. Cait hung back to look for Sadie, while Rook, RT, and Shep walked over to the agents.

"Cait! Over here," Sadie called.

Cait saw her friend standing in the gazebo and hurried over. "Have they said anything yet about the drugs?"

"No, but by the grim look on their faces, we're just another illegal drug trafficking problem for them. They've been talking to Luke since before I called you. You don't think they'll arrest him do you?"

"Rook won't let that happen," Cait assured her. "He's been here from the start. He knows you've done nothing wrong."

Sadie smiled. "When did RT get here?"

"Last night. Mindy's with him."

"I'd love to meet her."

"You will. She's with June and Jim right now." Cait saw the men enter the winery. "Let's see what's going on."

Inside the winery, Rook was saying, "I wanted to give you a heads up if you were already working a case involving Miguel Quintero. Don't know who his partner is."

Cait looked at Rook. "Did you tell them what happened yesterday when those guys came to my place?"

"Haven't gotten around to that yet," Rook said.

Cait raised her eyebrow. "What about the dead PI? Last name Thornton. His initials are RAT."

The agents stared at her but neither cracked a smile.

"Cait, these are DEA Agents Dunne and Turner, and Harrison Aimes from Homeland Security," Rook said.

Cait shook their hands. The two smart-suited DEA agents could have been twins—mid-thirties, square jawed, blue-eyed—except one had dark hair and the other was a redhead. Cait knew Homeland Security was involved because the cocaine had been traced back across the border to Mexico.

"The PI's name was Regan Alex Thornton," Rook continued. "He was legit as far as I know, but who hired him is still unknown."

The redheaded DEA, Dunne, pulled out a small electronic notepad from inside his suit jacket and tapped a few keys.

Turner looked at Cait with quick assessment. "Why would those men go to your house?"

"That's what I'd like to know," she said, "but I have a

theory. The previous owners, Pamela and Vince Harper, were either into drug trafficking or know who was. Quintero and his partner came looking for the drugs and discovered them missing. They decide to stake out this winery, but when Sadie left they followed her to my house. I'm guessing they think I have the drugs or know where they are." Her frustration built as she talked.

"Do you?" Turner asked.

Cait's jaw dropped. "*What?*"

"Hey!" RT said. "Back off! Cait is not involved, except as Sadie and Luke's friend. Look elsewhere for your drug couriers."

Cait, thrilled at the hard set of RT's jaw and his attack-ready stance, restrained herself from throwing her arms around his neck. Then she noticed the subtle smile on Shep's face and knew what he was thinking: *her navy SEAL to the rescue.*

"I can vouch for Cait," Rook said. "She was a cop and a crime analyst in Ohio before moving to Livermore. She knows what she's talking about and has excellent reasoning skills."

Praise from Detective Rook! Cait hadn't seen that coming.

Rook pointed to the disassembled boxes in the middle of the winery. "Those are the boxes of glass bottles where the cocaine was hidden. I assume you'll want to check to make sure we didn't overlook any."

Cait bit her lip to keep from laughing. *Way to go, Rook.*

"I don't think that will be necessary," Agent Dunne said after hesitating. "We've seen enough."

"Then I'll walk you to your cars." Rook handed each agent his business card.

"Wow," Luke said, after the agents left. "I'm glad Detective Rook is on our side."

"What happens now?" Sadie asked.

"Probably nothing," RT said, "at least as far as the DEA is concerned. They're more focused on dismantling high-level trafficking and terrorist organizations that are more notorious than what you've got going here."

Sadie squinted into the distance, a far away look in her eyes. "That Quintero guy and his partner are still hanging around. What are we to do about them?"

Shep smiled at RT. "I don't know about you, but I don't mind making my presence known around here. Hey, I'm on vacation and you're off duty, right? Let's kill time enjoying the wine and chasing bad guys."

RT nodded. "Agreed."

"What are you two up to?" Rook said when he joined them.

"Oh, just doing our jobs," Shep and RT said.

# Chapter 28

The drug couriers won't come today," Rook said. "Too many cars parked in front." He pulled his keys from his jacket pocket. "I'm on duty or I'd stay to enjoy a glass of wine with you. Instead, I'll do something useful, like contacting Pamela and Vince Harper for another chat."

Cait sat up in her seat. "Get their uncle's name and number. He helped the siblings finance this winery. I'm guessing he hired the PI guy to check up on them. I'd like to know why."

Rook stood over Cait and raised his eyebrow. "Is that so?"

Cait groaned. "I know that look. You're going to give me the old run around about wanting me to come work for the Livermore PD."

"Why not? Great benefits. Best bunch of cops around." He threw a wink at Shep. "Plus, you've had your nose in every investigation I've been involved with since you moved here."

"Only because I was the victim," she said. "And now my friends are."

Shep laughed. "You're not serious. You want to *hire* her?"

Cait glared at him. "Why is that funny?"

"Sorry," Shep said, a sheepish grin on his face.

"You can't be seriously considering it, Cait," RT said.

Cait looked at the men, all half grinning. Even Sadie wore a big smile. "Geez, you can't blame me for wanting to help. Someone should go to Sonoma where the Harpers lived and their uncle has his own winery. I wouldn't mind driving up there to check it out."

"Check what out?" Rook asked with a straight face. "Some wine tasting?"

Cait bristled a bit, but still, she thought it was a good idea to delve further into Pamela and Vince's background. And since they'd worked at their uncle's winery, somebody there might be willing to talk about them. When she was a cop, she wanted no question left unanswered. Right now, what bothered her the most was the identity of the person on Pamela's Facebook page. If Cait were a betting person, she'd bet he was either a partner in their winery or otherwise involved. There had to be a reason why his name was a secret.

Shep leaned forward in his seat. "Detective Rook, I'll volunteer to drive to Sonoma if you think it would do any good."

Cait gave him thumbs up before turning to Rook. "Holly Gardner, Sadie and Luke's realtor, should be able to tell you who their uncle is. He helped finance the sale. Who knows? She might even be able to identify the other partner, if there is one."

"Actually, I have a call into Holly," Rook said. "I'd prefer to invite their uncle to come here, meet with me at the police station to discuss the case. The Harpers might open up more in his presence."

Cait grinned. "Now you're talking. How long ago did you call Holly?"

"Before coming here this morning." Rook's golden-brown eyes sparkled. "Glad you approve."

She felt her face flush with embarrassment and sat back in her seat. "No disrespect meant, Rook."

"None taken." He smiled. "You'd make an interesting addition to the department, should you decide to get back into law enforcement. Which I hope you don't."

Cait frowned. "Why not? You're always hinting at it."

"You've got your hands full with the Shakespeare festivals," he said. "I like giving you a hard time whenever you interfere with my investigations." He turned to leave. "See you later."

"I like him," Shep said after Rook left. "Reminds me how you and I used to spar when we were partners."

"I'm sure you've got good tales to tell," RT said. "I'd like to hear them sometime."

Shep laughed. "Sorry, no tales out of school or Cait will send me on my way."

ᥱᕟᥱᕟ

Shep dropped Cait and RT back off at Cait's house.

"I'll get Mindy," RT said and turned toward the path leading to June and Jim's RV. "I want to spend time with her before we return to Sadie's, unless you want to go back by yourself, Shep."

"No, we can go later," Shep said.

RT nodded and left.

"Let's see if Grace and her students are still here," Cait said. "It might be fun watching them rehearse."

An engine noise caught their attention. Cait turned and recognized Kurt Mathews white pickup. She waved. "That's Kurt, my vineyard manager."

Kurt parked in front of the house and stepped out of his truck. "How's it going, Cait?"

"The vines look green and lush to me, but I admit I haven't spent as much time as I should in the vineyard. I count on you to let me know if we have a problem." She smiled.

"Kurt, this is Shep Church, my friend from Ohio. We were partners at the Columbus PD."

The men shook hands. "Nice to meet you," Kurt said. "Cait, does the offer still stand for me to continue working your vineyard, but on a part-time basis?"

Cait worried Kurt would find a full time job at another vineyard and leave her in the lurch. "Absolutely," she said.

Kurt crossed his arms and grinned. "I would be happy to stay on and manage your vineyard. Your vineyard is small enough to split my time between here and another vineyard."

Relief spread through Cait's body. She hesitated to bring up Marcus's interest in the vineyard because of his criminal background, a fact Kurt knew about. But Kurt saved her from the dilemma.

"If you don't mind," Kurt said, "I'd like to talk to Marcus. If he's serious about learning how to work the vineyard, I'll help him. We're grown men—no reason we can't get along. What's past is past."

"I'm happy to hear that," she said, remembering his distrust of Marcus. "Thanks, Kurt. I just got back, but Marcus is probably in the house if you want to go in and talk to him now. Or I can ask him to come outside."

"I'll wait out here for him."

Cait nodded. "I'll let him know. I hope it works out."

"What's that all about?" Shep asked as they walked around to the back of the house.

"I think I told you Marcus had grown up in this house and that he spent time in prison for breaking and entering. Kurt and Marcus knew each other in high school. That was years ago. When Marcus was released, Tasha hired him. She believed in second chances."

"I remember," Shep said. "He did everything for her, right?"

"Yes. From taking her to doctor appointments to maintaining her Jaguar. And because he is good with a hammer—" She smiled. "—he built my new gift shop." She tapped the app on her cell phone and unlocked the house. "He's invaluable to me."

Marcus walked in from his office behind the kitchen. "How'd it go?" Today, he looked "business casual" in a pair of khakis, a long-sleeved blue shirt, with sleeves rolled up. His blue eyes, Cait noted, were not as wary, his face not as creased with lines of tension and frustration as when they'd first met. He even walked with a lighter step. She hoped his meeting with Kurt wouldn't change any of that.

"It was a quick meeting. Then all those alphabets left."

Marcus stared at her. "Huh?"

"You know, the guys from the DEA, DHS, and all that," Shep said.

"Oh. At least Sadie and Luke weren't arrested—or were they?"

"No," Cait said. "Shep and RT are going back in case the bad guys return." Then she remembered Kurt. "Marcus, Kurt Mathews wants to talk to you. He's outside." She hesitated. "He's going to stay on as a part-time manager and, if you're still interested, he'd like to show you how he manages the vineyard. And you can still attend vintner classes at Las Positas if you want."

Cait watched as lines returned around his mouth and creases lined his forehead. "You had to twist his arm to agree to that."

"No, he brought it up," Cait said. "He's sincere, Marcus. Give him a chance."

"Hell. I don't know."

"It's an excellent opportunity for advancement," she said.

After a tense moment, Marcus let out a long sigh. "*Okay.*"

After he left, Cait said, "I hope it works."

Niki preceded RT and Mindy in the back door. "What's wrong with Marcus? He looks like he's seen a ghost."

Cait smiled. "Maybe he did." *Tasha's ghost.*

# Chapter 29

"This is for you," Mindy said. "Chocolate chip cookies." She handed Cait a basket shaped liked a bird's nest. "June said I can help her make more when these are gone."

Cait's heart melted like chocolate at the sight of Mindy. "Thank you. What a cute basket." She turned back the napkin lining the basket and offered cookies to everyone. "I forgot to ask Marcus if Grace Bishop is still here. It would be fun to watch her students rehearse. Who wants to come with me?"

Before anyone could answer, Marcus returned, a slight smile on his face. "I'm going to help Kurt in the vineyard."

"Oh, Marcus," Cait said, relieved. "That's wonderful." That Kurt and Marcus had sorted out their problems enough to work together was a monkey off her back. Now she could pick up where she'd left off with her own vintner classes. Hopefully, no one would threaten to kill her like before.

"Time will tell," Marcus said, "but I think we've come to a mutual understanding." He tugged at the collar of his shirt. "Hot out there."

This was one of those awkward moments when Cait wasn't sure what to do with RT and Shep, now that they were both here. "Is Grace still here, Marcus?"

"Nope. They've left. Be back tomorrow. Got plans for lunch?"

"I can make sandwiches, grilled cheese or BLTs. I'm starved, so decide quickly before I keel over."

"Grilled cheese!" Mindy shouted.

Cait grinned. "Grilled cheese it is. With avocado?"

Mindy turned her nose up and shook her head.

"I'll make the sandwiches," RT offered.

"I'll help," Marcus said.

RT reached in his jeans pocket, pulled out his keys, and handed them to Cait. "Mindy, recall what's in the trailer?"

Mindy jumped up and down. "Yes!"

"Get it and bring it back here."

"Okay. Come on, Cait," Mindy said.

Bewildered, Cait asked, "Can Shep come too?"

Mindy's eyes danced. "Yes."

"What are we going to find in the trailer, Mindy?" Cait asked as they left the big house and walked toward the parking lot where RT had parked.

"A playmate for Niki?" Shep guessed.

"Nooo. It's a secret."

Cait hadn't realized Niki had followed them until he barked when they reached the trailer. "It's okay, Niki. You're not going anywhere."

"Whoa," Shep said. "Will you look at that! A silver Airstream trailer. Must be from the 1970s."

"I think so," Cait said.

"The Hummer's not too shabby, either."

"I guess." She checked the key ring for the key to the trailer. When she got the door open, she helped Mindy up the steps.

"Would RT mind if I looked inside?" Shep asked.

"You can come in," Mindy said, "but Cait can't. She has to stay out here."

Cait sat on the bottom step with Niki and waited for Mindy and Shep to emerge. "I don't think they brought you a playmate," she said as she petted the dog.

"Let us out, Cait," Mindy said.

Cait stood and helped Mindy down. Shep jumped down and Cait locked the trailer. She couldn't tell what was in the wrapped package Mindy held but it was shaped like a book.

Mindy skipped along beside Cait and Shep on their way back to the house.

Cait sniffed as she entered the kitchen, savoring the smell of cheese sandwiches on the griddle. Chips had been poured into a bowl along with olives and dill pickle spears in another. A pitcher of iced tea sat on the counter.

"Here, Daddy," Mindy said as she offered the package to him.

RT turned from the stove and winked at his daughter. "Give it to Cait."

Cait assumed the package held RT's newest children's book. How he did his job and wrote was beyond her. "Can I open it now?"

RT turned his spatula over to Marcus to dish up the sandwiches and put them on the plates. "Sure, why not."

She untied the twine and pulled away the brown paper. "RT! I love it. *Sea Jewels*, a great title. The book cover is gorgeous." She smiled at him. "Thank you!"

Mindy grinned. "Open it."

Cait opened it to the first page. What she read didn't register for several seconds. *To Cait, a bright jewel in the sea and in my life.* Her heart lurched. She reread it. "How— why—" Overwhelmed with emotion, she ducked her head as her eyes teared.

"Look in the back, Cait," Mindy said.

Cait turned the book over and opened it. Inside was a small envelope taped to the back. She turned the flap up and pulled out a small stack of hand-written notes.

"You might want to read those in private," RT suggested.

She nodded and tucked the notes back in the envelope, but she could tell the first was a short poem. She closed the book and held it to her chest.

"You can kiss him now," Mindy said.

"Don't mind us," Shep said. "We'll start eating."

Cait's cheeks flushed as she stepped closer to RT. She hesitated and then wrapped her arms around his neck and kissed him on the lips. "Thank you," she whispered.

Mindy clapped. "Let's eat!"

∽∾∽

After lunch, Cait cleared the dishes but her mind was on the change in RT during lunch. While they all ate, he smiled, opened up to Shep about his work, and asked Marcus about his horse, all the time resting his hand on Cait's knee. Was this a lasting change? Was it an indication he wanted to take their relationship to another, perhaps more permanent level?

Cait's cell phone rang. She put the towel down and glanced at the screen. "Detective Rook. Got news for us?" She looked back at RT and Shep.

"Talked to Calvin Harper, the siblings' uncle," Rook said. "He'll be here tomorrow. Pamela and Vince have agreed to meet with us at eleven o'clock at the police station. After that, we'll go to Luke and Sadie's winery. Care to join us at Turtle Creek Winery about noon? RT and Shep, too?"

"Yes! You've been busy," Cait said. "I'm putting you on speaker." She drew close to Shep and RT. "Okay. What should we expect? Did Mr. Harper hire the PI?"

Rook chuckled. "You have good instincts, Cait. He did indeed hire the PI."

"Why?" she asked.

Another chuckle from Rook. "There was another partner, as you surmised. His name is Bill Reigo, and he's Pamela's soon-to-be ex-husband."

"There was a film, around 2005, about Reigo, a Deep Sea Monster," RT said. "Let's hope the real Bill Reigo isn't a monster."

"We may never know if we can't find him," Rook said. "Mr. Harper has no idea where Bill might be, but maybe Pamela does. We'll soon find out. Let's meet tomorrow at noon at Luke and Sadie's winery."

"Good," Cait said. "Can't wait. Maybe your investigation will be a short one and we can all live happily ever after."

"Dream on, Cait," Rook said. "See you all tomorrow."

"Wow," Cait said after she disconnected the call.

"I don't know Rook well," Shep said, "but you must have lit a fire under him."

Cait frowned. "He works at a difference pace than I do. Dang, I forgot to ask if Bill Reigo is the guy on Pamela's Facebook page."

"You can ask her tomorrow," RT said, "but today Shep and I said we'd spend time with Sadie and Luke. We could help clean up the scattered mess of glass bottles the DEA and Homeland Security guys made while we're there. Would you take care of Mindy?"

Cait grinned. "Are you kidding? I'd love to. Okay with you, Mindy?"

Mindy nodded. "We can help June make more cookies."

*Or maybe I'll have a chance to privately read the notes in the back of RT's new book, Sea Jewels.*

၆၁၆၁၆

RT and Shep were back at Cait's house by five-thirty, with a couple glasses of wine under their belts and in a jovial mood. Apparently, Cait had worried for nothing whether RT and Shep would like each other.

RT picked Mindy up, kissed her, and set her back down. "As Rook predicted, no bad guys showed up. We did spend time walking through their vineyard and found where we think the men disappeared to when Sadie flashed Luke's gun at them. There is a fence, but only to mark the property line. Easy to jump and then take off down the road on the other side."

"That's a nice piece of property," Shep said. "I almost wish I was a vintner. Did you know Luke still does free-lance work for *Outside Magazine*?"

Cait nodded.

"And Sadie's amazing," Shep continued. "Separation from the world is the Amish trademark, but to see Sadie now, how she's changed from when you introduced me to her at Dennison University, is remarkable."

"At times, I forget she's Amish, or rather, was," Cait said, "but occasionally it slips out in her speech, the way she phrases sentences. I'm sure she has moments when she misses her family."

"Yeah, she's bound to. Look guys," Shep said. "I'm going to take off and go back to the hotel to catch up on the work I brought with me. I'll see you in the morning. About ten okay?"

"Yes, but you could come for breakfast," Cait said.

"A cup of coffee would be good."

"Okay. I'll walk you out."

Shep and RT shook hands. "It was a good day," Shep said. "See you tomorrow. Hang onto RT," he said after they left the house. "He's a good guy, smart, and obviously devoted to Mindy. But it must be tough splitting his time three ways."

"Three ways?"

He grinned. "Sure. Work, being a dad, and being with you. Not to mention the long distance he has to travel to get here."

"He also has a vineyard to run and the children's books he writes."

"Makes me feel I'm going backward by comparison."

"Not you, never," she said. When they reached his car, she casually asked, "Anyone special in your life, Shep?"

"Maybe." He smiled. "See you tomorrow."

Cait waited until Shep's car disappeared from sight before returning to the house. Mindy and RT were munching on the newest batch of chocolate chip cookies Mindy had helped June bake.

There was a quick rap on the back door. Cait saw June smiling through the window in the door and opened it.

"I've got lots of pot roast left over from last night if you'd like to join Jim and me for dinner," June said. "We can sit outside in the shade and have wine and cookies for dessert."

"I'm famished," RT said. He looked at Cait.

"Me, too."

"Where's Shep?" June asked.

"He left. He'll be back tomorrow when we're all going to Sadie and Luke's to meet with Detective Rook, Pamela and Vince, and their uncle."

"Oh, that should be interesting," June said. "You can tell me how it came about while we're eating. Let's go. Dinner's ready."

After dinner and dessert, June asked Mindy if she'd like to stay and watch a video with her. "I have a drawer full you could pick from."

Mindy's head bobbed up and down. "Can I, Daddy?"

"Sure. Cait and I will take a walk."

It was obvious to Cait that June's offer was meant to give her and RT time alone. She knew exactly what she would do with the time. After they left, Cait said, "This is a chance to read the notes you'd written."

"Then let's not waste a minute of what time we have," RT said, his face serious.

In the kitchen, Cait grabbed the book and RT's hand and headed to the stairs. She hesitated on the second floor, but RT held his other hand out. "Wrong floor. Key?"

Cait fumbled in her jeans pocket for the key to unlock the door to her bedroom and handed it to him. He unlocked it and quickly slammed the lock firmly in place after they were inside the stairwell. Her skin tingled when RT took her hand and climbed the stairs to the third floor.

He pressed his lips to hers, walking her backward. He never took his eyes off her as he lowered her to the bed. Heat raged between them as they tore at each other's clothes. Nothing else mattered as they became reacquainted with each other's bodies.

Cait felt her life was finally unfolding exactly as it was meant to.

# Chapter 30

That was the best walk Cait could remember taking—into her bedroom with RT, where she still lingered the next morning. RT had left the previous night to rescue June, who'd volunteered her time to baking more cookies with Mindy after dinner. He'd been different, less cautious, and more vulnerable during their lovemaking. After RT left, she'd reread the nine poetic notes he'd written. She wondered why nine. Would a tenth note be a declaration of love?

With that question lingering on her mind, she took her time showering, dressing, and preparing for the day. Being with RT last night temporarily released the tight knot in her stomach, but she knew it wouldn't last. The drug cartel men hadn't been captured and the danger to her friends remained. She would go the extra mile to help Sadie and Luke.

She heard a soft knock on her bedroom door, and when she opened it Mindy grinned. "Daddy made eggs and toast."

Cait grinned. "Then let's not keep him waiting." She locked the door and took Mindy's hand. "How did you find my room?"

"It's the only locked door," she said, as if that explained everything.

RT and Marcus were eating at the kitchen counter when Cait and Mindy walked in. "You slept late," RT said. "Must have been tired."

Cait's cheeks flushed. "Thanks for fixing breakfast." She dished up the scrambled eggs and added two slices of toast to her plate. "I could get used to this," she said as she buttered her toast.

With a glint in his eye, RT pushed away from the counter. "I'll get your coffee, and then take Mindy to June's."

Cait settled on her stool to eat. "Thanks," she said when RT set a mug of steaming coffee in front of her. He leaned close and nibbled her ear, but not long enough for anyone else to notice.

"Ray Stoltz called," Marcus said. "He's in town and wants to stop by to see Grace Bishop and her students rehearse, if it's okay with you."

"He doesn't need to ask," Cait said, "but I think Lucky is who he hopes to see. Ray invited him to Oregon to attend the festival and for first-hand experience with stage management."

"That's good because I already told him to come," Marcus said.

Cait laughed. Then she sobered as she remembered Lucky's sad demeanor. Unfortunately, his parents were against his making the stage his life's career, similar to the resistance her Aunt Tasha encountered with her parents. *Maybe under Ray's guidance*, she thought, *Lucky will gain confidence with his decision to become an actor.*

The back door rattled. Cait glanced up to see Shep peering through the window.

"I'll get it," Marcus said.

"I'm early. Hope that's okay," Shep said when he walked in. "I smell coffee."

"Help yourself," Cait said. "Made any plans to meet your friends for golf?"

"No. I'll wait to see what happens with Sadie and Luke," Shep said.

"Shep—"

"My friends understand," he said. "I thought we were clear on that."

"He should use his vacation how he wants," RT said when he returned from dropping Mindy at June's. "Like when I choose to drive seven hours to come up here to spend a couple of days with you—and that's if I'm lucky and don't get called in." He drank his coffee and then got up for a refill.

Marcus shook his head. "I have work to do," he said and headed to his office.

Cait tried to suppress her grin. *Wow, RT and Shep standing up for each other?* "Okay, okay, guys. I get it. Now we need to focus on Pamela and Vince and their Uncle Calvin." She checked the time on the wall clock: ten. "We have a couple of hours to come up with questions for Calvin about this Bill Reigo person."

"Did you find out who the stuffed rabbit belonged to?" Shep asked.

Cait shook her head. "I suspect Vince. Maybe he and Reigo are close and he got some coke for turning his back."

"I hope they don't clam up when the three of us show up," RT said.

Cait sighed. "Then we'll push a little harder for answers. I've little experience with drug cartels. Now I wish I did."

RT frowned. "No you don't. It's a nasty business. Huge amounts of money are made shipping drugs all over the country to sell, backed by big time drug lords. This Bill Reigo must know someone at a higher level with connections south of the border. It's an ongoing nightmare, not exclusive to California or any other border state. Probably rampant in Ohio, too."

Cait rose. "Unfortunately, you're probably right." She stacked the empty plates and carried them to the sink.

Someone pounded on the back door, startling Cait. She turned as RT opened the door and ushered Ray Stoltz inside.

"Looks like the gang's all here!" Ray said.

"Hi, Ray," Cait said. She noticed he wore khakis and what appeared to be a new blue sports shirt. Even his dark, graying hair had been slicked back. "I haven't seen Grace or her students."

"They're here," he said. "Ran into them in the parking lot. Can you open the Blackfriars Theater for them?"

Cait grabbed her cell phone from the kitchen counter and found the app to unlock the theater. "Okay. Done."

He smiled. "Ain't technology grand?" He turned away. "I better get busy."

Cait's phone chimed. She glanced at the screen and answered. "Hi, Sadie."

"They're here, Cait. Detective Rook, Pamela and Vince, and their uncle."

Cait checked the time: ten-thirty. "They're early."

"They are, but I'm not sure why. Can you still come?"

"Yes. Right away."

"I assume you heard," Cait said to RT and Shep. "Let's go to Sadie's."

"Glad I was early," Shep said.

Cait stepped into Marcus's office. "We're leaving. Do you know where Niki is?"

Marcus stopped typing and looked at her. "He's outside, probably with June. Don't worry about Ray and Grace. I've got it covered." He hesitated. "Give the gang at Sadie's hell."

Cait grinned. "I'll do my best."

RT rode shotgun in Shep's rental, while Cait sat in back. "You know," she said, "meeting earlier could be good news."

"Or not," RT said over his shoulder.

They arrived at the winery, got out of the car, and headed up Sadie and Luke's driveway. Luke's burned Fiat was gone and Cait wondered if it was in the garage or being repaired.

Luke greeted them at the door. Cait couldn't tell by his

expression how things were going, but when she walked inside and saw a ring of people sitting in the front room looking glum, she didn't need to ask.

Sadie walked in from the kitchen with a tray of steaming coffee mugs. She smiled when she saw Cait. "Thanks for coming, Cait." While Sadie offered coffee to everyone, Cait's eyes rested on the one person she assumed was Uncle Calvin. Dressed in pressed blue jeans, cowboy boots, a short-sleeved white sports shirt, his silver hair combed back into a ponytail, Calvin sat cross-legged next to Detective Rook.

Detective Rook nodded to Cait and then introduced Calvin. "Cait owns the Bening Estate here in Livermore." Rook didn't elaborate on RT or Shep, leaving Cait to wonder if that was intentional. *Oh well, they'll figure it out when we start asking questions.*

"To catch you up," Rook said, "Mr. Harper hired the PI to keep his eye on Bill Reigo, Pamela's husband, because he has a criminal record. He didn't trust him."

"*Never* did," Calvin said. He stared hard at Pamela. "The man served time because of his drug addiction, yet you allowed him to handle the books. What were you thinking, Pamela?"

Pamela sat straighter in her chair, head held high, as if in defiance. "I gave him an ultimatum—go straight and we'll get married. He promised he was drug free and so we finally got married—seven years after we'd met."

Cait wondered how much of this conversation had already taken place at the police station. Pamela refused to look at Cait, but Vince shot darts of hatred at her.

Calvin was seated on a hardback chair. He shifted in his seat so he could look directly at Cait, RT, and Shep. "I don't understand why any of you are here. What does my family situation matter to you?"

"Yeah, I'd like to know what business it is of yours," Vince said.

"Is that a fact?" RT said. "We're here as Sadie and

Luke's friends. We care about what's been happening to them. Maybe that's something you can't understand."

Calvin raised his eyebrow. "No disrespect meant, Detective Rook, but it would have been nice if you'd mentioned them earlier."

"I could have," Rook said, "but whether they'd be here or not depended on what happened at the police station."

*Huh? Really, Rook?* Cait bit her lip to keep from smiling when she realized what he was up to. Rook could bend the truth when he had to.

"And since you refused to answer all my questions," Rook continued, "I knew Cait had some of her own."

Cait took the hint. She looked at Pamela and Vince. "Absolutely we do. Whose drugs were in the rabbit?"

Vince's jaw dropped. His face paled as he shook his head.

Pamela nudged Vince with her elbow. "Tell her."

He remained silent. Pamela slapped his arm. "Tell her."

"*Mine*, okay? I fell off the wagon—once. Pamela found out and hid the damn thing. I never tried to find it. I'm clean. Crap! If not for Bill Reigo, we'd still own this winery."

"Where's your husband now, Pamela?" Cait asked.

"I don't know," she said. "And that's the truth."

"You better find out," RT said, "because two drug couriers have been nosing around here and at Cait's place. They're armed. Someone else will die if this isn't stopped. Your husband must know these guys."

"The police confiscated the cocaine," Shep said. "There shouldn't be any reason for them to stick around. So I'm curious, what's keeping them here?"

As Pamela and Vince exchanged glances, they shook their head.

Calvin ran his hand through his hair, his earnest blue eyes on Pamela. "Did you know there were drugs stashed in the crates of wine bottles?"

Pamela worked the cuticles on her fingers. "I suspected."

"Why didn't you check? Or call the police?"

"I don't know," she said. "Maybe I didn't want to know."

Cait's impulse to act was at odds with Rook's calmer and more reasoned approach, but Pamela's answer shot to the core of Cait's stomach. "You don't *want* to know? You don't care if someone else dies? It could be you or Vince! Or Sadie and Luke! Think, Pamela, where would Bill Reigo go? His parents? Friends?"

"I don't know! Leave me alone!"

Cait's coffee had gone cold, but she drank it anyway.

Luke had remained silent up until now. "A dead PI was found in the winery. My car was burned. Pamela, will you at least think about where your husband *might* have gone? He's the answer to ending this fiasco."

"Pamela, that PI is dead because of you guys," Calvin said.

Pamela glared at her uncle. "You should have told us you'd hired a PI to watch our backs."

"Would it have made a difference?"

Detective Rook stood and set his coffee mug on the table nearest him. "Look, we're going in circles. I suggest we take a break. Calvin, let's go out to the winery. Pamela and Vince can come too or sit here and make up a cock and bull story about Bill Reigo. But no one leaves until I get answers to my questions."

Shep stood. "We'll come with you. RT and I were here yesterday. We can show you where we found how the men got into the vineyard and then escaped back over the fence. We also straightened up the mess left when the wine bottles were dismantled by the DEA and Homeland Security."

RT and Shep followed Rook and Calvin out the door. Cait stayed with Sadie and Luke, and the three of them left the house to sit in the gazebo, leaving Pamela and Vince inside.

"They're a strange pair," Luke said. "I wonder if she does know where her husband is."

"Or if she still loves him," Cait said.

"She knew him a long time before she married him," Sadie said. "Plenty of time to know if he's trustworthy. A sick kind of love, if you ask me, considering what's happened."

A cell phone rang. Cait's was set to vibrate so she knew it wasn't hers.

"It's yours, Sadie," Luke said.

Sadie reached in her skirt pocket and looked at her phone. "I have to take this." She jumped up, stepped outside the gazebo, but close enough for Cait to hear a few words.

"Gut." And then, "Ach, how could I have forgotten?"

Cait looked at Luke when she realized Sadie was speaking in German. "Who's she talking to?"

"Her mother," he whispered.

Sadie stepped out of Cait's hearing. When Sadie returned, she apologized. "Sorry. That was my mamm. She tries to call once a month, but has to sneak out of the house and go to a neighbor's. If found out, she would be punished for talking to me because I've been banned. Any contact with me is forbidden." A slight glint lit her eyes. "A nice woman from a Mennonite family lets her use their phone. She's the teacher I told you about who encouraged me to further my education and helped pave the way for me."

"Oh, Sadie, I'm so sorry. How difficult for your mother," Cait said.

"It's not the phone that worries me," Sadie said, "but the recession that hurt my datt's buggy business."

Cait frowned. Recession? With the Amish simple lifestyle, she wouldn't think they would be affected by a recession as much as most Americans.

"His business hasn't recovered like he'd hoped. He may have to find another line of work," Sadie continued. "It hurts that we can't talk about it."

Pamela and Vince walked out of the house and stepped in front of the gazebo. "I want to talk to Detective Rook," Pamela said.

"He's in the winery with your uncle," Cait said.

"Fine. You may want to hear what I have to say, and then I'm done."

Cait exchanged glances with Sadie and Luke. *Maybe Pamela does know where Bill Reigo is—and then we'll be done too.*

# Chapter 31

The men were standing inside the winery carrying on an animated conversation when Pamela, Vince, Cait, Sadie, and Luke walked in. Pamela went directly to Detective Rook. "I'll tell you what I know and then I'm out of here."

"Just tell the truth," Calvin said.

Detective Rook reached into his jacket pocket took out a pen and notepad.

Pamela took a deep breath, head held high. "Bill's a good man. He would never intentionally hurt me, but he has—had—a weakness. Cocaine. He has a previous conviction for cocaine distribution." She briefly glanced at Vince, as if for support, and then continued. "When he was released from prison, he went straight, never touching any drugs. He wanted to show me I could trust him, and we could finally get married." Her voice wavered. "All was good until a year ago when Bill was confronted by one of his drug pals, a drug courier from San Diego."

"Give me a name," Rook said.

"Rafael Carrillo." She turned to Cait. "You said two men were at your place. The other one was probably Miguel Quintero. Bad guys who would do anything for money, including drug trafficking. They're snakes. You'll never find them if they don't want you to."

Cait remembered Quintero. He'd posed as a realtor at her house.

"How do you know these men?" Rook asked.

"I don't *know* them. I asked Bill their names."

"Drug mules," RT said, "are easy to find but hard to catch. They're the lowest on a drug operation's ladder but indispensible to the kingpins and middlemen. The mules are the ones who carry illegal products for distribution."

Pamela stared at RT as if she'd forgotten he was there. "That may be, but it doesn't make them any less dangerous. They made Bill nervous."

"Have you ever seen these men?" Rook asked Pamela.

She hesitated. "I saw a couple of swarthy-looking guys talking to Bill in the vineyard, but when I asked him who they were, he said nobody important. I pressed him and he told me their names. Later, I noticed a couple of other names on his correspondence. Bill said those were code names for Carrillo and Quintero. I don't remember them."

Cait noticed Shep had also drawn a notepad from a pocket in his jeans. "How did Bill explain why they were at the winery?" he asked Pamela.

"He didn't, except to admit he'd met Carrillo in prison."

Rook looked up from his notepad. "Which prison?"

"I assume Folsom. That's where Bill was."

"The San Diego Tunnel Task Force discovered a tunnel which connected a warehouse in Mexico with another warehouse in a California industrial park," Rook said. Cait watched his pen move across his notepad. "Did Bill ever mention a tunnel or if Carrillo was involved?" he asked.

Pamela appeared dazed and shook her head.

"I know about that tunnel," RT said. "ICE, US Customs and Border Protection, and the DEA were involved. They seized over three hundred pounds of cocaine."

Cait knew SEALs' missions included direct action, combating terrorism, and foreign internal defense. She didn't know if RT had been involved in drug busts in the San Diego area or anywhere else in the States.

"No wonder your husband's in hiding," Shep said. "Once drug lords get their claws into you, there's no escaping."

Pamela took a deep breath. "My soon to be my ex-husband," she corrected Shep. "I can't live like this any more."

"Where is he, Pamela?" Rook asked, catching her off guard.

Pamela hesitated.

"Tell them!" Vince said. "You agreed to tell all."

"I don't want to lead Carrillo and Quintero to Bill," Pamela said. "He's not a bad guy. It's the company he keeps." She turned as if to walk away and then stopped and looked at Detective Rook. "All I know for sure is he's in the Bay Area. I'm guessing San Francisco."

"That doesn't help much, Pamela," Calvin said.

She turned on him. "I don't *know* where he is."

"Does he call you?" Rook asked.

She glanced off into the distance. "Sometimes. From a pay phone."

"Not many of those around any more," Shep said.

"He also uses a burn phone," Pamela admitted.

"Good old burn phones," RT said. "Use 'em once and throw 'em away."

"If you're afraid we'll lead Carrillo and Quintero to him, that tells me you know more than you're letting on," Rook said. "The sooner we find Bill Reigo, the faster we'll find his drug buddies and Sadie and Luke can get on with their lives. You do realize, don't you, you've put them in harm's way? They could lose their winery. Or worse, their lives."

"Christ!" Pamela kicked a wadded up piece of duct tape left on the floor. "If I had a phone number or address for Bill, I would give it to you. If those jackasses find him before you do, you can forget it."

"What do you mean?" Rook asked.

"What else? They'll kill him!"

Rook nodded. "Because we confiscated the cocaine before they got their hands on it?"

"Yes."

"Why did Bill run, Pamela? Why not go to the police?" Calvin asked.

"Do you have any idea what it's like to be blackmailed?" she asked. "Bill only agreed to one shipment of drugs going through here. He never meant to involve us. He knew he'd lose me and end back up in prison." Her voice cracked. "He stopped using drugs when he went to prison, vowing to get clean, but Bill is naïve. They blackmailed him, Uncle Calvin! He ran because he was scared!"

"Why did they blackmail him?" RT asked.

"Because he'd already allowed one shipment to pass through here. They promised this would be the last, but if anything happened to the drugs, they were coming after him. Bill thought if he disappeared, they wouldn't hurt me or Vincent."

"It doesn't work that way," RT said. "Have either of you been hurt physically?"

"No," she sobbed, as if unable to control her emotions. "Vince and I sold the winery because we were worried they'd take their revenge out on us."

*Instead, they took it out on Sadie and Luke.* Cait's barely contained anger finally spilled over as she glared at Vince. "You took a little cocaine off the top of the shipment as your reward for not reporting the drugs to the police? How did you do that? Why hide it in a child's toy rabbit?"

Vince hung his head. "The rabbit was my dog's toy. I couldn't bear to toss it out."

Momentarily touched by the look of pain on his face, Cait hesitated. *Did his dog die?* She shook off her pity for Vince. "Still, that makes you as guilty as those drug mules." She glanced at RT. The only evidence of his anger was a flutter of muscles in his clenched jaw.

"I never expected this to go as far as it has," Pamela said. "I'm sorry." She walked out of the winery.

Cait was far from calm, but her initial fury had ebbed. All that had been uncovered today was the name of the second drug mule and the fact that Bill Reigo might be in San Francisco. It wasn't enough.

# Chapter 32

The group dispersed shortly after Pamela left, but Cait continued to think about what she'd told them. Cait had been to San Francisco once—eight years ago when she got married. Searching for Pamela's husband, Bill Reigo, in San Francisco was not an option for her. She'd never met Bill and didn't know the city well enough to help look for him.

A faint scent of roses and wine wafted on the afternoon breeze as Cait, RT, and Shep stood outside the winery talking with Sadie and Luke. Cait wasn't surprised when Luke said he'd been offered a plum short-term assignment for *Outside Magazine*, his place of employment for ten years, but now with the winery he had a lot on his plate.

"Probably my last with the magazine," Luke said. "It's only for two days. The winery is in capable hands because I kept most of the help who'd worked here for the original owner. Sadie handles phones and orders." He squinted in the sun and swiped his hand over his sweating brow. "I said I'd let the magazine know today if I'd take the assignment."

Cait understood the somber tone in Luke's voice. She'd also given up a job she loved when she inherited the Bening Estate. She glanced over her shoulder at the winery. Luke had mentioned updates he wanted to make, and she assumed the extra money he'd make from this assignment would go toward improvements.

"Luke, I thought we'd agreed you would do it," Sadie said. "If it's me you're worried about, don't. I may not look like it, but I *can* take care of myself. Also—" She opened her hands toward Cait, RT, and Shep, "—these guys are no dummies. They're only minutes away if I need them."

Cait didn't know how long Shep or RT would be around, but she saw no reason for Luke not to accept the assignment. Besides, she felt the damage had already been done to her friends. The drug mules had to know the drugs were gone and the Harpers no longer owned the winery.

"Where's the assignment?" RT asked Luke.

"New Orleans."

"Ah, the Big Easy."

"Yeah," Luke said.

"Too bad you can't take Sadie with you," Cait said.

Sadie grinned. "When I go, it'll be for longer than a couple of days."

RT glanced at his watch. "I need to get back to the house and check on Mindy."

Cait loved Mindy and how she was always on RT's mind. Being a single dad couldn't be easy, especially considering his line of work. She didn't want to think about the day they'd both leave and return to San Diego.

છે આ છે

Back at the house, Cait suggested they look in on the rehearsal at the Blackfriars Theater and see if Ray Stoltz was behaving himself. At times, his overbearing attitude was hard to take.

"I need to rescue June," RT said. "Mindy may have worn out her welcome. We'll catch up with you."

Cait refilled Niki's food and water bowls and then entered Marcus's office. "How's it going?"

Marcus sat back in his chair. "Other than a couple small hang-ups, okay. Kurt Mathews stopped by. He wants to discuss the vineyard with you."

"Did he say what about?"

"Nope. And I didn't ask. Don't think he's ready to trust me."

Cait wondered if Kurt had second thoughts about working with Marcus in the vineyard. "I'll call him." She turned to go and then added, "We'll be at the Blackfriars."

"I was there a little while ago. Ray had everyone's attention with stories about how bad he'd been when he started in show business and stage management. I don't know how much rehearsing they got done, but those kids hung onto every word he said. I'd never seen that side of Ray."

"He's an interesting man," Cait said. She turned when she heard a commotion in the kitchen.

"Cait!" Mindy hollered.

"I'm here," Cait said. "Oh, what's that?"

Mindy held a paper plate with the biggest chocolate chip cookie Cait had ever seen. June stood behind her. "Wow!" Cait said.

"It's for you," Mindy said, "but it's okay to share it."

Cait laughed and broke off a piece and ate it. "Yum."

"Where's mine?" Shep said.

"Yours is here." June held a plate of normal size cookies. "But only if someone tells me what happened at Sadie's."

Shep snatched a cookie. "Pamela admitted her husband, Bill, is in the Bay Area, possibly San Francisco." He bit into his cookie.

June set the plate on the kitchen counter. "'Tell the truth, and shame the devil.'"

Everyone stared at June.

"*Henry the Fourth*," June said. "Do you believe Pamela?"

"I don't think she has reason to lie," Cait said. "She's ready to divorce him."

RT reached for a cookie. "I believe her, but it won't be easy finding her husband. He could be anywhere—on a boat or in a residential hotel—making it nearly impossible to find him."

Cait groaned just as her cell phone beeped. She pulled it from her jeans pocket and glanced at the screen. "What's up, Sadie?"

"Luke accepted the job in New Orleans and I'm going to Santa Cruz. Both of us will leave in the morning. Luke wants his graphic art supplies, and I need the rest of my summer clothes. Livermore is hot."

"I could check on the house and winery while you're gone."

"I don't think it's necessary. We have a security system and those new outside sensor lights. Maybe they'll help keep those bad guys away. Wallace Cranston, our wine master, has a key to the winery. I also told our neighbor at the other end of our lane we'd be gone for a couple of days. I'd prefer to go down and back the same day, but that depends on how much I accomplish. By the way, we got an offer on our house."

"Great. Too bad you have to sell, but it will make it easier for you living up here," Cait said. "Let me know when you're back."

After she disconnected the call, she said, "Luke took the assignment. Sadie's going to Santa Cruz for a couple of days. Looks like they sold their house."

RT leaned against the counter and crossed his arms. "Tell me how you feel about Luke taking off at a time like this."

Puzzled, she frowned. "Why shouldn't he go? Sadie will be in Santa Cruz."

RT took another cookie, thoughtfully dissecting it before taking a bite. "She wasn't going originally. I wouldn't have left you alone with drug mules hanging around."

She didn't know whether to be elated that RT cared about her or concerned he didn't trust Luke. She glanced at

Shep and saw a corner of his lips turn up, a look of humor in his eyes.

"There's is a different situation," she said.

"How so?" RT asked.

"They're married."

"You think that makes a difference in how a man treats his gal?"

"No, of course not. I thought you liked Luke."

"That's not the point, Cait. If the situation were reversed, I'd be in your pocket until those guys were caught. You have to understand the mindset of people like drug mules or any others mixed up with drug trafficking. They can turn on a dime and kill you without blinking. Never turn your back on them. That's an opportunity for murder."

Silence reigned over the kitchen until Jim walked in. He looked around at the serious faces. "Am I interrupting?"

Cait took a deep breath, relieved she didn't have to reply to RT, even though she knew he was right. She couldn't help but wonder if another shipment of drugs was on its way to the winery. That would explain why those men were still here. "We're going to look in on Grace at the Blackfriars. Want to come?"

"Sure." Jim gently pulled one of Mindy's blonde curls and watched it spring back.

When they reached the gate to the theater complex, Cait heard her name being called. Shading her eyes with her hand, she saw Fumié and Ilia coming toward her. She hadn't seen them since Sunday when the play at the Elizabethan Theater ended.

"Hi," Fumié said. She grinned. "We have a surprise to show you."

Ilia took her left hand and held it up for everyone to see.

It took Cait a few seconds to realize what she was looking at—a heart-shaped diamond ring. "Oh," she gasped. "Wow. You're engaged?"

"It's a promise ring, a symbol of our commitment," Ilia said.

Cait hugged Fumié and then Ilia. "Congratulations."

RT shook Ilia's hand and kissed Fumié's cheek. "You're a lucky guy, Ilia."

"I know." Ilia grinned. "She's leaving soon for Santa Rosa. I was afraid she'd meet a park ranger at that school and forget me."

"Not a chance," Fumié said.

Mindy looked at her dad and asked, "Are you going to give Cait a promise ring?"

Everyone, except RT, laughed.

Even Cait nervously laughed as her heart skipped a beat. *The eyes are the windows of the soul*, but she couldn't see behind RT's dark sunglasses.

"Uh..." RT said. He seemed to be tongue-tied.

Eyes wide open, Mindy asked, "You like Cait, don't you?"

Cait considered getting RT off the hook by changing the subject, but she was curious to hear his answer.

"Of course I like her," RT said.

Mindy looked at Cait. "Do you like my daddy?"

Cait smiled. "I like him."

Mindy grinned. "Good. Can I play with Niki?"

"Yes. Niki would like that," RT said. "We'll be in the Blackfriars if you need me."

June walked next to Cait. "You gotta love how a child's mind works. Adults tend to complicate everything."

Inside the theater, *Comedy of Errors* was in full swing. Ray sat in the front row with Grace. Cait held the door so it wouldn't slam and then stood in the back with the others and watched the play until Grace called the end of rehearsal.

Grace turned and then hurried up the aisle when she saw the group in the back. "Hi. How do you think the kids did?"

Cait had never seen the play, but she'd read a synopsis about it since her theater was being used for rehearsals. The plot was about identical twins accidentally separated at birth.

"I know the play," June said, "but I enjoy seeing college

kids perform. They could be the next super stars. I love slapstick humor."

Grace grinned. "Great. I can get you tickets."

Ray approached them. "They're good. They've learned how to work a small stage like this one."

"They'll be on a bigger stage at the college," Grace said, "but this is good practice for when they're up close and personal with an audience. Rehearsing here has been a blessing. Thanks, Cait."

"Any time the theater is available, you're welcome to use it," Cait said.

The door opened and Mindy and Niki came in. "I'm hungry," she announced.

"We'll have to remedy that," Cait said.

"We're leaving," Grace said. "You can lock up in about ten minutes. I'm not sure about tomorrow. Okay if I call to let you know?"

"Sure," Cait said. "You can leave your things here if you'd like. No one else will be using the theater."

When everyone left, RT walked beside Cait. "Uh, Cait? What's your take on promise rings?"

"They're sweet," she said. *Does he think I want a commitment from him?*

RT grabbed her arm, forcing her to face him. "Sweet?"

His dark eyes flashed. *From anger? Or hurt?* "I meant, Fumiè and Ilia are young," Cait said.

He let go of her arm. "We should talk about this."

She nodded. "I agree."

They caught up with the rest of the group. Cait saw Shep slip his cell phone into a pocket in his jeans. "Everything okay?" she asked Shep, recalling he had a case that concerned him.

"What would you think if I drove down to Pebble Beach tomorrow morning, hooked up with my buddies for a day of golf, and came back the following day? Luke and Sadie will be gone too, so I wouldn't expect trouble at their winery."

"Shep, that's why you came, to play golf, not work more

crimes," Cait said. "Go, have fun, and stay as long as you want. If we're lucky, the drug mules will be caught and we can celebrate when you return."

"You heard her," RT said. "Vacations are hard to come by. I don't know if I'll be here when you get back, but in case I don't see you again, it's been nice meeting you."

"It was nice meeting you too, RT," Shep said. "How about we all go out to dinner tonight? My treat."

"You don't have to do that," Cait said.

"I want to. It's settled."

Back at the house, RT suggested they have dinner at the Zephyr Grill & Bar in downtown Livermore. Cait made the reservations for six o'clock. When the time came to go, RT unhitched his Hummer from his Airstream trailer, the six of them piled in, and he drove downtown to the restaurant.

While the guys talked, Cait couldn't get her mind off what RT had said about a promise ring. Lately, he'd been hinting he had something to discuss. *Is he ready to make a commitment? Am I?*

# Chapter 33

Cait couldn't go back to sleep because of the heat. Apparently, Friday wouldn't be any different from the rest of the week—hot. Only two windows in the third floor bedroom opened and they seldom allowed enough of a breeze in to cool the room. Cait glanced at the bedside clock: six-fifty-five. She groaned and dragged herself out of bed and to the bay window. Looking down on the sun-dappled green grapevines, she wondered if she'd ever understand the process of growing grapes. If not for Kurt Mathews, her vineyard manager, those luscious-looking vines would be dead.

Cait squinted. Was that Kurt's white pickup? *Sure enough*, she thought. This was her opportunity to talk to him before Marcus arrived. After a quick shower, she pulled on shorts, T-shirt, and tennis shoes and, with Niki at her heels, rushed downstairs. She came to a dead stop when she smelled fresh coffee and saw RT and Mindy sitting at the kitchen counter eating cereal. Their heads were buried in a book and they didn't see Cait until Niki growled.

RT looked up and grinned. "Your hair's wet."

Cait fluffed her hair with both hands. "I didn't take time to dry it. You're up early."

"Mindy and I were starved," he said.

"So am I, but first I want to talk with Kurt. He's out front."

"The vineyard's looking good," RT said.

She nodded. "Yeah it does. Kurt comes almost every day. Marcus is interested in the vineyard, and Kurt's agreed to show him his routine. Working together might help improve their relationship."

"I'll have cereal and coffee for you when you're back."

Cait hurried out the back door and around to the front where she found Kurt chest deep in one of the rows studying the vines. The new growth was vigorously reaching toward the sky with pea-size grapes. A multi-wired trellising system with drip irrigation held the vines upright. "Your hard work's paying off, Kurt."

Kurt rose and smiled at Cait. "That's what it's supposed to do. The long sunlight hours help by motivating the fruit and adding richness to the wine."

Cait nodded. "Marcus said you wanted to talk to me."

"Yeah. Let's sit on the porch out of the sun. It's going to be another scorcher."

"Would the drought cause serious damage to the vineyard?" Cait asked as she turned to the house.

"Not necessarily. It means the roots have to go deeper in search of water. Might lose some grapes, but have better wines."

They settled in wicker rockers on the porch. "I should have brought water for you," Cait said.

"I have plenty in a cooler. I called because I wanted to know what plans you had for Marcus. He shows real potential in the vineyard."

"Oh," she said, relieved Kurt hadn't called to complain about Marcus.

Kurt laughed. "You thought I was going to refuse to work with him. I've put our problem aside, mostly *my* problem. When I knew Marcus in high school, he was a troublemaker. I didn't trust him, but now I have to admit prison did okay by him. He's serious about wanting to learn the process of growing grapes and possibly becoming a vintner."

"I'm happy he has other interests besides the festival," she said. "There's months where there's not much for him to do, except building things, which he loves doing."

Kurt smiled. "This is a good place for him to start. Marcus isn't a scientist, and he has a lot to learn, but I sense he's a quick study."

"I agree. What do you have in mind? It's a little late for summer classes at the college."

"I'm here most days. He can help me on my daily routine. I'll explain what I do as we work together and he can ask questions. He shouldn't wait too long to sign up for classes. Vintner classes are popular. Can you spare him time from your Shakespeare festivals?"

"I don't see a problem," Cait said. "There are only two more festivals this year—August and September—and that's for only one weekend each. We'll work around that."

"Then I think we've got a plan." He stood. "In the meantime, I better get back to work."

Cait rose. "I'm glad we had this talk, Kurt." After they parted, she went back inside the house.

"Going to be quiet around here today," RT said when Cait entered the kitchen. "Sadie and Luke are gone, and I assume Shep's on his way to Pebble Beach. You got plans?"

"No, except a talk with Marcus. He's going to help Kurt in the vineyard."

"Won't be long before harvest. It usually begins around the end of August. That will keep them busy."

"And you've got your own vineyard to worry about." It was one of many things she and RT never had time to discuss.

"Yeah, but I have a good friend and his dad who help when I'm gone. My folks handle much of the business end of it and watch Mindy when I'm working. It will help when she starts school in September."

"Grandma and Grandpops let me help in the vineyard," Mindy said. "When I grow up, I'm going to take over for you, Daddy."

Cait grinned. "And you'll be good at it."

"You better grow up fast, sweetheart," RT said, "because your grandparents aren't getting any younger."

Cait loved watching the interaction between RT and his daughter. *She has the same closeness with RT as I had with my dad.*

RT reached for the box of cereal sitting on the counter, filled a bowl, and added milk. He handed Cait a spoon. "Eat. I'll get your coffee."

"Thank you," she said.

He set a steaming mug of coffee in front of Cait and then reached in his jeans pocket for his cell phone. "I have a call to make." He walked into Marcus's office.

"Want me to read to you while you eat?" Mindy asked as she opened a book on the counter. "Like I read to Daddy?"

"I would love it." Cait pulled out a stool and sat down. She watched Mindy's face over the rim of her coffee, amazed how dramatic she got as she read. *She must be gifted to read before she even starts first grade.*

RT returned and tucked his phone back in his pocket. "You practically have that book memorized, Mindy. You'll be ahead of other kids in your class."

"I have more books in the trailer, and June has some too," Mindy said. "Can I go see June and Jim now?"

"Sure," RT said. "Take Niki with you."

After Mindy left, RT said, "I hope you don't mind, but I'm going to meet Rook later today. It's the anniversary of his brother's death. I'll take Mindy with me."

"Of course I don't mind." RT still carried guilt over the mission that killed Rook's brother. He held himself responsible for everyone—family and friends. A good trait—not necessarily a healthy one. "Mindy could stay with me while you're gone," she said.

RT leaned over and kissed her on the lips. "Thanks, but I

want her with me as much as possible. I'll take her for ice cream afterward." He took her hand in his and massaged her palm. "What are we going to do about us?"

Cait's heart skipped a beat and she felt heat rise in her cheeks as she thought what she'd like to do right now. Instead, she said, "Enjoy the time we have together."

"That's the problem. There's too little time." He pulled her to him and kissed her until she could barely breathe. He reached his hand under her shirt and started to pull it up.

"Uh...excuse me."

Startled, Cait almost fell off her stool.

"Your timing sucks, Marcus." RT said.

"I'm sorry."

෴

Later that afternoon, the house was quiet. Marcus left for the Bening Ranch to ride his horse. RT and Mindy went to meet Detective Rook. June and Jim Hart planned to watch an old movie in their RV, trying to stay cool from the stifling heat. Cait had a long conversation with her friend Samantha about Sadie and Luke's situation until Sam had an emergency in the ER where she was a doctor.

Restless, Cait decided to check on Turtle Creek Winery to be sure it had been secured. She hurried upstairs to change her clothes. Tucking her Glock in her waistband, she grabbed her keys, shoulder bag, and sunglasses, and went downstairs, where she found Niki spread out on the cool kitchen tiles. She secured the house and then went to the Harts' RV to let them know where she was going. Finally, inside the garage, she settled behind the wheel of her Saab.

Five minutes later she pulled into Post Lane, waved to the neighbor working in his yard, and then parked in Sadie and Luke's driveway. The house was partially shaded by large oak trees, while the long wraparound porch looked cool and inviting. Cait wasn't expecting trouble, but she wanted to make sure no one was sniffing around the house or winery while her friends were away.

She tried the doors of the house and, finding them secure, headed to the back. She stood for a few moments to admire the lush green vineyard before trying the doors to the winery. As she reached for the door handles, she noticed one door was cracked open. Adrenalin surged through her body. She pulled her gun and backed against the building as caution warred with fear.

Cait listened, but all she heard were birds in the trees. She inhaled deeply and then nudged the door open with her toe. The hinges creaked as she pushed it. She slipped inside, swept the large space with the muzzle of her Glock.

She heard a metallic click—the sound of a pistol being cocked.

Then another click.

Realizing she wasn't alone, she turned her head at the slightest hint of movement—a muffled sound, maybe feet hitting the cement floor. Thoughts rushed through her mind, like storm clouds passing over the sky.

She was on her own.

She could be in serious danger.

Cautiously, she took a step to her right and then another. Her eyes scanned the inside of the dark building, the stacks of wine barrels.

A bullet hit the concrete floor inches from her tennis shoes.

She darted across the open space and ran behind stacked boxes of glass bottles. Bullets slammed into the concrete floor behind her and then into the boxes, dogging her tracks, spraying shards of glass and pieces of cardboard at her. She returned fire, catching blurs of movement of a man running between rows of wine barrels. She started after him. Shots from the opposite side of the building flew over her head and plowed into a barrel. She crouched, instantly aware of her situation.

There were two of them.

Odds were not in her favor.

The next rounds were deafening and echoed throughout the winery. Her best hope was that the neighbor, at the far end of the lane, heard the shots and called nine-one-one.

Cait hunkered down, ready to spring into action, cursing herself for not knowing how many bullets she had left or how many shots the shooters had taken. A shadow moved across the floor a few feet in front of the wine barrels she hid behind. She leaned on one knee, left hand bracing her right, and pointed her Glock, eyes intent on the shadow. The shadow vanished into the dark corner like a ghost.

Whispered Spanish reached her ears, but she couldn't understand the words. A man in jeans and a white muscle shirt materialized from the shadows, turned in Cait's direction, and fired his gun. An empty barrel partially exploded a few feet from Cait, giving her a clearer view of the shooter. She thought she recognized him as Carrillo, the one who'd shot at her own vineyard several nights ago. Without hesitating, Cait aimed and fired.

The man screamed and crumpled on the spot.

Cait took a shooter's stance, her eyes scanning her surroundings, waiting for the man's partner to show himself. Her cell phone vibrated in her pocket, its ring on mute. With her left hand, she reached in her pocket and pushed a key to keep the line open, hoping whoever was on the other end would hear and call the police.

Tension clamped around her shoulders and neck as she waited, openly exposed. The second man spun in front of Cait so fast she almost fell back into the barrels. She got off a couple wild shots, sending him for cover. A quick glance around told her she had nowhere to go but up. The barrels were stacked five high, a climb she wasn't sure she could make without being hit. When the shooter stepped out into the open and got off one shot, Cait fired one back in response then took her chances, dashed behind the barrels, and started climbing. If she could reach the top, she'd have the advantage of seeing the shooter. She had no doubt she could kill him before he pulled the trigger. As a cop, she'd scored in the top three of the best in the country in all shooting competitions she entered but one, a feat she was proud of.

The man laughed, as if he'd read her mind. "Give it up. Make it easy on yourself."

Determination and a whole lot of adrenaline helped her set her feet on each barrel as she climbed. They were offset enough to give her leverage and reach the next barrel. She didn't dare set her gun down or tuck it in her waistband and nearly slipped as she struggled to wrap her arms partially around each barrel as she climbed. She didn't know if the barrels were full or empty until she tried to shove one and discovered it was immovable. She gasped for breath when she finally reached the top barrel. Looking down into the dark eyes of the man below, she feared she'd lost the battle. He fired a volley of bullets in her direction.

Clinging to the barrel, her lungs on fire, Cait ducked and crawled behind it, using the barrels below as a platform. Wine spurted from numerous holes in the barrel, soaking her shirt and jeans. Hope surged through her. If she could push the damaged barrel onto the man below, she'd have a chance. After several shoves, the barrel gave way and tumbled down with a crash. Her adversary was momentarily distracted as he jumped to the side to avoid being hit. Cait emptied her gun until she heard him gasp and collapse on the floor.

Cait used her remaining strength to climb back down the wine barrels, careful not to slip in the wine.

The door flew open, spilling sunlight into the winery. RT charged inside, his gun sweeping the building, then settling on the groaning man on the floor. "Cait! You could have been killed!"

"But I wasn't." She stood over the injured shooter, her empty gun down by her side, breathless from the encounter.

"You're bleeding," he said.

She grinned. "No. It's the wine."

RT pulled his cell phone from his pocket and tapped a key. "There's been a shooting at Turtle Creek Winery on Post Lane. We need medics." Next he called Detective Rook. "I'm at Turtle Creek Winery. Cait's been shot."

# Chapter 34

After securing the man's hands and ankles with duct tape that RT found in the winery, he examined Cait's shoulder. "You're lucky it's only a graze, but it still needs attention."

Cait touched her shoulder and swore under her breath. She'd been unaware of the injury until now—and now, the burning sensation was almost unbearable. She'd assumed her clothes were stained red from the wine that had spilled from the shot-up wine barrel, not blood. Sirens wailed off in the distance.

"What the hell were you doing here?" RT asked.

Cait saw tenseness around his eyes, and knew he was worried about her. "Making sure drug mules weren't here looking for more cocaine. I guess they were." She looked around. "Where's the other guy?"

"What other guy?"

"The other one I shot?"

"There were two?"

"Yes!" She ran around the building, behind wine barrels and boxes of glass bottles, frantic when she didn't see the other shooter. "Damn it, RT. He's gone!"

Commotion outside the building told her help had arrived. Detective Rook was the first in the door. "Cait?"

"I'm okay." She wasn't about to admit the burning in her shoulder had intensified.

Rook stared at her red-stained clothes. "RT said you were shot. Where are you hurt?"

"My shoulder. It's barely a scratch."

Rook motioned to the EMTs. "Check her out."

The female EMT hesitated beside the injured man on the ground. "What about him?"

"He's been shot. Have a look, but it doesn't appear to be life threatening," RT said.

Despite his injuries, the shooter's eyes shot darts of anger at RT, but he remained silent.

"Who is he?" Rook asked.

"One of the bad guys," RT said. "A second one got away—after Cait shot him. Good idea to check hospitals for a wounded man walking into their ER."

Cait sat on top of one of the empty wine barrels while the male EMT attended to her shoulder. She grimaced when he cleaned it.

The EMT smiled. "Count your lucky stars. It's only a surface wound. The bullet barely pierced the flesh."

Still, she thought, it burned like hell. Or was it anger she felt at losing the second shooter?

RT ran his hand over his closely cropped black hair as he watched the EMT clean Cait's wound and then wrap it. "Cait, did you recognize either guy?"

"Not conclusively. Too bad Shep isn't here. He saw both men at my house while I was in Santa Cruz."

"You'll be good as new in a couple of days," the EMT told Cait. "Use soap and water to clean it, an antibiotic ointment, and apply a loose dressing."

"Okay. Thanks."

"Let's get you home," RT said.

"I have my car."

"I'll follow you."

Cait pointed to the guy in duct tape on the floor. "What about him?"

"Not our problem," RT said.

"The other guy, he has to be in bad shape," she said. "I thought I'd killed him. The grounds should be checked in case he's lying wounded in there. Or maybe find a blood trail."

"We actually do know what we're doing," Rook said.

Cait swallowed a sharp comment in retaliation and let RT lead her out of the winery and to her car. He opened the car door and helped her in. "Damn smart you left your cell phone open. Hate to think what might have happened if you hadn't."

Cait turned the engine on and rolled the window down. "I'm lucky you were listening in."

"Thank the neighbor for calling it in first. Drive carefully."

❦

June, Jim, and Mindy were sitting outside their RV drinking lemonade and eating popcorn when Cait and RT joined them. Mindy jumped up and ran into RT's arms. "We have popcorn."

"I know, I can smell it," he said. He set her down and patted Niki's head.

Jim stood. "Cait, what happened to your shoulder?"

"She got shot," RT said. "Mindy and I are retiring to my trailer. Cait can explain. We'll see you in the morning."

Feeling guilty for causing so much trouble at her friend's winery, Cait watched RT walk away. Still, something good had come from it—one shooter had been arrested and the other injured. But their replacements would be easy to come by, which could lead to even bigger problems for Sadie and Luke.

"Cait," June said, "sit down and tell us what happened." She filled a glass with lemonade and handed it to her.

Cait sank into the nearest chair and sipped the lemonade,

wetting her parched lips. She couldn't believe how good the tart liquid tasted. "It was probably stupid of me not to expect someone to show up at the winery." She told them everything, including her concern about the one that got away.

"I'm relieved that's wine you're wearing," Jim said.

She'd almost forgotten how she must look. "I hope the one who got away doesn't die. One killing was bad enough, even though it was in the line of duty." Two years ago, she'd saved another officer's life when a bank robber held a gun to his neck.

Jim nodded in agreement. He'd had a similar experience years ago.

Cait reached for the popcorn. "The winery's a mess with spilled wine and the shooters' blood. I'll go back in the morning to clean it up before Sadie and Luke come back."

"Let me know when you're going and I'll go with you," Jim said.

"Thanks, Jim. I appreciate the offer. Now I need to get out of these clothes and take a shower. Thanks for the lemonade and popcorn. They hit the spot."

"Don't worry about RT," June said. "He'll get over his anger." She smiled at Jim. "Like someone I know."

Jim grunted.

"I'm not worried," Cait lied.

June smiled. "'The web of our life is of a mingled yarn, good and ill together.'"

*Shakespeare understood life*, Cait thought, *and his words still ring true today.* She remembered another one of his quotes: "Make use of time, let not advantage slip." She prayed RT wouldn't get called back to work before they resolved their issues.

# Chapter 35

Cait was groggy when she awoke the following morning. She'd tossed and turned all night and had considered getting up and going downstairs to watch TV to get her mind off the shooting at her friends' winery. But she stayed in bed and thought about the two men she'd shot. Like parts of a big jigsaw puzzle, bits of information moved about in her mind, as she tried to make them fit into the whole picture.

Her cell phone rang. She rolled over and grabbed it from the nightstand. "Hello."

"It's Rook. Didn't wake you, did I?"

"No. Anything new on the guy who got away?"

"Only that I don't think he was anywhere near to dying. Very little blood where you said he was when you shot him, but forensics did collect enough for DNA. So far, no one's gone into any ER needing to be patched up from a gunshot wound. As for Rafael Carrillo, the guy we arrested, the only talking he's doing is to complain about his free lodgings."

"I've had time to think about the one who got away. I'm sure he's Miguel Quintero, the guy who posed as a realtor at my house. He was dressed all in black both times, wearing a Marco Polo jersey with the familiar horseman emblem."

"That's a start. When's Shep coming back?"

"Today or tomorrow. Why?"

"He could probably identify Carrillo as one of the men who shot up your vineyard, since he confronted them."

Cait sat up on the edge of the bed. "Shep still has the keys he took from one of them."

Rook chuckled. "How's your shoulder?"

"A little uncomfortable." She hesitated. "RT's unhappy I went to the winery but, honestly, I didn't expect those men to show up, not after the police had confiscated the cocaine."

"Then why did you go there?"

"I was restless," she said. "I wanted to be sure everything was locked. I'm still glad I went."

"Maybe they were expecting another shipment of drugs."

"I wish we knew," she said. "Pamela didn't seem to think so. Have you found any paper to indicate otherwise? A second bill of lading?"

"No. That's another reason to find Bill Reigo. He handled that part of their business."

"Any leads on Reigo's whereabouts?"

"No. Look, I have to go. I'll be in touch. Try to stay out of trouble."

"Yeah, yeah," she mumbled.

After doing a series of yoga exercises, wincing and moving slower than usual, Cait showered, treated her shoulder wound, dressed, and went downstairs to let Niki outside. The house was quiet. She made a pot of coffee and filled a bowl with cereal and milk. As she ate, she wondered if RT and Mindy had food in their trailer.

When someone tapped on the back door, Cait assumed it would be RT. Instead, Jim smiled through the window. She opened the door to let him in.

"I'm ready to help clean up Turtle Creek Winery whenever you are," he said.

"Jim, you don't have to do that. It's a real mess."

He laughed. "You'd be surprised what I've had to clean up. The art recovery business isn't excluded from murder and mayhem. Do you have a key to get in the winery?"

"No. I didn't think to ask Detective Rook about a key. I'll call him."

Rook answered on the first ring. "What's up?"

"Is the winery locked? I want to clean up before Sadie and Luke return."

"No. I've got a couple of officers watching the place. I wondered if it'd been alarmed because the neighbor at the other end of the lane said he only heard gunshots."

Cait sighed. "I'm sure it was. Those guys must be pros at dismantling alarms."

"Yeah, among other misdemeanors and felonies. The place isn't all that bad. Only one wine barrel got shot up and there's a little blood."

"What about all those broken wine bottles?"

"The officers swept most of the glass up and tossed it in the trash, but if you want to take a look, have at it. Wallace Cranston, the Sloanes' wine master, has been notified. You may run into him."

Cait heard a quick rap on the back door before it opened. RT and Mindy walked in. No sign of last night's anger on his face. Relieved, she told Rook, "I still want to go. I'm responsible. I don't want Sadie and Luke returning home to a mess. Jim Hart's going with me."

"I'll let the officers know you're coming." He disconnected the call.

"Good morning, you two. There's a fresh pot of coffee," Cait said. "Mindy, would you like orange juice?"

"No thank you, we already had breakfast."

"Jim and I are going to clean up the mess at Turtle Creek Winery," she told RT. "Rook's officers are there."

"I'll come with you," RT said. "Then I'm taking Mindy to the ranch." He smiled. "She has gifts for Joy—my children's books."

Joy and her parents, Bo and Khandi Tuck, lived on the Bening Ranch in Livermore. Bo, a veterinarian, and his family had been on the ranch for several years. When Hilton

Bening died four months ago, Bo was allowed to remain on
the ranch for as long as he liked. Hilton was Cait's aunt Tasha's husband.

"What a wonderful idea," Cait said.

"You can go with us," RT said.

"I don't know," Cait said. "I thought I'd take Shep to the
ranch before he leaves."

"Go with them, Cait. You need a break," Jim said, "especially after what happened yesterday. You can go again
when Shep's back. June can watch Mindy while we're
cleaning up the winery," Jim said. "Okay with you, Mindy,
if you stay a little while with June?"

Mindy bobbed her head up and down.

"You sure, honey?" RT asked. "We won't be too long,
and then we'll go to the ranch."

"Okay," Mindy said. "I can read to June and eat cookies."

"You're turning into a cookie monster," RT said.

*⁂*

Two unfamiliar officers met them in front of Turtle
Creek Winery. "Detective Rook said to expect you," one of
the officers said when Cait introduced herself. "We cleaned
up the broken glass and bagged the shell casings."

Cait smiled as she read the officer's nametag: Brokaw.
"Thank you."

She expected yellow crime scene tape, but assumed there
wasn't any because the winery hadn't yet opened to the
public. She entered the building, looked around, expecting
total chaos. What she saw was one busted wine barrel and a
sticky river of dried wine that had run down over other barrels and finally settled on the concrete floor.

"Not so bad," Jim said. "I don't think crime scene clean-
ers are necessary. No bodies—no blood. A little mopping
and it's as good as new."

"It seemed much worse at the time," Cait said. "But then that's probably because I was alone and embroiled in a battle with a lot of bullets flying around."

A tall, heavy-set older man with silver hair smiled as he approached Cait. "Excuse me," he said. "Are you Ms. Pepper?"

Cait looked at the man. "Yes."

"I'm Wallace Cranston," he said. "Detective Rook may have mentioned me."

Cait smiled and held her hand out to shake his. "Yes, he did. Nice to meet you."

"I started working here years ago, back when it was first called Spring Haven Winery," he said, "but this is the first criminal investigation I've ever been involved in. I like the Sloanes. Good people. Sad what's happened to them, being new vintners and all."

"I agree," Cait said. "They're friends of ours. We're here to clean up the mess from yesterday."

Cranston shook his head. "From what I'm told, you had your hands full last evening. Not much left to do here, thanks to the police officers."

"If you're sure..."

He smiled. "I am."

"Then if it's okay, we'll walk around, make sure nothing was left behind."

"Help yourself. I'll get a mop and start cleaning up."

"Looking for anything in particular?" Jim asked Cait.

"Evidence." She assumed the police would have found any, but she liked to satisfy herself. She knew exactly where the shootings took place. While RT and Jim separated on their own search of the winery, Cait turned to her left, where she'd shot Carrillo and the second man. She stepped over the stickiness on the floor, threaded her way through the stacked barrels, visualizing everyone's position when the shooting started.

Cait stood behind the stack of barrels she'd climbed yesterday and stared up at the top. No way was she tempted to try again. *How did I manage that and not get killed?* She stepped out from behind the barrels and was about to rejoin RT and Jim when something caught her attention. Partially hidden under a piece of cardboard was a pendant and key-chain.

Cait nudged the cardboard away with her toe. She crouched, picked up the keychain, and turned the pendant over in her hand. A sticker covered the pendant.

"What's that?" Jim asked as he came up beside her.

"A keychain but no key. Just this." She rose and handed it to him.

"Looks like a John Deere logo," he said. "Probably had one of their pieces of equipment here at some time, maybe a tractor."

"Could be. Let's show RT."

They skirted the sticky floor and caught up with RT. "Found this," Cait said. She handed the keychain to him.

RT stared at it for several seconds. "Where'd you find it?"

"Where Carrillo and the other guy were shooting at me," she said. "It was under a piece of cardboard similar to the boxes the bottles came in. It could have fallen out of one of their pockets."

When RT didn't say anything, she asked, "Is it important?"

RT looked at her and nodded. "Sometimes when drug cartels are in the United States, they'll place stickers like this one on their rear windshields. It's a way to distinguish themselves from other cartels. You'll also find them on their clothing, leather jackets, or jewelry. Also on key chains, like this one. So yes, I'd say this is significant."

"Why John Deere?" Jim asked.

RT shrugged. "A few years ago, they used the MGM lion; another time the Ferrari logo. Don't know what they use today." He pocketed the keychain. "I'll turn it over to Rook. Ready to go?"

Cait couldn't imagine a worse job than border patrol between the United States and Mexico. A thankless job. They could never pay her enough.

*Chapter 36*

Seeing Bo and his family again always lifted Cait's mood. As soon as Bo's two golden retrievers ran over to greet everyone, Niki was out of the car and off to play. Tall, slender, Bo looked every bit the cowboy in jeans, dusty boots, and plaid shirt with sleeves rolled up. He tipped his Stetson back as he smiled at Cait, RT, June, and Jim. "Howdy. 'Bout time you came to visit."

Cait grinned. "Oh, Bo, you know how it is."

"Sure do." Bo shook hands with RT. "You're looking good, RT, considering what you do for a living." He smiled at Mindy. "Who's this little lady?"

"Bo, this is my daughter, Mindy," RT said. "Mindy, Bo is a veterinarian and has lots of animals on his ranch."

Mindy's blue eyes sparkled. "Can I see them?"

"Sure can," Bo said, "as soon as you meet the rest of the family."

"Hi, Bo," June said. "Good to see you again. This is my husband, Jim. He's heard all about you."

"You been telling secrets out of school?" Bo asked.

June grinned. "Only the good stuff, because that's all I know."

"Let's go inside. Khandi's always happy for company."

As they crossed over the dry creek on their way to the

house, Cait hesitated, as always, to admire the single-story log house snuggled against the base of a hill. External stairways on both sides of the house led up to a pencil-reed balcony across the front.

Inside, Bo called, "Khandi, we've got company."

Everyone turned at the sound of a soft whooshing noise. Joy, Bo's ten-year old daughter, rolled her electric wheel-chair into the room, a big grin on her face. "Cait!"

Khandi, Bo's wife, followed Joy into the room. Her soft cocoa skin glowed from the sun pouring through the sky-lights. Her braided hair hung part way down her back. "It's about time you came to see us," she said.

After Jim and Mindy were introduced, Cait kneeled, hugged Joy, and ran her hand over the halo of dark curls. "Mindy's been eager to meet you." She turned to Mindy, who stood beside her dad.

"Joy," RT said, "Mindy brought you a present."

"Here," Mindy said. She handed a gift-wrapped package she'd been holding to Joy.

"For me?" Joy asked. She tore the wrapping paper off and squealed, "I love books. Thank you."

Mindy tapped her finger on the cover. "That's my daddy. He writes kids books. Do you like to read?"

Joy grinned. "Yes."

Cait dug in her purse. "I have something, too." She handed Joy a package of black licorice, her favorite candy.

"You remembered!"

"Always do," Cait said.

"Can you sit for a while?" Khandi asked. "I have iced tea."

"Maybe later," RT said. "I promised to show Mindy your horses."

"Can I go too?" Joy asked her dad.

"Sure, sweetheart," Bo said.

Outside, everyone walked slowly to accommodate Joy's wheelchair. "Let's go through the barn," Bo said. "You can see my horse, Cash."

"This is a great spread you have here," Jim said.

Bo nodded. "I'm lucky. I assume you know Hilton Bening built the house. When he died, he left it to me to live in. If I leave or die, the property reverts back to his family's estate in Colorado." He smiled. "Sealed the deal with a handshake."

Jim nodded. "That's good enough. Hilton was my cousin, the most honest man I've ever known." He winked at June. "She introduced Tasha and Hilton."

"We wouldn't be standing here if I hadn't interfered and brought them together," June said.

Inside the barn, Mindy ran to the first stall and horse she saw, a big, black stallion. "Look how pretty he is, Daddy."

"This is Cash," Bo said, offering the horse a sugar cube.

Cait's eyes locked onto an empty stall she knew to be Faro's. Hilton's leather saddle still hung on a hook next to the stall, a sad reminder he was no longer there to ride his horse.

"Let's go out the back," Bo said, as he pushed Joy's wheelchair outside.

"Where's Faro?" June asked Bo.

"Not far. He'll come when he sees us."

Mindy walked beside Joy, sharing the licorice with her until she saw horses in a pasture behind a white fence and ran toward them.

"Ride Faro much?" RT asked.

Bo smiled. "Sure do. He's a changed horse since Hilton's death, but he's come around. Joy wants to ride him, but I haven't decided yet."

Mindy stared at Joy's wheelchair, as if she'd just noticed it. "Can you ride?"

"I used to ride by myself. Got lots of ribbons to prove it," Joy said. "I used to teach my horse tricks. Now I ride double with my daddy."

Cait's heart ached for Joy. Horses had been the center of her world up until her accident three years earlier—and still were.

"I write stories about horses," Joy continued. "I'm real good on a computer. My doctor told me to never stop believing in myself, that things will come my way if I work hard."

Cait's mind began to drift, back to yesterday, the shootings, and the guy who got away. She wanted to go back to Turtle Creek Winery and look for him. What if he died in the vineyard? What if Sadie or Luke stumbled upon him? They'd freak out, with good reason. And Cait would be responsible because she was the one who shot him.

"The bond between animals and children can be a powerful healing medicine," Bo said. "Joy understands horses, probably better than I do."

Faro ventured over to the fence, his silky bay coat glistening in the sun, long extended neck reaching out to them. Cait leaned over to stroke the horse, struggling to reconnect with the peacefulness of the farm and her friends, while at the same time she revisited the events from last evening. What was the matter with her? Why couldn't she let it go?

"Cait?"

Startled, she asked, "What?"

"Your phone's ringing," RT said. "Are you okay?"

She reached in the back pocket of her jeans, glanced at the screen, and saw it was Sadie calling. She drew a deep breath and answered the call. "Sadie, is everything all right?"

"You tell me. Two cops are here. What happened?"

"They didn't explain?"

"They said there'd been a break-in, and that I should talk to Detective Rook. There's more to it than a break-in, Cait. There's blood outside the winery, near the vineyard. Luke's going to flip out when he returns."

"Sadie, we're all at the ranch. We'll swing by when we leave and explain what happened. Okay?"

"Okay, but if another body turns up at this winery, I'm moving back to Santa Cruz."

"You can't. You sold that house," Cait said.

"Then Sugarcreek, Ohio."

Trying to ease the tension, Cait chuckled. "Can't go there either. You've been shunned. And you're married to an Englisher."

Sadie attempted a laugh. "I know. Isn't it ironic? I'm heading full circle, back to my roots. The Amish believe in keeping their problems from the outside world." She rambled on. "Think of what would happen to us if another body is found at our winery. The wine community, like at home, would ex-communicate us. Luke would be devastated. His dream of owning his own winery gone."

"Sadie, please. You're not Amish now, or at least not in the way you used to be. You're—"

"I'll always be Amish at heart."

Stunned, Cait didn't know what to say to help Sadie. So far, Sadie had taken the unfortunate incidents at their winery in stride, calming Luke when a body was found in their winery, and again when his Fiat was set on fire. Cait understood Sadie had reached her limit. She glanced away and saw RT watching her.

"Come soon. I want to know everything that happened while I was gone," Sadie said.

"Okay."

The golden retrievers barked at a flock of ducks crossing behind a flatbed loaded with bales of hay. Cait watched and thought how simple their lives were.

"Sadie's back?" RT asked when she slid her cell phone into her back pocket.

"Yes," Cait said. "She's upset and wants to know what happened while she was in Santa Cruz." She glanced at the peaceful scene, the horses grazing in the pasture, and envied Bo and Khandi and their lifestyle. Then she looked at Joy in her wheelchair and knew their lives weren't without heartache. "Let's go. We need to check the Turtle Creek vineyard."

RT's blue eyes bored into hers. "We can do that. You want to tell me why?"

"To look for a body."

Bo raised his eyebrows. "You can explain that another time, but you might want to watch for a black SUV on the road," Bo said. "According to my neighbor who came by earlier, some guy was driving haphazardly on Mines, nearly forcing him off the road."

Cait and RT locked eyes. *Could it be the shooter who got away? He's alive? If so, what's he doing on Mines Road?*

છાગ્ટગ

RT and Cait took June, Jim, and Mindy back to Cait's house before going to see Sadie. When they arrived at the winery, Sadie was standing outside engaged in animated conversation with the police officers.

Sadie held her hand out to Cait, palm up. "Look what I found."

Cait stared at the shell casing and then at the officers and saw resignation on their faces. "Detective Rook was unavailable, but she knows everything we know," Officer Brokaw said.

Sadie gasped, reached out to touch Cait's bandaged shoulder, then pulled her hand back and stared at the shell casing. "Were you shot?"

"Only a graze. Nothing to worry about," Cait said. "I probably don't need the bandage."

Tears flooded Sadie's eyes. "I shouldn't have gone to Santa Cruz." She turned on the officers. "You forgot to tell me she was shot."

Before Cait could speak up, RT slipped his arm over Sadie's shoulder. "Cait was luckier than the men *she* shot. One's in jail."

Sadie looked at RT. "There were two? What happened to the other one?"

"He got away," Cait admitted, "which probably accounts for the blood you saw near the vineyard."

"You think he's hiding in there?"

Cait looked at the officers. "Have you checked?"

"Yesterday, but not today," Officer Brokaw said. "We didn't want to leave the winery unprotected after it was broken into. We'll look again to see if there's a trail of blood, and call for backup if we need to expand our search."

Cait shook her head, still in disbelief the other guy she'd shot had disappeared. "I thought I killed him," she said.

# Chapter 37

RT's cell phone buzzed. Cait froze. Not now, she thought. Please don't let it be a call for him to report back to work. Time stood still as she watched him pull his phone from a back pocket of his jeans, study the screen, and then answer.

"Tanner." He looked at Cait as he listened to the caller. Then he turned away, his back to her as he talked. She recognized his frustration by the way he ran his hand over his hair and paced. He raised his voice enough for Cait to hear "Impossible. My daughter's here with me." After a couple terse words, RT ended the call.

Cait waited for him to turn around and face her.

"I don't have a choice, Cait," he said as he slowly turned back. "I'm sorry."

She squinted as a glint of sunlight glanced off a metal drum next to the winery and into her eyes. "Don't apologize. I understand. It's your job, your career." She didn't bother asking when he'd be back.

RT took her hand and led her away from the two officers and Sadie. "I'll be at sea, on a container ship." He brushed the tips of his fingers across her cheek. "I shouldn't have told you that much." His phone rang again. He checked the screen and answered. "Tanner."

When the call ended, he said, "We're on a direct flight tomorrow morning from San Francisco. They'll send a car to pick us up."

"You and Mindy?"

He nodded. "Okay if I leave my trailer and Hummer here?"

"Of course," Cait said. She wanted to say Mindy could stay with her while he was gone, but then thought better of it. What if other men from the drug cartels were sent in to replace the ones she shot? If they recognized her from the night they shot up her vineyard, they knew where she lived and she could be vulnerable.

"I know what you're thinking," RT said. "I'll bring Mindy back with me another time."

Sadie walked over to them then hesitated. "I'm sorry to interrupt, but has something happened?"

"Mindy and I are leaving in the morning," RT said.

"Oh, no," Sadie said. "Another navy mission? Where to?"

"Not sure."

Sadie glanced over her shoulder at the winery and then crossed her arms over her chest. "I think the government should send you as liaison to the US Embassy in Mexico City to confront the Mexican drug cartels. You have special skills and experiences in counterterrorism activities and could surely handle the drug problem."

RT smiled. "That's an interesting idea. Thanks for your confidence in me, but the decision is not mine to make."

"I'm a news junkie," Sadie said. "I read where navy SEALs helicoptered into the mountains in Mexico in search of a cartel kingpin. If people like that are captured, then folks like Luke and me wouldn't be in the situation we're in now."

"I couldn't agree with you more, Sadie," RT said.

Cait watched the exchange between her friends with great interest. It was clear to her why Sadie left her family and community to further her education. Her interest in the

outside world was voracious and could not have been satisfied in her closed Amish community.

"Listen to me," Sadie said, "selfishly thinking of myself
when you're going off on a dangerous mission. I'm sorry."

"I'm the one who is sorry to leave while you're in a
tough situation, but you have law enforcement—local and
national—behind you on this," RT said. "I hope the crisis
will be resolved quickly, and you and Luke are back to running your winery by the time I return." He smiled and
winked at Cait. "And Cait and I can pick up where we left
off."

Cait almost melted from the sexy look RT sent her way.
She braced herself sternly. There was no time for that. She
needed to check the vineyard to be sure the guy she shot
hadn't died there. Better if she or the officers found him
than Sadie and Luke. She turned to the officers. "I'll go
with you to check the vineyard."

"We've got it," Officer Brokaw said. "Wait here. If we
find the guy, it may not be pretty."

She swallowed her sharp response, thinking he probably
didn't know she'd worked in law enforcement. "Until recently, I was a cop. It wouldn't be my first dead body. Let's
go."

"Sorry. Detective Rook didn't share your background
with us," he said. "Let's do it."

Cait smiled at Sadie. "This shouldn't take long with the
four of us scouting the vineyard. Try not to worry."

Sadie wrapped her arms around herself and turned toward the gazebo. "I'll wait here."

The trail of blood spots were the obvious place to start,
but they soon disappeared. The dry ground between the
rows of sun-dappled grapevines had been carefully main-
tained. Cait walked down the rows, careful not to get
snagged on the wire supporting the vines and their heavy
clusters of grapes. Her chest ached with worry at the possibility of finding a body. She knelt occasionally, checked the
leaves and then the ground for signs of blood. She sighed

with relief when she found nothing to indicate the man had bled in the vineyard.

Cait heard rustling around her as the officers and RT made their way through parallel rows. Tension gripped her shoulders and neck. She expected, any second, to hear the words, "FOUND HIM." The vineyard wasn't large—fifty acres—and it didn't take long to reach the road, turn back, and go up another row. An hour later they met up where they'd started their search. Cait's relief was apparently obvious to RT because he leaned over and whispered in her ear, "Told you so. Now relax."

Sadie rushed over to the group. "Well?"

Cait grinned. "Nothing but clusters of beautiful pea-sized green and purple grapes. You're going to have a terrific harvest."

"Ma'am," Officer Brokaw said, "we'll be leaving. Call nine-one-one if you're concerned and an officer will come."

Sadie nodded. "Thanks."

After the officers left, Sadie offered Cait and RT iced tea. RT declined. "Thanks, but I need to let Mindy know we're leaving tomorrow." He hugged Sadie. "Take care. See you when I get back."

"You're welcome to come stay with me, Sadie," Cait offered.

"Thanks, but I'll be fine staying here. Luke will be back tomorrow."

"Then make sure all alarms are set after we leave," Cait said. "Call if you need anything and I'll come." She gave her a hug, reluctant to leave her friend alone.

Inside RT's Hummer, disheartened over his leaving in the morning, Cait felt her independence slipping away. Determined to hang onto her freedom, particularly since her divorce, she'd clung to it like a shield. But RT had unintentionally ripped it away, a little more each time she saw him, rendering her soul open to be hurt. She recalled her dad saying, "You can't be brave if you've only had wonderful things happen to you."

She sighed. Sometimes the greatest pain grew out of the best things in life, she thought. Facing the unknown with an open heart took a lot of courage. Cait determined she would find that courage in herself.

*Chapter 38*

E arly the next morning, Cait was awakened by a knock on her bedroom door. She glanced at the clock as she slipped out of bed—six-thirty. She threw on a robe and quietly descended the stairs. On the landing, she waited for another knock.

"Cait, it's me," RT said.

Relieved, she slid the lock back and pushed, careful not to shove the door into RT in her haste to see him.

"Come here." He reached out, pulled her close, buried his head between her shoulder and her neck, and kissed her behind her ear. His warm breath raised the fine hairs on her body. She sucked in her breath when his hand slipped under her robe and beneath her razorback cami, cupping her breast. She went limp when he ran his finger beneath the waistband of her shorts.

RT lifted his head, kissed her hard. "Wait for me. I'll come back as soon as I can." The strained look on his face said more than words about how he felt about leaving her.

Then he was gone.

Cait laid her hand flat on the wall for support. She sank onto the bottom step, wanting more from RT than he could give at that moment. His absence plucked at her heart-strings, tight as a fiddle. Vibrating in every nerve of her body, she rose and went up the stairs, absently leaving the bedroom door at the bottom of the stairwell wide open. She stood at the window in the bay area and stared down at the empty driveway, the car that had been sent to pick up RT and Mindy, gone.

She settled on the wicker chaise lounger and curled into a tight ball, as if to protect her body from her cravings for RT and fell asleep.

∽∾

"Cait! Wake up!"

Cait stirred, unsure where she was. She opened her eyes, then quickly shut them against the sun streaming through the windows.

"Cait!"

She recognized the voice: Marcus. She pulled herself up to a sitting position and turned to see him standing over her. "What time is it? How did you get in here?"

"Eight-thirty," he said. "You left your bedroom door open."

She shook her head to clear the cobwebs and stood, a bit wobbly on her feet. "I never leave it open or unlocked," she said and then remembered everything: RT knocking on her door, a moment of fiery passion between them, and then how spent she'd felt when he'd left. "Why are you here?"

"To get my saddle. I'm going riding at the ranch with Bo," Marcus said. He tried not to stare at her skimpy sleepwear. "You better get dressed. A couple strangers are out front."

She gasped. "What? Why didn't you tell me?" She ran to her closet to get dressed.

He turned his back while she hastily pulled on sweats over her nightwear. "I tried. Do you know how hard it is to wake you? Any idea who those men might be?"

"Maybe. I hope I'm wrong."

"Should I call the police?"

She hesitated. "Not yet. Give me a minute and I'll come down." She ran into the bathroom.

When Cait went downstairs, she found Marcus staring out the kitchen window. He turned when he heard her. "Now they're in the back. I'm calling the police."

She'd stuffed her Glock in the back waistband of her sweats before coming down. She now pulled it out, its weight and the familiar shape a comfort in her hands. "Probably a good idea," she said as she stared out the window and studied the two men standing in the meditation garden. She didn't recognize either of them, but they reminded her of Rafael Carrillo and Miguel Quintero in their appearance: average height, stocky build, black hair, and swarthy skin. She ducked to the side when they looked her way.

"Police are coming," Marcus said. He stared at the gun in Cait's hand. "You're not thinking of going out there, are you?"

"It's my house. I'm going to find out what they're doing here. But first, call Jim and ask him to come over here and bring his gun."

"Got it." He hurried back to his office.

Cait watched as one of the men pulled his cell from his jeans pocket. Using his phone conversation as a distraction, Cait opened the back door and stepped outside, saying in a loud, commanding tone, "What are you doing here?"

Startled, both men turned and stared at Cait.

"We were told this property was for sale," the taller of the two said.

"You heard wrong," Cait said. *Stupid idiot*. She remembered Quintero had used that same excuse when confronted by Detective Rook. "Now get out of here and don't come back."

One of the men laughed. "Not very hospitable, Cait. Why don't you come over here and talk to us?"

Cait saw a movement out of her peripheral vision and as-

sumed it was Jim. Assured by the proximity of reinforce-
ments, she decided to chance a close-up confrontation. She
brought the gun out from behind her back so they could see
it.

Their eyes widened.

"Okay. I'm coming, but don't make any sudden moves."

The man who laughed reached inside his windbreaker.

"I wouldn't do that if I were you," she said. "I could
shoot your balls off before you could pull the trigger."

He slowly pulled his hand back, empty.

Cautiously, she approached the men, her gun leveled at
them.

Cait saw Jim coming from behind the men, his gun in
one hand and the other hanging onto Niki's collar. "How's
Miguel Quintero? Is he dead yet?" she asked.

He glared, daggers in his eyes. "Lucky for you, he sur-
vived."

Cait wiggled her gun. "Good to hear. Your names?"

The men exchanged looks. "Go to hell, bitch," the short-
er one said.

"You heard the lady," Jim said. He stepped out from behind the willow tree. "Or should I let the dog loose to help
you remember your names?"

As if on cue, Niki growled.

The men swung around, their guns now in their hands
and pointed at Jim.

Cait's heart thudded in her chest. "You're not going to
win this one. The police will be here shortly. Put your guns
on the ground and kick them away."

The men mumbled words undecipherable to Cait, but
they lowered their guns.

"I said drop your weapons on the ground."

The minute they did as Cait asked, Marcus ran outside.
"I'll get their wallets."

Cait's jaw dropped when she saw Marcus charge toward
the men. "Marcus!"

Marcus kicked the guns out of reach and checked their

pockets. He read off each name: "Diego," and "Mateo," and then tossed the wallets on the ground. "See how easy that was?" he asked the men. He walked back and stood with Cait.

Cait heard sirens. "Police. See what happens when you show up uninvited?" She smiled. She couldn't understand the words the men were spitting at her, but she suspected they were swearing in Spanish.

"I'll let the police know you're back here," Marcus said.

Cait knew the police couldn't hold the men for long, but maybe long enough to get to the bottom of why they were here. Did they want revenge for her shooting their buddies, Quintero and Carrillo? Or were they looking for Bill Reigo, Pamela's husband?

Detective Rook rounded the corner of the house, along with Officer Brokaw and another officer unfamiliar to Cait, their guns drawn. Marcus followed. Rook quickly took in the scene—the men, the guns, and the wallets—and said, "Looks like you got everything under control."

Cait told Rook about their real estate excuse for being there. Privately, she wondered if they were expecting another shipment of cocaine and wanted to take her out before she could interfere. If so, maybe they'd have second thoughts about that now. She'd already proven she could shoot to kill.

"By the way," she told Rook, "Quintero's alive."

"Good to know," Rook said. "Can't wait to interrogate him."

Brokaw went over and picked up the guns and wallets. He handed the guns off to the second officer but kept the wallets and flipped them open. "You're not going to need these for a while."

The men were put in the back of the police cruiser. The second officer found keys to the Land Rover parked at the side of the house already in the ignition. "I'll call to have this towed to the station," he said as he pulled his phone from his belt.

Detective Rook nodded and then turned to Cait. "We can detain these guys for a while for trespassing. We might put a tail on them, once they're released. By the way, its good Marcus and Jim were here, but I was surprised to see Marcus today. Does he usually work on Sunday?"

"Only during the festival. He's going riding with Bo," Cait said as she glanced over at Marcus. Marcus continued to surprise her, but today he scared her when he charged those men and grabbed their wallets. At least he hadn't done anything really stupid, like attacking them. Then he'd be in serious trouble, and so would she. She would be lost without his skills for managing the Shakespeare festival.

# Chapter 39

"Y ou going to be okay?" Marcus asked Cait after Detective Rook and the other officers left.

"Sure. Those guys aren't going anywhere any time soon," she said. "Did you get your saddle?"

"I'll get it now. A strap had worn off and needed fixing," he said. "Isn't Shep due back today?"

She smiled. "Yes. He's not going to be happy he missed all the action here and at Sadie and Luke's place. I think Luke is due back today also."

He nodded. "Glad to hear that. I'll see you tomorrow. Keep your bedroom door locked," he added.

Her skin tingled thinking about the passion between her and RT when he came to say goodbye. No wonder she forgot to lock the door when he left.

"Marcus proved himself when he charged out the door and pulled the wallets off those men," Jim said. "I'm glad you didn't tell Detective Rook what Marcus did. I don't think he's ready to trust him."

"He does, but won't admit it," she said.

"Just sayin'. By the way, I heard most everything those guys said," Jim said, "and most of the Spanish. What a lame excuse saying they came because this property was for sale, and then in the next breath admitting they knew who you were. I think the real reason they came was because you worry them. You shot their friends. You're not safe until the situation at Sadie's is resolved and the bad guys are all in prison."

"If you're suggesting I hide until this is over, think again. Oh, look," she said to change the subject, "there's June."

June rushed up, stray locks of blonde hair falling about her face. "Will somebody tell me what happened?" She eyed Cait and Jim like a hawk. "I don't see any bullet holes, so I assume you were on the winning side."

"For now," Jim said. "Let's go home and I'll tell you about it."

"Wait," Cait said. "How did you keep Niki quiet when you snuck up behind those men?"

"I promised him a playmate, a female one." He smiled as he grabbed hold of June's hand and left.

Cait laughed. Jim had been hinting Niki needed a canine friend. Her stomach clenched, a reminder she hadn't eaten breakfast or had her usual two cups of morning coffee. She almost tripped over Velcro when she turned back to the house. The cat rubbed against her leg, turned her china blue eyes on Cait, and purred. Cait picked her up and carried her into the house, while Niki sprawled in the shade of the willow tree.

Cait settled on a bagel with cream cheese. The coffee pot was full, apparently prepared by Marcus. She took her breakfast outside and settled on the bench in the meditation garden under a crystal clear blue sky. The tiered fountain, a new addition to the garden, flowed gently in a melodious rhythm, surrounded by the sweet scent of roses and lavender. By all appearances, a perfect day.

She tried to relax in the calm surroundings but was too keyed up. Her mind vibrated with pent-up energy. Jogging usually helped to clear her mind, enabling her to find traction for any scattered thoughts. She downed her coffee, finished the bagel, and then went inside to change into shorts, razorback tank top, and running shoes. She tucked her gun in the waistband of her shorts, slipped her cell phone into a pocket, and grabbed her sunglasses. Before she left the house, she got a water bottle from the refrigerator. She started jogging as soon as she went through the gate and crossed the theater courtyard. As she traversed the long, steep hill to Cross Road, the rocks and tree roots required her focused attention.

It wasn't long before she found her rhythm and turned her thoughts to the men who had boldly come to her house that morning. Obviously, they were replacements for the two she'd shot: Carrillo and Quintero. The new recruits were temporarily out of commission with their arrest, but could be released later today. That worried her. She was convinced a second shipment of wine bottles was coming, with more cocaine wedged between the boxes. She saw no other explanation for why these men were here.

She slowed to catch her breath and found a stump to sit on. She opened the bottle of water and drank deeply as she thought about Bill Reigo. He had to know why the drug dealers remained in the area, even after the winery had changed ownership. Would he be willing to talk to the police? As she screwed the lid back on the water bottle, she had an idea she knew Detective Rook wouldn't like—a private visit with Pamela and Vince. She wanted to ask them if they had kept any of the winery's files after they sold it, files that would incriminate Reigo. A plan began to take shape in her mind. All she needed was cooperation from everyone involved.

Cait also intended to ask Sadie and Luke if she could look through their files. Surely, Pamela and Vince had left most of the files intact for the new owners. Wallace Cranston, Luke's viticulture technician, might be willing to answer some questions about Bill Reigo.

Excited about her plan, she stood and started the long hike back up the hill. Near the top, a shadow crossed her path. Heart pounding, she removed her sunglasses, hooked them at the neckline of her shirt, reached for the butt of her Glock, and slowly continued her climb.

"I've been looking for you," Shep called to Cait.

Relieved the shadow had morphed into her friend, she gasped, "You don't know how happy I am to see you. You too, Niki." Niki stood beside Shep.

Shep held his hand out to help her crest the hill. "I talked to Jim and June. Apparently, I missed a lot while I was gone. How's your shoulder?"

"Better," she said. "Shep, I've got a plan. But first, I'd like to take a shower, and then I'll explain."

"Okay. Sorry to hear RT had to leave. I saw his trailer and Hummer; I assume he'll be back."

She nodded. "The timing sucks."

"For a relationship to work, you have to overlook a lot of things," he said.

"I'm beginning to learn that."

"Come on, let's walk back. I'll hang out while you get cleaned up."

"How was golfing with your friends?" she asked as they walked toward the house.

"Pebble Beach is not too shabby, my friends were fine, and the weather perfect, but my game stank." He smiled at her. "I think my mind was on Sadie and Luke's problem. I came up with a plan too, but with RT gone I don't think it will work."

She stopped walking. "Let me guess. You and RT were going to San Francisco to look for Bill Reigo."

He smiled. "You're good. Something like that."

"I know you, that's all. Want to tell me about it?"

"Of course, but it will wait until you're all cleaned up."

She tipped her head. "Tell me this: Is it legal?"

"No comment. Now get."

She ran the rest of the way to the house, excited they both had plans. Like old times.

እ⁄ᕤ⁄ᕤ

It was nearing noon when Cait and Shep joined June and Jim outside their RV. The Harts shared their barbecue chicken wings with them but refused to share their recipe.

"It's not a secret if I share it," June said.

"If I'd known you cook like this," Shep said, "I'd have been here sooner."

"Come any time," June said. "Now let's hear your plans. I assume they will end the mess Sadie and Luke are in."

"You go first," Shep said to Cait.

Cait sipped her ice tea. "I'm going to ask Pamela and Vince to show me what files they may have taken from the winery when they left. If they refuse, I'll ask Detective Rook to get them. Pamela said Bill Reigo handled the business end of the winery but, unfortunately, we can't ask him. I'm betting the siblings kept all paper work pertaining to that shipment of bottles with the cocaine." She set her glass down. "What do you bet a second shipment is coming? Why else would all those drug dealers hang around here?"

"Do you know how to reach Pamela or Vince?" Shep asked.

"No, but their realtor does."

"I don't know, Cait," Shep said. "You should talk to Detective Rook first. You're going over his head if you go directly to the Harpers. I wouldn't like it, and I'm damn sure he wouldn't either."

"You're right. I was only looking for a shortcut," Cait said. "Sadie and Luke could get seriously hurt, or even killed. I proved that the other night." She tapped her wounded shoulder. "Those men mean business, and they won't leave until they get what they came here for—the cocaine."

"I'll go with you tomorrow to see Detective Rook," Shep said. "That's the place to start. I appreciate you're worried about Sadie and Luke. I am too."

"Shep's right, Cait," Jim said. "The siblings would probably turn over what they have if Detective Rook asks."

Cait sighed. "Okay, Shep, let's pay Rook a visit in the

morning. Then we can talk to Sadie and Luke and see what their files show."

He grinned. "It's a date, partner."

"Wait. Shep, you haven't told us *your* plans," June said.

Shep refilled his wine glass and started to refill Cait's. She covered her glass with her hand. "I've had enough."

Shep sat back in his chair. "I happen to have a police connection in San Francisco. I'll contact him about Bill Reigo. I was hoping RT would be here so we could follow up on any leads my contact may turn up."

Jim drank from his glass and then cleared his throat. "I'm available. Can I help?"

June put her hand on Jim's arm. "Jim's a shark in sheep's clothing. Don't underestimate him."

Shep laughed. "I've learned to never underestimate anyone. Sure, Jim. I'll see what my contact says."

Cait smiled, happy Shep and her friends could work together, leaving her free to spend more time with Sadie. Her cell phone buzzed. Sadie's name showed on the screen. "Hey, Sadie."

"Luke's back," Sadie said. "He's confused. Officer Brokaw called to let us know two men had been arrested this morning at your place and were released an hour ago. He told us to take precautions in case they showed up here. What's he talking about, Cait?"

Cait massaged her temple. "Didn't he explain?"

"Only that the men were arrested at your house. What's this got to do with us?"

"Those men are probably here to replace the two I shot," Cait said. "I'm surprised he didn't explain."

"He was in a hurry when he called, but he did say Detective Rook would contact us later."

"Shep and I are going to the police station in the morning to see Detective Rook," Cait said. "We planned on stopping by to see you after that. We'll explain everything then." She caught Shep's eye. "Sadie, did Pamela and Vince leave all the files pertaining to the winery?"

"As far as I know, but I wouldn't know if any were missing."

"Would you mind if Shep and I came over and had a look?"

"Of course not. What are you looking for?"

Cait hesitated, not wanting to make Sadie more worried than she already was. "It's possible a second shipment of bottles is on its way."

"Oh, God," Sadie said. "We don't need more bottles." Then she caught on to what Cait meant. "Are you saying there could be *cocaine* in the next shipment?"

"I'm sorry, Sadie, but it's the only explanation for why those men are still here," Cait said.

After a long silence, Sadie sighed. "Luke and I will go through the files tonight. You can have whatever is here. In the meantime, I'm sleeping with Luke's gun under my pillow."

"Sadie—" Cait said, but Sadie had hung up. *What about Luke? Does he have another gun?*

Cait sighed and stood. "Tomorrow can't come soon enough."

# Chapter 40

C ait couldn't sleep. She'd spent half the night staring out the window, waiting for morning to come. When she finally did grab a few winks, her dreams were troubled. A tower of glass bottles shattered and, in slow motion, fell to the ground, almost burying her. The man who was arrested in her meditation garden shot the bottles and then continued shooting, even after the last one blew apart. Then he laughed.

Cait woke up, her own scream echoing in her ears, with a startled Niki at the foot of her bed. She sat up, rubbing her arms, half expecting to find bloody cuts all over them. She blinked at the sun streaming through the stained glass panels and at the walls awash in tones of yellow, green, red, and orange. She glanced at the bedside table and was surprised to see it was eight. She climbed out of bed and headed to the bathroom.

The cool shower not only cleared her head, it refreshed her mind. She remembered what she'd found last night while skimming Pamela Harper's Facebook page. Cait thought it was a waste of time looking for a secret message to Bill Reigo until she'd clicked on a link and found a collection of Pamela's poems.

Cait's dad, a university history professor at Ohio State,

had loved literature, especially poetry, and encouraged Cait to read it. One of the greatest gifts she received from her dad was her love of literature and language. He told her writers created poems to reflect what was important to them—the world, nature, adventures—and love of family.

Pamela's poems bespoke of hope. As Cait read, she tuned into Pamela emotionally and the hurt she must have felt when her husband betrayed her belief in him with his failed rehabilitation. It helped Cait understand where Pamela was coming from when she refused to talk to Detective Rook about Bill's disappearance, despite being left to face the consequences of his deceit.

When Cait stepped out of the shower, she wrapped herself in an over-sized towel, tipped her head to listen to a pinging noise, and went in search of her cell phone. Sadie's name appeared in the window. "Good morning, Sadie."

"Cait, Luke and I stayed up late looking through the files. We found a bill of lading dated mid-May from Mexico to American Canyon for pallets of bottles. The carrier was Wardell Trucking Company, but I think it's a copy of the one Detective Rook took with him when he was here."

"If there is a second shipment, the date would be later. I'll ask Rook when Shep and I see him this morning."

"I left it out for you when you come. If there is another shipment, Pamela and Vince must have the paperwork."

"If they do, then they're hiding something," Cait said. "If I'm wrong about a second shipment, there's got to be another reason why those men are still here. A scary thought."

"Maybe they want Bill Reigo."

"Then let's hope the police find him first." Cait tightened the towel around her. "I'll see you later."

&#x267A;&#x267A;&#x267A;

Shep was working on a steaming mug of coffee when Cait entered the kitchen. "Morning, Sunshine."

The scene felt familiar to Cait, like old times in the break room at the police station where she and Shep worked— Shep with a mug of coffee in his hand and Cait straggling in, dying for one of her own. She smiled. "Excuse me while I get a little nostalgic."

He filled a coffee mug and handed it to her. "You're entitled. I even stopped for bagels and cream cheese. They're in the bag on the counter."

"I already snatched one," Marcus said as he walked in from his office. "Hope you don't mind." He opened the back door to let Niki out and Velcro in.

"Does Detective Rook know we're coming?" Shep asked.

Cait sipped her coffee. "Not yet. I should call him now." She reached in her pocket for her phone. "We are telling him our plans, aren't we?"

"Absolutely. By the way, I called my contact at SFPD last evening," Shep said. "I'm still waiting to hear back from him."

"You have contacts everywhere," she said. "Sadie called. She and Luke spent last night searching their files for anything that might indicate another shipment of bottles. Nada. I still want to look." She called Rook.

"Rook," he answered.

"Okay if Shep and I stop by?"

"Sure. What's it about?"

Cait smiled at Shep. "Our plans of action."

Silence.

"Did you hear me?" she asked.

"I was waiting for you to continue. Whatever it is, is it legal?"

"Have faith, Rook. We'll be there after breakfast. Bye."

Shep laughed. "Same old Cait."

Ten minutes after leaving the house, they parked Shep's rental car in front of the police station. "That didn't take long," he said. "There are times when I wish I lived closer to work."

Inside, Detective Rook stood at the kiosk talking to a clerk. He smiled when he saw them. "Welcome to the LPD, Shep," he said as they shook hands. "We can talk in the interview room."

"Nice setup," Shep said when they were seated.

Rook nodded. "Cait's been in here a few times." He withdrew a pen and pad from his jacket pocket. "So, what's on your mind, Cait? Or do I want to know?"

"Funny. Any news about Bill Reigo?"

"No."

"Then I want to talk to Pamela and Vince," she said. "Do you have their phone number or should I call their realtor?"

"I have their number," he said.

"Good. I want to know if they kept any of the winery's files," Cait said. "I'd like to look through them. I've suspected there was another shipment for a while now. If I'm right, can it be stopped? The Harpers' might have kept the paperwork, thinking they wouldn't be implicated if another delivery of cocaine arrived at the winery. It's also a good reason for them to sell the winery." She took a deep breath. "If those drug guys are looking for Bill Reigo, I hope the police find him before they do. It's a worry for Sadie and Luke. They're planning their open house."

"I understand their concern," Rook said. "We *are* looking for Reigo, but without a definitive direction to look in, it could take time."

"That's where my plan comes in," Shep said. "Do you know James Forrester, former SFPD?"

Rook smiled. "Yes. How do you know him?"

"He's a friend," Shep said. "I called him and mentioned Bill Reigo. He didn't know of him, but he may be able to help locate him if he's still in the city."

"Good. Let's hope Reigo's still alive," Rook said. "I certainly want to talk to him."

"Before I went to bed last night," Cait said, "I looked at Pamela's website again. She writes poetry. If you read between the lines of her poems, she's still in love with Reigo, although she's hurt by how badly he deceived her. I think she knows exactly where he is. Do you know where she and Vince are staying?"

"In Dublin with friends," Rook said.

"Will you call and ask her to meet with us?" Cait asked.

"My last call to her went unanswered. I couldn't even leave a message."

Cait frowned. "You don't think she and Vince skipped town, do you?"

"Wouldn't surprise me," Rook said.

Cait sank back in her seat. "Maybe she left with Reigo. Have you tried Vince?"

"Of course. I left him a message to call."

Cait sighed and sat up. "Shep and I are going to see Sadie and Luke when we leave here. I want to look at their files, maybe find evidence of a second shipment or...I don't know...anything else."

Rook rose. "Let me know what you find. I'll call if I hear from Pamela or Vince."

Shep's phone rang. He looked at the screen. "Hey, James. Got anything for me?"

Cait watched Shep's face for a reaction to what his friend was saying, but he was as unreadable as stone.

"Okay, thanks. Appreciate it." Shep closed his phone. "James has a minor lead, but who knows? Could mean something, or maybe nothing."

Detective Rook walked them out to the lobby. "We'll talk soon."

Outside, Cait slid into the Toyota rental, disappointed Rook hadn't heard from Pamela or Vince.

"Cheer up," Shep said. "At least no bad guys are breathing down your neck. Maybe they left town after they were released."

"Yeah, maybe. Or they're working on their next devious plan."

"That's why I may take you up on your offer to stay in your apartment," Shep said.

Cait stared at him. "Really?"

Shep grinned. "Nah. I'm kidding. What if RT returned and found me sleeping one floor below your bedroom? How awkward would that be?"

"I wouldn't worry about it," Cait said, but actually did wonder what RT's reaction *would* be.

# Chapter 41

Cait knocked on the Sloanes' front door. When no one answered, she called, "Sadie, it's Cait." She tried the doorbell, forgetting it wasn't working. "I wonder where they are," she said to Shep.

As they were about to leave, the door opened and Luke let them in. Cait noticed his hair looked disheveled. "Sorry about that," he said. "We didn't hear you knock. Sadie will out in a minute. She set out a file for you in the office. Search through whatever you want. Oh, here she is."

"Hi," Sadie said, entering the front room.

Cait wondered if Sadie was ill. Her freckles appeared more pronounced on her pale face and she held her hand over her stomach. "Sadie, are you sick? We can do this another time if you are."

Sadie and Luke exchanged looks. Then Sadie smiled faintly. "This is a good kind of sick. I'm pregnant."

Cait stiffened. Chills raised the hair on her arms. She closed her eyes for a second to calm down and then hugged Sadie. "Oh, Sadie. I'm so happy for you and Luke."

Shep glanced at Cait and then smiled at Sadie. He clapped Luke on the back, shook his hand, and kissed Sadie's cheek. "Couldn't happen to a nicer couple. Congratulations!"

"When's the blessed event?" Cait asked.

"End of January, early February," Sadie said.

"That's why we're so concerned about the crazy turn of events here at the winery," Luke said. "The stress on Sadie has been rough, but I think she's holding up better than I am. Good grief, she's pregnant, yet she's confident all will turn out fine in the end."

Sadie smiled. "It's in God's hands, Luke. We haven't done anything wrong. How can it not work out for us?"

Luke frowned. "Your family would blame me for our troubles." Then, he sighed. "I'm sorry. I shouldn't have said that. They would be happy you're going to have a baby."

Sadie touched Luke's arm. "I know. Family is the foundation of the Amish way of life."

"And a fine baby it will be," Shep said. "So, how about Cait and I take a look at those files?"

"Good idea," Luke said. "Let's go back to the office."

One wall in the office was lined with black file cabinets. The rest of the walls were filled with books. "There's another office in the winery," Luke said, "but these are current files and more convenient for Sadie. We haven't had a chance to go through the others, but we will if you think it would help. Of course, you're free to do so."

"I doubt it will be necessary," Cait said. "If Bill Reigo is found, he could clear up our questions about why those men continue to hang around."

"Yeah, including how he got into drug trafficking in the first place," Shep said. "I have a friend in San Francisco. He's looking into finding Reigo."

"This guy pisses me off," Luke said. "Disappearing in the middle of a crisis."

"I feel guilty," Sadie said. "This is no way to spend your vacation, Shep."

"I've had my play time," Shep said. "Now let's see that file."

"Have a seat," Luke said.

An hour passed while papers were exchanged and each

had a chance to peruse them. Sadie got up and went into the kitchen. When she returned, she set a pitcher of iced tea in the middle of the table and then went back for glasses. Minutes later, she set a tray of frosted glasses on the table and filled each with tea. "Help yourself," she said.

A half hour later, Cait sat back in her chair. "This is a waste of time. There's nothing to indicate another shipment of bottles. I was so sure. If Rook hadn't released those two felons, I would pump them for information."

Cait's cell phone beeped. Rook's number showed on the screen. "Are your ears burning? I was just talking about you," she told Rook. "Do you know where those two guys you released are staying?"

"I know what they told me. I don't want you near them," Rook said.

Cait rolled her eyes. "Has Pamela called you back?"

"No, but Vince did. Pamela's missing."

"Oh great."

"Vince can't find her and his calls go directly to voice mail. He wondered if Sadie or Luke had heard from her. Are you still with them?"

"Yes. Hold on. I'll ask." Cait looked at her friends. "Has Pamela contacted you?"

Sadie shook her head, as did Luke. "Why would she?" Luke asked.

"She's missing. Rook says they haven't heard from her," Cait said. "Do you think she's gone into San Francisco to meet up with her husband?" she asked Rook.

"That's my guess," he said. "Vince got worried when she didn't return to their friends house in Dublin last night."

"He waited until now to tell you?" Cait asked. "I thought they were close."

"Apparently not. Can I talk with Shep?"

"Sure." She passed her phone to Shep. "Rook wants to talk to you."

While Rook and Shep talked, Sadie whispered, "You don't think something's happened to her, do you?"

"No. I always thought she knew where her husband was. She probably spent the night with him."

Shep returned Cait's phone. "I have to call James." He turned to Sadie and Luke. "He's a friend and former SFPD. Rook wants me to add Pamela Harper to the list of those missing."

"I wonder if the men Rook released had anything to do with Pamela's disappearance," Cait said.

"Their full names are Jesus Diego and Angel Mateo. Rook doesn't know where they are," Shep said. "He sent officers to their hotel, but they'd checked out."

"Doesn't mean they left town," Cait said. She stood. "I think we've taken up enough of our friends' time, and Sadie needs to rest."

Sadie shook her head. "How do people like that have names like Jesus and Angel? Do they mean something different in Spanish?"

Shep laughed. "Your guess is as good as mine."

"Will you let us know if the police find Pamela?" Luke asked.

"Of course," Cait said.

"Stay safe," Shep said as they left.

As soon as Shep and Cait were in the car, he said, "I'm sorry, Cait."

She frowned. "Sorry? For what?"

"About Sadie's news that she's pregnant. That must have hurt hearing another one of your friends was having a baby."

Cait glanced back at her friends' house. "Was I that obvious?"

"Only to me."

"I'm *extremely* happy for them, Shep. They've been married a long time."

"I know. One day you'll have a family of your own, even if you have to adopt a child."

"The doctor didn't know why I never conceived. After seven years of marriage, Roger blamed me."

Shep clasped Cait's hand. "I'm a firm believer that if your marriage had been a good one, you would have gotten pregnant. Mind over matter, Cait. Roger was a sorry excuse for a police chaplain."

"He definitely was a different man behind closed doors." She shifted in her seat. "Thanks. I'm better now. We can go."

"Let's have lunch at one of the wineries. Any idea where you'd like to go?"

"I've heard Garré Winery has a great café."

"Then that's where we'll go. I'll call James when we get there."

eↄeↄ

Cait and Shep sat at an outside table under an umbrella, surrounded by panoramic views of Livermore Valley vineyards, an Italian garden, and wine barrels overflowing with flowers. She tried to let the worries of the day disappear. While Cait studied the menu, Shep called his friend James in San Francisco. After she chose a salad with grilled chicken, she tuned into Shep's phone conversation.

"Her name is Pamela Harper, Bill Reigo's estranged wife. I've never met her but I was told she's tall and willowy, blonde, and blue eyed. She has an engineering degree from San Francisco State and an MS in Viticulture from UC Davis." He laughed. "Yeah, a lot of blondes in California. Pamela's brother Vince said they have friends who own a large sailboat docked in Sausalito. He tried calling but couldn't reach them. He did leave a message." He nodded. "I agree. Okay. Thanks."

He disconnected and said to Cait, "James also owns a sailboat and belongs to a sailing club. He may be former SFPD, but he consults with them at times. He'll make inquiries, check the club's membership list, and then get back with me when he has something to report."

"Your friend must have money other than what he made as a police officer," Cait said.

Shep smiled. "He was a captain. He married into money but has never forgotten where he came from—the skids of Detroit. I'm starved." It only took him a minute to glance at the menu and decide on the Cowboy Burger.

They had just finished their lunch when Rook called Cait. "Vince called. He wants to talk to Luke and Sadie. I let them know he'll be at their house shortly. You might want to be there when they talk. I have a meeting I can't miss."

"Thanks for letting me know," Cait said. "Of course we'll be there. Did he say what he wanted to talk to them about?"

"Bill Reigo."

"That should be interesting. I can't wait to hear what he has to say," she said.

After the call, Cait told Shep why they had to go back to Sadie and Luke's.

Shep reached for his wallet and left money on top of the bill. "Let's go."

෴

Vince's Subaru was in the driveway when Cait and Shep arrived. "He must have been around the corner when he called Rook," Cait said.

"What he has to say must be important," Shep said as he opened his door and got out.

The front door of the house was open. Cait tapped on the screen then opened the door. "Hello."

"Come in, Cait," Luke said. "Vince Harper is here."

Shep and Cait entered to find Vince sitting on the sofa. He rose when he saw them.

"What are you doing here?" he asked.

Cait smiled innocently. "We stopped by to see our

friends. Why are you here?" She glanced around the room. "Where's Pamela?" she asked, pretending she didn't know Pamela was missing.

"I don't know," he said. He stared at Shep.

"Vince," Luke said, "this is Shep Church, a friend of ours visiting from Ohio."

Shep smiled and held his hand out. "Nice to meet you."

"I don't shake hands." He sat back down and ran his fingers through his perfectly groomed blond hair.

"Vince," Sadie said in a soothing voice. "It's okay to talk in front of Shep. He knows the situation we're all in."

Vince clasped his hands together, elbows planted on his knees. "Pamela's missing. She's probably with Bill. If so, I hope she can convince him to come back and talk with the police. I thought Bill was a deadbeat until I got to know him. He's weak, easily influenced." He glanced up at the ceiling as if looking for answers. "When he was released from Folsom, he had every intention of going straight. But then, Rafael Carrillo found him in San Diego. They knew each other from their time at Folsom Prison. Bill has a big mouth—he likes to talk. He told Carrillo about this winery. You can guess the rest." He shifted in his seat. "Can I have a glass of water?"

Sadie jumped up. "Sure." She went into the kitchen, returned with a glass of water, and handed it to Vince.

"Thanks." He drank most of the water and then continued. "Long story short, Carrillo hooked Bill back on cocaine, a habit Bill had gone through rehab for. You know how easy it is for someone who isn't strong-willed to begin with. Bill thought he could do it recreationally without becoming addicted. Yeah, like that was going to happen." He stood and paced. "I should know. I thought I could do it recreationally too. Bill gave me a little cocaine. I hid it in that damn rabbit! Stupid!"

"Vince," Cait said, "do you think Bill might have gone on a drug binge and is holed up somewhere in San Francisco?"

"Hell, I don't know. If he called Pam, she'd rush to his side."

"Would he hurt her? Physically?" Shep asked.

"*What*? No."

After a couple of tense moments, Cait asked, "Do you know if Bill agreed to a second shipment of bottles and cocaine?"

Vince shook his head. "I asked him. He said no. I wanted to believe him, but I knew he was afraid of Carrillo and the other guy, his partner."

"Miguel Quintero?" Cait asked.

"Yeah, that sounds right."

Cait didn't know how much Detective Rook had told Vince about her shooting the men or that they'd been replaced by two other mules. "If there isn't another shipment, why do you think they're still hanging around here?"

"I don't know. Revenge? They'd want their money, drugs, or Bill—in that order."

Cait thought about that. *If they didn't get their money or the cocaine, it made sense they'd go after Bill.* "So why did you want to talk to Sadie and Luke?" Cait asked. "To make up for your part in this?"

Vince glared hard at Cait. "The only part I have in this mess is trusting Bill as a partner when Pamela and I bought this winery. He's not even educated. Uncle Calvin had a share in the business too." He looked off into the distance. "Pamela refused to marry Bill until he proved he was reformed. You can see how that turned out. Now they're both missing and I don't know where to turn to next."

"I have a friend in San Francisco," Shep said. "He's former SFPD. At my request, he's looking in the city for Bill Reigo."

Vince stared at Shep. "Why do you care?"

"I care about Sadie and Luke, as does Cait. Do you have contact information for your friends in the city, which might help the police locate Bill?"

"There's the boat our friends own. We've stayed on it a

couple of times." He hesitated. "My sister and I are close, we're best friends, but she doesn't always keep me in the loop about what's going on. The investment in this winery meant a lot to her. She had hopes of being here a long time. I thought she'd finally accepted that Bill wouldn't change. She filed for divorce. Then he disappeared. I don't know if he's hiding from Pamela or the drug mules. Either way, I'm worried for her."

"What do you mean? You think she could be killed?" Shep asked.

"Not by Bill." He stood and looked at Sadie and Luke. "I'm sorry for the trouble we've caused. I hope it works out for you."

"Sadie and I are sorry you've been drawn into a situation that isn't your doing. I'll walk you out," Luke said.

As soon as they left, Cait asked Shep, "What do you think?"

"I think Vince is worried about his sister, but I believe there's more he's not willing to share. He's caught in a web of deceit."

"I agree. Although his coming here today has raised my impression of him," Cait said. *And now I'm concerned for Pamela's safety.*

# Chapter 42

There was the strangest phone call a while ago," Marcus said when Cait and Shep walked into the kitchen. "Some guy looking for Pamela Harper and Bill Reigo. Do you know who they are?"

"What?" Cait asked in disbelief. "I don't suppose he gave his name."

"Nope. He sounded angry and hung up," Marcus said. "So who are they?"

"The previous owners of Sadie and Luke's winery," Cait said. "I wonder how they got this phone number."

Marcus rolled his eyes. "Well, duh. Bening Estates is listed in the phonebook. The name is also at the entrance of the driveway. Why would they think the siblings were here?"

"Because Pamela and Bill are missing. Let's hope whoever called doesn't find them before the police do," Cait said. "If he calls again, play dumb."

"Ha. Like I need to act dumb. You need to keep me informed about what's going on. Do you think the caller was one of the guys who was in the backyard?"

"Yes," Cait said. She sat down at the counter, exhausted, head pounding.

"I don't think there's anything else we can do right

now," Shep said. "Why don't you rest while I follow up on a case of mine?"

"Are you sure—"

"I am. My briefcase and laptop are in the car. I'll get them and set up a spot on the counter, if that's okay with you."

"Of course," she said.

"And I'll be in my office," Marcus said.

"What about Grace and her students? Are they coming today?"

"She called and said they'll be here tomorrow," Marcus said.

"Where's Niki?" Cait asked.

"With June and Jim," Marcus said. "They like having him around and giving him extra treats."

Shep laughed. "I'm thinking of getting a dog when I return home."

"I hope you do," Cait said. "Everyone should have a pet to love and care for." Her cell phone beeped. "Darn. Every time it rings it usually means trouble." She reached in her pocket and looked at the screen. She smiled, relief pouring through her body. "RT," she answered. "Where are you?"

"I'm coming home," he said.

"To San Diego?"

"No. To you."

Cait's heart skipped a beat. "How soon can you be here?" She felt Shep's and Marcus's eyes on her.

"Tomorrow," RT said. "Anything new with Sadie and Luke?"

*Oh, yes, but I'll let them tell you their good news.* "Pamela's missing," she said.

RT groaned. "She's probably with Bill Reigo."

"That's what we all think," Cait said. "Even Vince. Shep has a friend who was with the SFPD. He's offered to look for them in the city." She heard background noise over the phone.

"See you soon." RT hung up.

"RT's coming tomorrow," she said, hoping his plans didn't change at the last minute.

One corner of Marcus's lips turned up. "Hey, that's great."

"Yeah it is," Shep said, "since I'm leaving tomorrow."

Disappointment swept over Cait. "Not already."

He smiled. "Time flies when you're having fun."

"But you haven't had fun, except when you played golf with your friends."

"Cait, I did what I wanted to do. Seeing you and giving what little support I could to Sadie and Luke. I wish I could stay to see how it ends. I'll have to count on you keeping me posted. Okay?"

"Of course I will." She sighed. "But you won't be here when RT returns."

"We already said what needed to be said before he left. Look, he's a good guy. I can honestly see you and RT as a couple. It won't be easy, him in San Diego and doing his SEAL work and you in northern California with your Shakespearean theaters. But don't give up. Love conquers all. Hey, isn't that Shakespeare or something? Anyhow, it will work if it's supposed to. Trust me."

Near tears, Cait hugged Shep. "Thank you."

Cait's cell phone rang. She answered when she saw it was Sadie calling. "Hi."

"Cait, Pamela and Vince are here. Can you come over right away?"

"You're kidding. Of course we'll be there. What about Detective Rook?"

"He's on his way."

"Okay. See you soon." Cait told Shep what Sadie had said. "I wonder what that's all about, and where Pamela's been."

"We'll soon find out. Let's go."

"You will let me know what's happens, won't you?" Marcus asked.

"I promise." Cait grabbed her purse and tucked her cell

phone in her pocket. "Maybe Pamela and Vince are ready to confess everything."

❧

Vince's green Subaru and Rook's unmarked Ford were in the Harpers driveway when Shep parked on the road in front of the Sloanes' house. Cait rapped on the screen door.

Luke held the door open for them. "Come in," he said, rolling his eyes.

She glanced around the front room and noted the strained look on Pamela's face. Vince looked somber but nervous as he shifted in his seat. Detective Rook nodded to Cait and Shep as he leaned against the fireplace. His demeanor told Cait how angry he was. She could only guess why— Pamela's disappearance.

"Now that we're all here," Rook said, "where is your husband, Pamela, and why isn't he here with you?"

"He's in San Francisco," she said then corrected herself. "Actually, Sausalito. He's staying with our friends on their boat."

"How long is he planning on staying there?" Rook asked.

"Until he feels it's safe, I guess," Pamela said. "For some time, I couldn't quite wrap my mind around the idea Bill would lie to me like he did, or how he would let Mexican drug cartels insert themselves into my life. I haven't done anything wrong, but I feel like a criminal."

"You withheld information from the police," Rook said.

"You should have told me where you were going," Vince said. "I would have gone with you and dragged him back here to face the consequences of his stupidity."

"Exactly why I didn't tell you," Pamela snapped. "Your temper would have gotten in the way. You probably would have tossed him overboard."

"He deserves it," Vince said.

"He can't swim!"

"Pamela," Rook said, "what did you tell Bill? Does he know there are two more drug mules looking for him?"

She shook her head. "Not until I told him. He wasn't surprised. He hadn't completed his end of their bargain."

"And that would be what?" Rook asked.

"He was to receive another shipment of cocaine. He would get to keep the partial payment he'd already been given. The other half would apply to the second shipment, providing the police didn't impound it," Pamela said.

"And if the police did seize those drugs?" Rook asked.

Before she could answer, Shep's phone rang. He glanced at the screen and answered. "Hey, James." He frowned, nodded, listened for a while before finally speaking. "Got it. Thanks."

Cait stared at Shep and knew whatever the news was, it wasn't good. "Shep?"

"That was James," Shep said. "I told you he was looking for Bill Reigo at my request. He found him." He looked at Pamela. "I'm sorry, Pamela. Bill is dead."

# Chapter 43

S hock waves swept through Cait and, apparently, everyone else in the room as indicated by the expression on their faces. *What's going to happen now? Will Bill's death end the fiasco for Sadie and Luke?*

Pamela buried her face in her hands and sobbed. Vince tried to console her by wrapping his arm over her shoulder and whispering words in her ear. After a few moments, she looked up and wiped her tears with her palm.

"But I just saw Bill. Why would anyone kill him?" Pamela asked.

"Perhaps it's their way to get at you," Rook said.

She frowned. "Me? What did I do except sell the winery? Bill screwed up royally—our finances and all of our lives."

"By selling, you cut off the opportunity of more drug trafficking through the winery," Rook said. "That's motive enough to kill Reigo and then come after you."

Pamela's jaw dropped, her eyes full of fear. "Are you saying I'm next? They'll kill me? I knew nothing about any drugs until that drug-sniffing dog found them."

Rook watched Pamela closely. "The drug dealers probably assumed it was you who alerted the authorities to look into the next shipment bound for this winery. It *was* you who called the authorities, wasn't it?"

Sadie gasped.

When Pamela refused to answer, Rook shrugged. "I talked to Homeland Security. A female called to report her suspicions about cocaine in that shipment. Thanks to the caller, the shipment was grounded and the cocaine located." He stared at Pamela. "Why didn't you tell me?"

Pamela shook her head and looked away.

Rook glanced at Luke and Sadie. "You can relax. There will be no further shipments of drugs sent here."

"Thank God," Luke said.

Vince glared at his sister. "*You* made that call?"

Sadie stared at Pamela. "Thank God you did, but it must have been difficult for you."

Vince looked at Shep. "I don't suppose Bill's death was suicide. Remorse? Fear of facing the consequences?"

Shep shook his head. "I don't know all the details, but I can assure you from what James told me, it was not suicide. Detective Rook can ask James if you want to know how Bill died."

"I found that bill of lading," Pamela admitted. She looked at Sadie and Luke. "I'm sorry. I kept one file, the one with the second lading document. I wanted to believe there was only the one shipment, but by then I didn't trust Bill." She turned to Rook. "That's why I went to see him. When I confronted him with the file, he admitted there was another shipment on the way. He begged me to try to stop it before it was too late. Believe it or not, he *was* looking out for Sadie and Luke."

"And got murdered for it," Rook said.

Pamela broke down. "Yes."

৩৩৩

"What do you think Pamela will do now that Bill is dead?" Cait asked Shep as they drove back to her house.

"I'm more worried what the drug cartel will do if they

find her." He glanced at Cait. "It's not over. And you need to be careful. I'm glad RT will be here."

She nodded. "Still, I wish we'd had time to do something fun while you were here."

"Hey, you know I'm a workaholic," he said. "And I have something to tell the guys back at the station. They think you're basking in the sun, drinking wine, and dancing around on the stage in Shakespeare costumes. Then again, I might let them continue to think that. It paints a prettier picture than murder and mayhem, right?"

Cait grinned. "Right."

Shep parked in front of the house. "I got a direct flight from Oakland to Columbus tomorrow. I need to leave by seven."

She nodded. "Okay. I'm sorry to see you go."

Niki ran around from the side of the house and greeted them. Shep leaned over and ruffled the dog's fur. "Wish I could take you back with me," he told the dog. "I might get a lab like you when I get home."

"It's nice to have someone to greet you after working all day. I wanted a dog, but Roger wouldn't allow it. He didn't even like live plants in the house because of germs."

"You're exactly where you need to be in your life, Cait. I'm glad I was able to come and see that for myself."

June and Jim rushed over as if they'd been waiting for them. "Inquiring minds want to know what happened," June said. "Marcus said you shot out of here like a bullet and went to Sadie and Luke's. Haven't the police caught those bad guys yet?"

"You mean the two they released?" Cait asked.

"They're the ones," June said. "Why is Detective Rook dragging his heels?"

"He's not," Cait said, although she didn't always agree with Rook's studied approaches, even when he didn't have a choice. "Let's sit in the meditation garden. We'll tell you what's happened."

Marcus came outside and joined them. He sat on the

ground with Niki beside him. "Tell all," he said.

Cait glanced at Shep.

"You can explain better than I can," Shep said.

Cait and Shep settled on the grass beside Marcus while June and Jim sat on the bench. "Pamela went to see Bill Reigo in San Francisco, but now she's back. We just met with her, Vince, and Detective Rook at Sadie and Luke's place." She explained what Pamela said about seeing Bill, and that Shep's friend, James, had called informing them that Bill Reigo had been murdered." She glanced at Shep.

"We think Pamela could be next," Shep said.

"Wow," Marcus said.

"Why am I not surprised?" Jim said.

June rolled her eyes. "So much trouble over drugs. Will it ever end?"

"Not as long as there's someone to cultivate the drugs, sell them, and traffic them," Shep said. "It's a universal nightmare."

After a short silence, Cait said, "Shep leaves in the morning."

June gasped. "But you just got here."

Shep smiled. "A week ago."

"You should stay until Cait and the police wrap up the case," Marcus said. "Save her from getting shot again."

"RT will be back tomorrow," Shep said. "He's all the help she'll need." He winked at Cait.

Cait ducked her head to hide her flushed cheeks.

"Still, we're sorry to see you go," Jim said. "It's been nice knowing you."

"You too," Shep said. "You can count on my coming back."

"Why don't we finish off the leftover ribs from last night," June said. "I'll toss a salad and open the wine. You too, Marcus. You miss out on too much fun around here."

Marcus grinned.

Cait couldn't help but think the celebration was a bit premature.

*Those killers are still out there. They haven't gotten what they want, so who's to say they won't kill again?*

# Chapter 44

It was early morning as Cait stood in the driveway at the edge of the shade and watched Shep drive off. At her request, he stopped by for a cup of coffee before flying back to Ohio. She felt the loss as soon as his rental car disappeared down the driveway, but she was grateful he was able to take the time from work to visit.

Cait went back inside the house and poured herself another cup of coffee. She was still sitting at the kitchen counter when her cell phone rang. Her friend Samantha's name popped up in the window. "Hey, Sam."

"How's everything?" Sam asked.

"Shep left, he's on his way back to Ohio," Cait said. "I miss him already."

"I know. Family and friends mean a lot to you. What did you do while he was there?"

Cait chuckled. "Not what I had planned on, for sure. But he did spend a couple days in Carmel golfing with his friends."

"Good," Sam said. "Give me the latest on Sadie and Luke's situation. How are they doing?"

Even though Sam and Luke were only cousins, Sam worried about him. "They're hanging in there, even with the bad guys dogging them." She caught Sam up on the latest—

Bill Reigo's murder, how Shep's SFPD friend helped find him, and that Pamela called Homeland Security to stop the second shipment of cocaine. "Other than that, nothing new."

"Are you kidding? I hesitate to visit with all that's going on out there."

Excited, Cait asked, "Sam, are you seriously planning to visit?"

Sam, an ER doctor, led a busy life. She and her husband and their teenage son spent their winter vacation skiing in Vermont and their summer vacation on Martha's Vineyard. Cait doubted Sam had time left for a trip to California.

Sam hesitated. "Not this year. I have news."

"Okay. This sounds serious. You're not sick, are you?"

Sam laughed. "Not exactly. I'm pregnant."

Cait almost dropped her phone. "You're joking."

"No. Judd and I had mixed feelings about it, but once we got used to the idea, we're excited. Mark is embarrassed. What doesn't embarrass a fifteen year old boy?"

"I suppose," Cait said. "Uh...have you talked to Luke or Sadie?" She thought they should tell Sam their good news, but now Cait was tempted to let Sam know.

"No. I wanted to tell you first."

"Maybe you could call them today," Cait urged. "They would welcome good news."

"I will. Cait, are you okay? I mean—"

"I'm more than okay, Sam. I'm surprised, is all. How far along are you?"

"Four months."

Cait was surprised Sam hadn't told her about her pregnancy sooner, but then Sam knew how sensitive she was because she couldn't have her own baby. "I'm happy for you and Judd. And Mark will make a great big brother."

"That's what I told him. I'm being paged, Cait. The ER's been a zoo all morning."

"Don't forget to call Sadie. It's important."

After the call ended, Cait refilled her coffee cup. A sudden loneliness overwhelmed her. She needed company and

went outside to look for Niki. She told herself her tears were
tears of happiness for Sam and Sadie, but when Niki trotted
over she dropped to her knees, wrapped her arms around his
neck, and let the tears fall.

That's how Marcus found her.

"Cait!" Marcus said. "What's going on?"

She swallowed hard, then rose and swiped at her tears.
She smiled. "No one died. My friend Sam is going to have a
baby. And so is Sadie."

Marcus stared at her and then sighed. "Aren't babies
supposed to be good news?"

Cait smiled. "Oh, yes, they certainly are."

He shrugged then turned and went inside.

♥∽♥∽

That afternoon, as Cait was walking in the garden, RT
surprised her when he slipped up behind her and wrapped
his arms around her. "The warrior has returned," he whispered in her ear.

Heart pounding, she swung around and hugged him.
"I'm so glad." She kissed him deeply.

"Wow," RT said. "That's the best welcome home I've
ever received. Are you sure you're okay?"

Cait relaxed her hold on him and smiled. "I'm sure."

A golden brown eagle soared overhead, its seven-foot
wingspan mesmerizing against the blue summer sky.

"See that?" RT pointed. "An omen. I wonder what's in
our future."

She grinned. "You tell me."

"Hey, when did you get back?" June asked as she and
Jim entered the meditation garden. "Jim and I were just
talking about you. We had a mini send-off last night for
Shep. We should have a welcome back celebration for you."
She crossed her arms and rested her chin on her fist and
glanced heavenward. "Shakespeare said 'Make use of time,
let not advantage slip.'"

RT and Cait looked at each other and smiled. "You read my mind," RT said. "Where's Shep?"

"He left this morning," Cait said.

"I like him," RT said. "How come you two didn't become a couple?"

*Whoa*, Cait thought. "Why spoil a great friendship?"

"Good point. So tell me about Sadie and Luke."

"Why don't we go inside?" Cait said. "I'll catch you up on what I know."

Marcus was in his office, pounding on his keyboard, when they entered the kitchen. "Grace and her students are at the Blackfriars Theater for a couple of hours," he called out to Cait. "They're coming back tomorrow, too."

"Good to know," Cait said, although she had an uneasy feeling about it. *What if Mateo and Diego return while Grace is here?* "I'll stop by to see them. Coffee anyone?"

"No thanks," June and Jim said.

"Me neither," RT said.

After they settled around the counter, Cait told RT that Bill Reigo was murdered and the guys who were responsible were still out there and dangerous. "Pamela could be next."

"Sounds like it. I'll talk to Rook," RT said.

Cait chose not to think about how long RT would be around this time, but was just happy he was there. Together, maybe they could help end their friends' predicament so they could get on with their lives.

"When you call Rook," Cait said, "ask if Mateo and Diego could learn the shipment had been stopped. If they think it's still on its way here, maybe a trap could be set. This needs to end before anyone else gets hurt."

"Why wouldn't they just leave if they knew they weren't getting the cocaine?" June asked. "Why risk the chance of being caught and arrested?"

"Your top traffickers tend to fixate on the concept of risk," RT said. "But they spread the risks around to avoid a catastrophic loss, like the separate shipments sent to Sadie and Luke's winery. That doesn't mean these guys aren't scared."

"So we sit and wait for the next shoe to drop," Cait said.

"Or we force their hand," RT said.

Cait smiled. "I like how you think. What do you have in mind?"

"I'll call Detective Rook. Then we'll see."

"Sounds good," Jim said. "Count me in. I'd rather help than sit and twirl a glass of wine."

RT smiled and reached in his jeans for his cell phone.

"Whatever we do," Cait said, "I hope it's safe for Sadie. She's pregnant."

RT grinned. "Wow! Don't worry. We'll keep her safe." He tapped on his phone. "Hey, Rook. I'm back."

Cait glowed inside as she watched the intensity on RT's face as he talked to Rook. "The stakes are raised," RT said after the call ended. "Pamela is scared. She thinks she's being followed and wants to leave town."

Marcus walked into the kitchen. "I've been listening. Why not a showdown at the winery? Draw those drug guys in and take them down before they can hurt anyone else."

Everyone stared at Marcus.

"What?" he said.

"Were you listening in on my phone conversation with Detective Rook?" RT asked.

Marcus frowned. "No way!"

RT smiled. "Then you *are* brilliant. That's what Rook suggested. It's in the works."

Marcus grinned. "Cool."

"Rook already called the American Canyon warehouse in San Diego and asked if anyone had called to inquire about the grounded shipment. He'll let us know when he hears back. If not, those drug traffickers are still expecting it. Rook will then order the truck to continue up here, minus the cocaine, of course."

"Oh, no," Cait said. "More bottles! Luke will blow a fuse."

"He can return the bottles," RT said, "but to look legit, there's no other way. I think it's a perfect solution."

"What if they already know the shipment's been busted?" Jim asked.

"Then we'll have to come up with another solution," RT said.

"Rook should tell the people at the warehouse to say the shipment's on its way here," Cait said.

"I think he's already taken care of that," RT said. "Now, you got anything to eat in this house?"

සාළ

Later that evening, Cait and RT curled up on the leather sofa in front of the TV. They made love, ate popcorn, drank wine, and made love again. Cait had never felt so content. With RT she felt anything was possible. She loved his brain, his courage, his body, and his body's reaction to her enthusiasm for him.

It was still dark outside when they dragged themselves upstairs to Cait's bedroom on the third floor. When they climbed into the bed, RT pulled her against him and kissed her forehead. He was big and warm, his heartbeat steady against her chest.

When she opened her eyes later in the morning, RT was standing over her. She stretched and yawned. "What time is it?"

"A bit after eight. How are you feeling?"

"Like a million bucks." Her body hummed as she studied his.

"Rook called," he said. "The shipment from American Canyon should arrive at six this evening."

She sat up and pulled the sheet over the top of her breasts. "Good. It will still be light."

"Good thing Rook didn't waste time calling the warehouse. The drug guys called this morning asking for a delivery time."

"Oh, wow. Is it possible this whole situation could be over by tonight?"

"Hard to tell, but we need to be ready for anything," RT said. "Rook will let Sadie and Luke know." He tugged on the sheet, exposing Cait. "There's still time for this," he said as he dropped his shorts and lowered himself on top of her.

Cait smiled and sighed.

# Chapter 45

I'm uncomfortable having Grace and her students here while those drug traffickers are on the loose," Cait said as she and RT sat at the kitchen counter, polishing off their breakfast of ham and eggs.

Marcus poked his head out of the office. "Do you want to call Grace, or should I? What excuse should we give her?"

"You call her," Cait said. "All you need to say is we have a situation that needs resolving, and that we're concerned for their safety." She sipped her coffee. "Say that it should only be a day or two and that you will let her know when it's safe to come."

"Got it," Marcus said. He returned to his desk.

"That's optimistic," RT said.

"Maybe not. I think I finally have the answer to the last piece of the puzzle," Cait said.

RT smiled. "Are you thinking what I'm thinking?"

She smiled. "Tell me what you're thinking."

He brushed the crumbs from his toast into a neat little pile. "How did those drug guys know where to find Bill Reigo?"

"Exactly! Nothing adds up unless—"

"Unless *they* didn't kill him," RT said.

"We need to call Detective Rook. If the shipment arrives as planned, it would be the perfect time to invite Pamela and Vince to the winery. They can rejoice in the capture of the traffickers. I wonder if Rook is tracking the shipment."

"One way to find out." He picked up his cell phone from the counter.

Cait smiled. *I love working a case with RT. I also love— enough. Save those thoughts for later.*

"Detective Rook," RT said, "Cait and I think we've solved your case. Here's what we've come up with."

While RT talked, Cait cleared their dishes, rinsed them, and put them into the dishwasher. Her mind was going a mile a minute. Patience was not one of her virtues. She returned to the counter, anxious to hear what Rook thought of their plan, but the conversation continued for several more minutes. When RT finally ended the call, she asked, "Does he agree with our solution?"

"Yeah. And he's been tracking the shipment. It should arrive at the winery about six o'clock."

"I hope that's not cutting it too close," Cait said, "between when the shipment arrives and when those drug guys show up. They're probably tracking it too and could be waiting around the corner. We need to time our arrival so as not to interfere too soon. The police will want to catch them in the act of recovering the cocaine. We should coordinate the time with Rook. What about Sadie and Luke? I think we should let them know what's going to happen this evening and get them to go elsewhere."

"What we *think* will happen," RT corrected her. "Give them a call if it will make you feel better, but Rook was also going to call them. If they won't leave the premises, they should stay locked inside their house, preferably all day, in case they get "unexpected" visitors. But at this point, the drug guys will want to get in and get out, without creating chaos."

"I agree. I doubt they'd park right out front and wait for the truck to arrive. That would look suspicious. My guess is they'll drive past Post Lane several times and then park somewhere when the truck arrives, probably the road behind the winery." She smiled. "In the meantime, what do you want to do while we wait for tonight to happen?"

RT grinned. "You need to ask? But I suggest we pay June and Jim a visit, let them in on our adventure. And we shouldn't keep Marcus in the dark either."

"I heard that," Marcus said from his office. When he joined them, they briefly explained what was going to happen that night.

"Cool," he said. "I left a message for Grace. I said I'd let her know when it was safe to come back."

"Thanks, Marcus," Cait said. "I don't know what I'd do without you."

"I hope you never have to find out." He returned to his office.

When RT slid off his stool, Cait noticed his gun tucked at his back. "I left my Glock upstairs. I should get it now."

"Not a bad idea. I'll call Rook and coordinate the time, and then we can head over to the RV. I didn't think to ask Rook about taking Jim along with us tonight, but he did offer to help."

"Let Jim decide if he wants to go," she said. "As long as he has his gun with him. And he should wear a colored vest to show he's helping the police." She hurried upstairs for her Glock and returned seconds later.

They found June and Jim sitting at an outside table eating cut-up fruit. "Good morning," June said. "You two look bright and cheery."

"We have news," Cait said. She and RT took turns explaining what was going down that evening.

"Thank God," June said. "Poor Sadie and Luke have been through hell."

"No matter how it turns out, no one wins in a situation like that," Jim said. "I'd like to be there, but I don't want to be in the way. Sounds like the police will have the winery covered."

"They better," RT said. "There's always the unexpected in situations like this."

June grinned. "Cait, you and RT make a great team. You think alike."

Cait agreed, in more ways than one.

"So what are you going to do to kill time?" Jim asked. "It's a while until six."

Cait and RT exchanged looks. "Hang out," RT said, "rehearse what *should* happen tonight, and what to do if all goes haywire."

"Yikes," June said. "Let's hope not. The suspense is killing me."

Velcro darted across the open area and under Cait's chair. Niki bounded through the trees and drew up in front of her.

June laughed. "Look at that. I think they're adjusting to each other."

"Then why is Velcro hiding?" Cait asked.

"Just being playful. That's what cats and dogs do," RT said.

❧❧❧

That afternoon, Cait's cell phone pinged. Shep's name appeared in the caller's window. "Hey," she said. "You must be happy to be back at work."

"Ha. Work stacked up while I was gone." Shep said. "Is RT back?"

"He got back yesterday afternoon. If all goes as planned, Sadie and Luke's problems will end tonight." She recapped the plans without any interruption from Shep. When she finished, she wondered if he was still on the line. "Shep?"

"I'm here," he said. "I was taking it all in. I wish I could be there to see it happen. As you talked, I tried to find a flaw, but couldn't. It's a brilliant plan if everyone shows up."

Cait glanced at RT as he played with Niki. "Why wouldn't they? Everyone involved has something to gain—or at least think they do. The satisfaction of seeing those drug traffickers arrested should be incentive enough for all the players to show up."

"Just saying. It sounds like your plans are as air tight as possible. You'll have to call and let me know how it goes."

"Of course," she said. "Shep, thanks for coming here. It meant a lot to me."

"And to me," he said. "Good luck to you and RT. Think positive thoughts."

Cait smiled at RT, wrestling on the ground with Niki. "Thanks. I'll be in touch."

"What did Shep have to say?" RT asked after Cait slid her phone into her pocket. "I bet he wishes he were here to help take down the bad guys."

"He does," she said. "He wished us luck." She sat on the grass beside him. "I always found it hard to take part in a case, like Shep did here, only to have it turned over later to a different police department. I like to see a case through from beginning to end."

He shrugged. "Unless it's your case, that won't happen. And it depends on your expertise. My team and I are usually brought in to finish a job. It's a critical part of our capabilities. I understand my skills are likely to be employed on a regular basis. That's why I'm usually called away when I'm here." He ruffled Niki's fur. "I train for that."

"I know. Still, it must be difficult for you and Mindy. But I must say, Mindy seems to be a well-adjusted child in spite of your erratic schedule."

RT grinned. "She's a great kid." He glanced at his watch. "It's almost five. Want to grab a bite to eat before we go?"

"Good idea." She got to her feet. "Ham sandwiches coming up."

RT rose, grabbed Cait around the waist, and kissed her, taking her breath away.

"Don't start what you can't finish," she said.

"Oh, I'll finish it—later."

*Then we better end what lies ahead of us as quickly as possible*, Cait thought.

# Chapter 46

The truck of glass bottles was late. No sign of the drug traffickers either, unless they were hiding nearby or in the vineyard. If so, where was their car? As Cait and RT drove around, Cait pondered. When she and RT had driven down the road behind Sadie and Luke's vineyard, they didn't see a car parked there. If the drug guys had parked elsewhere, it would be a long walk in, and Cait couldn't see them doing that.

"Where do you think everyone is?" Cait asked RT.

"Don't worry," RT said. "They'll show as soon as that truck pulls in. I suspect a cop or two are hunkered down inside the winery and maybe in the house as well, so the scum haven't got a chance."

"We should have used my car. Your Hummer is too obvious."

"It is, but I'll drive around until we're instructed to go in."

Cait's cell phone pinged. She glanced at the screen. "It's Rook," she said. "Where is everyone?" she asked the detective.

"The drug dealers' green Land Rover just passed Post Lane for the third time," Rook said. "I'm in my unmarked vehicle directly across from it. SWAT is nearby waiting for my summons. I assume that was you and RT in the gray Hummer."

"Yes, you nailed us. What about Pamela and Vince? They will be here, won't they?"

"Oh, yeah. Pamela appeared to gloat and said she wouldn't miss the showdown for the world."

"And Sadie and Luke? Is there an officer in the house with them?"

"Cait, do you think I don't know how to do my job?"

"Sorry, I'm nervous. So much depends on the outcome of this plan."

"It does, but you can relax," Rook said. "Everyone will be here." He paused. "A truck is slowing in front of Post Lane. No, it went on by. You should park some distance from me. I'll let you know when the truck arrives and it's time to go in."

"Okay." She disconnected the call and relayed Rook's instructions to RT.

A half hour passed.

The truck was now an hour late.

"Maybe the truck driver stopped for dinner," she suggested.

"Possible," RT said. "It's a long drive from San Diego, especially when hauling a trailer. There's no reason for the driver to have been told about our situation. The haul would be business as usual."

"In that case, we could sit here all night," Cait said.

It was eight-thirty the next time Rook called. "The truck's here. It's pulling into the lane. We wait, and give them time to unload. I'll call when the truck pulls out." He hung up.

Cait perked up, energized and ready to go. "The truck is here," she told RT. "Rook will call when it leaves."

Thirty minutes later, Rook called again. Cait tapped the speaker button so RT could hear. "The truck left," he said. "An officer reported a green Land Rover pulled over on the road behind the Sloanes' vineyard. Like before, that's how

they'll go in. I told Pamela to park at the foot of Post Lane.
You park there too, but be sure to leave room for the SWAT
vehicle to get by. Then walk in. I'll do the same. We want
to give those men enough time to start cutting the shrink-
wrap. Remember, no heroics."

"Copy that," Cait said as she rolled her eyes.

RT started the Hummer and pulled out onto the road.
"Hang on."

They were quiet as they drove, each with their own
thoughts.

RT parked on Post Lane behind Rook's unmarked Ford.
Vince and Pamela pulled in behind them. It was growing
dark as they stealthily made their way to Turtle Creek Winery. Cait touched her Glock to reassure herself it was still in
place.

"I don't like it," she whispered. "It's too quiet."

"Not for long," RT said.

Pamela and Vince caught up with them. "Detective Rook
suggested we stay out of the way in the gazebo," Pamela
said.

"You should be okay there," Cait said.

They walked ahead and reached the foot of the driveway.
"I don't see Rook," RT said. "Stay close to the trees and
shrubs until we reach the winery. Be ready if you hear shots
fired." He took the left side of the driveway while Cait
made her way up the right side.

She was tempted to glance at the house where Sadie and
Luke were holed up, but it was a distraction she couldn't
afford. When she reached the end of her cover, she darted
across the open area to the winery and backed against the
wall near the doors. RT joined her on the other side of the
double doors as officers swarmed the building from all directions.

SWAT had arrived.

Officers yelled commands.

Rapid-fire gunshots ensued.

RT nodded to Cait. He held up three fingers, then two,

then one. They swung around and slipped into the building, their guns drawn.

Cait thought she saw a man dart behind a stack of wine barrels. When no one else appeared to have seen him, she took off after him. She darted around stacks of barrels, but when she didn't see anyone, she decided it must have been her imagination and returned to where RT stood.

More gunshots.

RT grabbed her hand and pulled her toward the door. "They don't need us. Let's not get caught in the line of fire."

Silence fell over the winery. One of the drug traffickers was standing, arms up in the air. A second followed suit.

After the officers cuffed the men, Rook approached Jesus Diego and Angel Mateo. He pointed to the new shipment of bottles. "No drugs. No cocaine. Only bottles." He turned and walked away.

Cait couldn't believe it was over in what seemed like a matter of minutes.

But there was one more arrest to be made.

Cait and RT followed Rook and another officer to the gazebo where Pamela and Vince waited.

"Wow, that went down fast," Pamela said. "So it's over."

"Not quite," Rook said. He drew handcuffs from his pocket. "Pamela Harper, you are under arrest for the murder of Bill Reigo. Turn around and put your hands behind your back."

"*What*?" Vince yelled.

Pamela straightened, chin up, her voice even. "It was a risk of getting caught, but I had to do it."

Cait shivered at the cold edge of her words.

She and RT watched as Pamela Harper, Jesus Diego, and Angel Mateo were led away. The officers regrouped and stood in the driveway talking to Detective Rook.

*Now it's over*, Cait thought.

She glanced back at the winery, now quiet, and caught movement in the vineyard.

*Or is it my imagination?*

She nudged RT. "Look over there." She pointed. *Could it be the man I thought I saw in the winery?*

He turned toward the vineyard. "What?"

"Someone or something is in the vineyard. Let's check it out."

With no moon and visible stars, Cait felt as if a cloak had been drawn over the vineyard. She stooped low, waiting out a silence that seemed like a physical presence. Her senses primed for any motion, she gripped her Glock. Her head swiveled toward RT and saw him grip his gun.

A sound like shuffling feet a short distance away had Cait adjusting the sight on her gun.

"Come out of there! Now!" RT yelled.

A lone figure rose from the dark.

The man, vaguely familiar to Cait, made no movement toward her or RT, except to raise his left hand and press a cigarette between his lips with his right. "Light?"

The gesture was so humorous to Cait she barely kept from laughing.

"On the ground!" RT demanded.

"No have gun," the man said.

"I said down!"

The man flipped his cigarette away and slowly sank to his knees, but not until he smirked at Cait.

She pressed her gun hard into his neck. "If it isn't Miguel Quintero. I shot you once. I could finish the job now. Yes?"

He rattled off in Spanish.

"How'd you like to see your partner?" she asked. "He's in jail."

Rook approached. "I got him," he said as he reached in his pocket for handcuffs. "I hope he's the last because I'm out of handcuffs."

Cait smiled and wondered how Rook had found them, but she was grateful.

The sudden screech of a night owl assaulted the air, startling Cait. RT took her hand. "Let's go home."

"Sounds good, but let's see Sadie and Luke first."

"Cait," Rook said after he handed off his prisoner to an officer. "How did you know he was hiding in the vineyard?"

"I didn't, until I caught a movement at the edge of a row at the vineyard. I'm not surprised Quintero or someone else would be here. Two to collect the drugs doesn't seem like enough for an operation like this, especially after they lost the last shipment of cocaine, don't you think?"

"Let's see," Rook said. "There were four, until you incapacitated one, at least temporarily, and sent the other to jail. That left two."

She grinned. "Oh, yeah."

"We're going to see Sadie and Luke and then head home," RT said.

"Good idea," Rook said. "Tell them I'll be in touch."

Sadie swung the door wide open as soon as Cait and RT stepped onto the porch. "Oh, God. Is it over?"

Cait nodded. "It's over."

"We were watching out the window," Luke said. "Was Pamela really arrested?"

"Yes. She murdered her husband, Bill Reigo," RT said. "I guess she'd reached her limit of pain and distrust. We'll probably never know at what point she decided to pull the trigger, shoot Bill, and toss him overboard, but when he got out of prison, he promised her he was off drugs. So she married him. Unfortunately, he fell back into his old habit when he reconnected with Rafael Carrillo, a fellow cellmate."

Luke and Sadie looked stunned by RT's revelation. "I never guessed Pamela killed her husband," Sadie said.

"It took me a while," Cait said, "but she was the only one it could be. Those drug guys didn't know where Bill Reigo was or about the boat in Sausalito. It's Vince I feel sorry for."

"I don't know," Sadie said "It will take a while to forget and forgive."

"Understandable. Cait and I are going home for much needed R and R," RT said.

Cait and Sadie hugged, while RT and Luke shook hands, promising to get together soon. "Sadie, I think Samantha is going to call you soon."

"That would be great. Is she okay?" Sadie asked.

"I'd rather she tell you. But don't worry. It's good news for a change."

"So, Cait," RT said as they walked to their car. "What are we going to do now that the bad guys have been arrested?"

Cait grinned. "Do you have to ask?"

He put an arm around her waist, pulled her toward him, and smothered her with lingering kisses.

## The End

## About the Author

Carole Price is a Buckeye! Born and raised in Columbus, Ohio, she attended The Ohio State University. She and her husband live in the San Francisco Bay Area where she graduated from Livermore's Citizens Police Academy and is an active volunteer for the Livermore PD. Carole fell in love with the Bard after attending plays at the Oregon Shakespeare Festival in Ashland. *Vineyard Prey* is the third in her *Shakespeare in the Vineyard* mystery series.

You can learn more about her at
http://carolepricemysteries.com.

CPSIA information can be obtained
at www.ICGtesting.com
Printed in the USA
FSOW01n1624030318
45252FS

9 781626 947658